# LITTLE BEACH BUNGALOW

# ALSO BY JOANNE DEMAIO

**The Seaside Saga**
*Blue Jeans and Coffee Beans*
*The Denim Blue Sea*
*Beach Blues*
*Beach Breeze*
*The Beach Inn*
*Beach Bliss*
*Castaway Cottage*
*Night Beach*
*Little Beach Bungalow*
*Every Summer*

**Countryside New England Novels**
*True Blend*
*Whole Latte Life*

**Wintry Novels**
*First Flurries*
*Cardinal Cabin*
*Snow Deer and Cocoa Cheer*
*Snowflakes and Coffee Cakes*

# little beach
# bungalow

A NOVEL

# JOANNE DEMAIO

Copyright © 2019 Joanne DeMaio
All rights reserved.

ISBN: 9781090956859

Joannedemaio.com

*To the little beach bungalows*
*of Connecticut's Point O' Woods Beach*

*Yes, every shingled cottage tells a story.*

# *one*

---

## *Early Monday Morning*

THE COTTAGE IS A STONE'S throw from Long Island Sound—and looks it. Years of standing beside that salt water have left the old beach house seaworn. The shingles are weathered. The cream trim paint, peeling. A narrow walkway made of boardwalk planks leads from the driveway, through scrubby dune grass alongside the cottage, to an open rear porch.

Jason Barlow briefly turns his architectural eye on that sparse porch, which is simple as can be. Seven painted steps lead to its entry. There, a sloped roof extends from the back of the cottage. And the porch floor? Its painted boards are the same dusty olive as the steps. The porch has no windows with screens and glass. Instead, open-air views fill that window space. At first, Jason thinks that if it were up to him, he'd redesign the porch to be the cottage's focal point.

On second thought, he realizes it already is.

Because those expansive views look out onto the sweeping blue waters of the Sound. Standing on that unassuming porch, you'd no doubt feel like you boarded a ship, with nothing but the sea before you. Actually, that wide back porch might be architectural perfection. Its simplicity lets a coveted blue view take center stage. If anyone were to sit on the porch ledge and lean against one of the tall wooden posts, wouldn't it make the perfect seaside seat, custom-made for daydreaming. Or relaxing. Or just breathing.

Which Jason needs to do—breathe. Slowly and deeply. He has to inhale that salt air just to lower his spiked blood pressure. Because as perfect as that cottage porch is, something's also wrong. Horribly, undeniably wrong.

That would be the man apparently staying at this cottage. The man who stands on that sandy, planked walkway and just now hoisted his packed duffel up over his shoulder. Hoisted and heaved that duffel right through the air to land on the wooden porch floor—the same way his duffel must hit the deck on a lobster boat.

The man who, in his jeans and tee, returns to his salt-coated pickup and lifts a carton from the truck bed.

A man who Jason damn well knows—Shane Bradford.

And a man synonymous with trouble.

A man who Jason also doesn't need seeing him drive slowly past while watching him unpack. So Jason gives the SUV a little gas and hurries by with only a glance in his rearview mirror. Enough of a glance, though, to see the *For*

*Rent* sign propped in the cottage's front window.

So that's that. The cottage is obviously rented now. By Shane.

One more glance back confirms it. Jason sees Shane climb the porch steps, all seven of them, and drop his packed carton there. Yes, it's painfully apparent Shane's about to settle into that little beach bungalow by the sea.

What that does—the biting realization of it—is one thing and one thing only. It gets Jason to drive around the block to be absolutely sure. To leave not one stinking shred of doubt that trouble is about to park itself at this tranquil New England beach community.

It is, all right.

There's no denying it after Jason rounds the cottage-lined block. When he sees that one little bungalow again, he also sees Shane carrying another box to the back porch. His arms support the large carton as he crosses that planked walkway.

The sight of it all leaves Jason no choice. He has to stop. Angry now, he pulls over to the side of the road, hits the steering wheel and again reminds himself to breathe.

Which he does. One long inhale, one slow exhale.

When he gets out and steps onto the street, Jason closes the SUV's door and breathes again. Salt air in, pause, and out. Tactical breathing, like his father was trained to use fighting in 'Nam. Funny, because it feels like Jason's headed off to battle now.

Raising a hand to shield his eyes from the early morning sunlight, he squints at the sight he still can't believe. But

3

also can't ignore. So drawing one more breath, he walks around his vehicle and approaches Shane Bradford in the cottage driveway.

"What are you doing here?" Jason calls out.

Shane, standing at the rear of his pickup, looks back over his shoulder. After lifting a second duffel from the truck, he turns to Jason. "No *hello*, Jason? No friendly greeting for an old beach friend?" Shane sets his duffel on the ground and steps closer.

Jason steps closer, too. Because as much as he wants an answer to his question, he also wants to take that damn loaded duffel, throw it back into Shane's truck and get him the hell out of Stony Point.

"How about this?" Shane asks. He stops and lifts dark sunglasses to the top of his head. "How about … *Hey, Shane. Good to see you, man. Nice of you to come by for Kyle and Lauren.*" He steps even closer, his head tipped. "*How's life treating you?*"

"Cut the shit, Shane. If you're staying on here to get a rise out of everyone, congratulations. You've done it." Jason looks from the truck bed partially filled with more cartons and brown shopping bags, to the shingled bungalow beyond, to Shane again. His eyes look tired. His face needs a shave. His tee is ragged at the shoulders— from the sleeves being ripped off, actually. Giving clear view of his tattooed arms, which rival his brother's in size. Lifting lobster traps from the sea will do that, Jason figures. He looks long at Shane before dropping his voice. "So what do I have to do to get you to leave?"

"You say that as though you're making a deal with the devil."

Jason raises an eyebrow. "It's just best for everybody if you move on. Which doesn't seem likely," he says while motioning to the duffel at Shane's feet. "How long you staying *here* now?" Jason asks, hitching his head to the rented cottage.

"One fishing trip."

"What's that supposed to mean?"

"It means there's a lobster boat that pulled out of a harbor in Maine a few hours ago this fine Monday morning." Shane checks a heavy watch on his wrist. "Boat's headed well out into deep waters right about now. And the crew's got me covered for the excursion, so I'm good for this leave."

"And exactly how long's an excursion?"

Shane squints at him. "Hang on, my friend," he says. "You're all questions today. *What are you doing here? How long are you staying?*" Shane turns back and slams the pickup's tailgate closed. "You know something, Barlow?" he calls over his shoulder. "I have a question for you, first."

Jason throws up his hands. "Go ahead."

So Shane turns, waits a second, then looks him straight on.

As Jason stands there in his short-sleeve button-down and cargo shorts, he sees it. Shane can't seem to help it, the way his gaze travels from Jason's face, to his prosthetic leg that must be startling to realize, then back to Jason's face. What Jason *never* sees coming, though, is the one question thrown his way.

"What are you doing marrying my fiancée?" Shane asks. "What?"

And there it is. That short laugh of someone who just caught you in his web, right before he goes in for the kill. "Maris never told you, did she?" Shane continues, squinting over at him. "We were engaged to be married, your wife and I. Maris was going to be Mrs. Shane Bradford." After a moment's pause, Shane picks up the duffel at his feet. Heading toward that open back porch, he calls over his shoulder, "Looks like you'll have an interesting dinner conversation tonight."

# *two*

---

## *Later Monday Morning*

EVERY AUGUST FIFTEENTH, MARIS KNOWS that something unexpected happens to the sea. As she crosses the beach with Eva, just behind Celia and Elsa, she listens to her aunt explain.

"Sailors refer to the North Star as the Stella Maris. *Stella* is Latin for star, of course. And *Maris*?" Elsa turns and pats Maris' wrist. "It means *of the sea*. So the North Star is the star of the sea, because it's a crucial guide to sailors as they navigate their ships."

"But I still don't understand why people dip their feet in today," Celia says as they near the water. Holding her baby close, she walks beside Elsa.

"Well, the Blessed Mother is *also* referred to as Stella Maris because she guides us through *life's* seas. And today's the Blessing of the Waters," Elsa continues, "marking the Assumption of Mary into Heaven. So it is believed that if you step into the sea today, you might experience the water's healing powers."

"I like that thought," Celia quietly says, looking out at Long Island Sound.

"Me, too." Elsa, in a black tunic-tank over side-striped capris, stops on the sand. "Me, too," she says again while slipping off her sandals.

The August air is warm and the sun bright. And okay, what Maris thinks is that this morning couldn't be more perfect. Because as they approach the water's edge, ocean stars, *thousands* of them, shimmer on the Sound. It's as though they're shining even brighter on this special day.

"Elsa, look!" Maris touches her aunt's shoulder.

"Oh, I never tire of that sight." Elsa lifts her cat-eye sunglasses to the top of her head and takes in the sparkling view.

"Tell us the story again?" Celia asks as she bounces her daughter in her arms. "I want Aria to hear it straight from her *nonna*."

Elsa steps closer and adjusts her granddaughter's white sunbonnet. "*Ocean stars*," she whispers as she takes Aria from Celia. Holding the baby close, Elsa wades barefoot in the small breaking waves. Sunlight ripples on the sea. "Do you see those pretty stars on the water, my little love?"

As Elsa asks, Maris can't help but smile. The baby, in her pink romper, looks out at the water from beneath the brim of her bonnet. Celia also steps barefoot into the water and inches close beside Elsa to hear the magical story. It might as well be a secret fairy tale, with the way Elsa's voice holds such wonder.

"Those are ocean stars," Elsa continues softly as she shifts the infant in her arms. "You see them in the morning because they are actually stars that fell there overnight. Twinkling stars that dropped from the sky and now float on top of the sea, flickering on the waves. What they're doing is regaining their strength to rise back up to the night sky much later today. And tonight?" Elsa asks, looking upward now. "Well ... Tonight those stars will shine again in all the skies above."

As if the baby understands every single word of Elsa's enchanted tale, she coos and reaches her fisted hands toward the water, all while squirming in Elsa's arms.

"Here," Celia says, taking her daughter from Elsa. "Since today is the Feast of the Assumption, I'd like Aria to have her very first toe-dipping." With that, Celia walks deeper into Long Island Sound and bends to touch her daughter's feet to the water.

"Look!" Elsa whispers to Maris and Eva. "She loves it."

Maris watches little Aria laugh again and again, every time Celia dips her toes. The scene couldn't be more peaceful. Especially after the tumultuous weekend they all had, with the arrival of Shane Bradford. That he'd left yesterday, just as suddenly as he'd arrived, has them all feeling relieved. Now, they're relishing the glorious sunshine and cool sea of this hot August morning.

"Come on, Maris," Eva says as she slips off her sandals. Wearing a sleeveless linen shirtdress, she takes her first steps into the blessed water. "Oh! It's always colder than you think."

After kicking off her flip-flops, Maris wades in. She takes Eva's hand in hers and gives a brief squeeze. In this moment, Maris couldn't be happier. Here she is, living at the beach with her sister close by, and her aunt Elsa about to open a seaside inn only blocks away. Oh, it's true. Life *is* good at the beach. Today, it feels like she's living the dream, that good life.

"Aunt Elsa," Eva calls out, raising her dress hem to keep it out of the gentle waves. "Do you think there's any chance of Kyle and Lauren's vow renewal ceremony ever happening?"

"I know." Maris sloshes through a low wave toward Elsa, too. "What a shame that it was called off. I mean, it breaks my heart that Lauren never even had the chance to walk the beach in that gorgeous wedding dress. It looked so amazing on her."

Elsa squints to the sandy spot where just two days ago, white chairs were set out on the sand for the big event. "When all the dust settles now that Shane's gone, I hope to convince Kyle and Lauren to give the ceremony another go. But we'll let them calm down, first."

"They're at their honeymoon cabin right now." Celia sweeps her baby's feet into the water as she talks. "They're unplugged, with no cell phones. No interruptions. Oh, I hope those two can work things out."

When Aria squeals with laughter as Celia hovers her tiny feet ankle-deep, the others rush over. Something about the baby's pure joy has them *all* cooing, and touching Aria's silky hair peeking out from her sunbonnet, and lightly hugging Celia. Leave it to the innocent child, Maris thinks, to remind them of life's simple pleasures—after a weekend when theirs were all stripped away.

Eva checks her watch then, before stepping out of the water and smoothing the hem of her dress. "I'm showing two cottages later this morning. So it's time for me to get home, ladies."

"Me, too," Maris says, following her onto the sand. "I told Jason I'd be writing all morning. Gosh, it seems ages ago when I set aside my manuscript, and it was only Friday," she adds. "After this crazy weekend, I'm so ready to pick back up with the story."

"I've got your writing nook all set up in the turret," Elsa tells her. "It'll be quiet at the inn today."

Maris nods, then glances out at all those twinkling ocean stars beyond. And what she knows is this: Her life took such a fortunate turn two years ago when dear, sweet Elsa showed up at Stony Point for her wedding. Especially after she and her aunt had been separated for thirty long years. Having Elsa nearby is as good as having her mother here, the mother Maris lost when she was just a child. So Maris is not one to dismiss any good fortune that comes her way. A sunny day spent writing in the inn's turret, then dinner at home later and a quiet evening with her husband? Her life can't get any richer.

"Okay, Aunt Elsa. I'll be there soon. Just let me pack a few things with my laptop. And leave a note for Jason."

"Good, good. I'll put on coffee for us, and we'll have pastry," Elsa tells her with a wink.

"I've got to get going, too," Celia calls out while tucking the baby into her sling. "I'm taking Aria for a quick walk down the beach before her checkup at the pediatrician's."

"Then I'm sure she'll have a nice nap this afternoon," Elsa says, turning toward her granddaughter. "With that warm sea breeze coming through the windows …"

"I'll help organize the inn's linen closet when she's sleeping," Celia adds. "We'll take care of some odds and ends before our grand opening."

"Wonderful." Elsa walks to Celia and leaves a kiss on little Aria's cheek. "You'll stay for supper later? Plenty of vow-renewal leftovers in the fridge."

"I'd love that." Celia hugs Elsa, then waves to Maris and Eva before turning away. Casual in faded denim cutoffs and a blue top, Celia walks down the beach. Small waves splash at her bare feet; wisps of hair fall from her topknot as the warm sun shines on her and her baby.

All Maris hopes while watching Celia is that, yes, it's as easy as that to get life back on track. This weekend, Shane Bradford surprisingly arrived at Stony Point—and it felt like a rogue wave crashed over them. Old memories surfaced. Anxieties hit full force as they grappled to make sense of his presence. Now that Shane's gone again, all Maris wants is for life to be easy once more.

Easy like Celia wading along the water's edge.

As easy as a walk on the beach.

# *three*

---

## *That Same Morning*

THIS IS THE FIRST MONDAY in fifteen years that Shane Bradford is not on the deck of a lobster boat. Not feeling the ocean spray on his skin, the salty breeze in his hair.

First time in fifteen years that he's not wearing his waders, and is instead wearing blue jeans while wading into the calm waters of Long Island Sound. After emptying the boxes and duffels from his pickup truck, *and* dealing with Jason Barlow, he felt it. Felt that urge to be out on the vast sea. What is it they say? Absence makes the heart grow fonder? Today, he's truly missing being on the lobster boat.

So he'd walked to the beach, climbed the granite steps, cuffed his jeans and crossed the sand—passing families setting out sand chairs, and opening umbrellas, and spraying on sunscreen. He tipped his newsboy cap to some, but kept walking right past them all, straight toward the

Sound. Its seawater is about as calm as he's seen since lobstering for more than a decade off the New England coast.

And he's no fool. Days like this, still and placid, are few and far between in his life—on the water and off. So he takes a deep breath of that salt air, feels the sun's warmth on his skin and soaks it all in. Because on any other Monday morning in August, he'd be aboard that lobster boat on the waters of the sea. Somewhere on the Gulf of Maine. Every muscle in his body would be working, going through one string of buoys after another, then another. The routine is so rote, so utterly familiar, he rubs a hand up along an arm—almost feeling the strain in his muscles just thinking about it all.

Just thinking about hauling up the dripping traps on each buoy, removing and measuring the lobsters before tossing some back in and banding the keepers.

Just thinking about rebaiting the emptied traps with sacks of netted herring before stacking the heavy, wet traps again. All while being covered in salty sea spray and fish bait.

Wading in the Sound, he thinks about the boat he's *not* on right now. The offshore wind might be blowing, the sea rolling, the occasional wave washing over the deck, the talk among the boys sparse as they keep the work routine moving at a quick pace. Quick, fast and efficient to get the seafaring job done. Really, Shane's typical days and hours are almost memorized, the way they don't much change.

The thing that changes is the sea itself. And in one way

or another aboard the boat, every day he's got to face down the sea and her moods.

Not today, though.

Today, he's wading and waiting.

Waiting to hear from one person in particular—Lauren—*if* Cliff delivered his letter to her as promised. Shane had done all he could: penned the private note to his sister-in-law, then left it in Cliff's beach-commissioner mailbox for his personal delivery. Now, if only Lauren would read the letter and agree to talk to him.

In the meantime, as a few teens swim out to the raft and as a woman floats past in an inflated tube and as a father tosses his young son off his shoulders and into the water, Shane's life comes down to this.

To wading and waiting. It's all he can do at this point.

~

"Shane?"

He turns when a woman's voice calls his name. And he's surprised when he lifts the brim of his newsboy cap to see Celia approaching. Wearing faded denim shorts with a navy tank top, she's also wading ankle-deep in the Sound. Wisps of her auburn hair fall from a messy bun, and her hand cradles her baby strapped to her chest.

"Celia," he says, walking through the lapping waves toward her. "Good to see you."

"What are you doing here?" Celia asks as he nears.

"You're the second person to ask me that today."

"It's just that, well …" She turns and briefly looks back down the length of the beach. "Elsa said you'd left here. Yesterday."

"I did leave," Shane says, squinting through the bright sunlight.

"And you're back? Did you forget something?"

"No." Shane can't miss how Celia's step slows, her sudden caution apparent. "I left the *inn*," Shane explains. "But I wasn't ready to leave Stony Point yet."

"What do you mean?"

"I'm staying on for the time being."

"Really. Whereabouts?"

"Place down on Sea View Road. Rented a cottage right in the dune grasses. Nice spot. Looks out on Long Island Sound." Stepping to where Celia stands in the shallows, Shane adjusts Aria's sunbonnet. "Good morning to you, too, little one," he says, his finger brushing across her cheek.

"Wait a minute." Celia moves back a step and eyes him closely. "You mean you're staying in the white two-story?"

"No, a few cottages beyond that one."

As Celia tries to pinpoint the cottage, Aria begins squirming in her strap-on baby sling. Her hands reach out and she anxiously coos.

"Oh, my little mermaid wants to go in the water again." Celia lifts the baby from her sling and sits her on a folded arm. "I dipped her feet in the sea to get the blessing of the waters and now she can't get enough of it."

"That's right. The blessing of the waters. Today's the

Feast of the Assumption?"

"It is!" Celia looks over at him as though surprised that he'd know.

"An important day in my line of work. I've seen lobstermen, and plenty of fishermen, jump right off their boats, straight into the sea on this day."

"Really?"

"The ocean's a rowdy place. Risk to life and limb is unsurpassed out there." Shane dips his fingers in the water and vaguely blesses himself. "So today, the boys all hope for some of the waters' blessing on their fishing trips."

"You're telling me they jump right into the ocean?"

"Some do."

"How do you like that …" Celia shifts her hold on Aria and dips the baby's toes in the water. "So," Celia says, looking up at Shane then. "I'm still trying to place your cottage."

"Okay, let's see … It's got a big open porch around back. When you stand there, it feels like you're looking out from the bow of a boat."

"Wait a minute. I think I know the place. It's that shingled one, right? With an old wooden walkway around the side. That … that … little beach bungalow?"

"That's the one." He stands beside Celia, but looks out over the sparkling water. Beyond the big rock, a Jet Ski blows past, leaving a plume of silver spray rising behind it. "Already had a visitor this morning, too."

"Really! Kyle, maybe?" Celia bends and dips the baby's toes again, gently swinging Aria's legs in the cool froth of a breaking wave. "Were you able to reach him, to patch things up?"

"No. Not my brother. Try Jason Barlow."

"Jason?"

"Yep. Seemed mighty agitated about my being here, too."

Celia straightens and positions Aria against her so that the baby faces the blue water. "Well. Didn't you date Maris? Years ago?"

"What?" Shane asks. "Now how would you know about that?"

"Oh, come on. You summered here all your life." With a slight smile, Celia starts to leave, walking backward down the beach. "Surely you know there are no secrets at Stony Point."

"I'm finding that out now, anyway."

Celia stops, the lapping waves splashing at her bare feet. She waits as a young mother and her two children carrying pails and crabbing gear walk past. "But if Jason was agitated, it must be something else," Celia finally says. "Because I doubt he would be tense about his wife's old boyfriend coming into town. Jason and Maris are rock solid, believe me."

When Celia lifts Aria into her sling, Shane steps closer and helps slip the baby's legs through the fabric. They pause then, standing right there, ankle-deep in the sloshing water.

"Nothing," Celia quietly insists, squinting up at Shane while she settles in Aria, "and I mean *nothing*, can break up those two." Slowly walking backward again, she gives a small wave.

Shane watches her leave, tossing one question her way as she goes. "Now that sounds like it's coming from someone who might've tried?" he calls out.

"What?"

He only looks at Celia for a long second, holding back his own smile before finally tipping his cap, turning and wading into the shallows once again.

# *four*

---

JASON SWIRLS THE DREGS OF a shot of whiskey, then downs the liquor. Sitting in his chair in the living room, he can tell Maris just got home. The dog gives it away. Madison runs to the kitchen, and first Jason hears only the German shepherd's feet prancing and clicking on the floor. Moments later, the slider scrapes open and Maris comes inside from the back deck.

"Maddy!" Maris says, laughing as she's apparently setting down packages on the counter. "Easy! I know, I'm excited to see you, too."

Still sitting, Jason only listens. From the sound of Maris' words, the dog must be circling her legs, tail wagging, all happiness at the sight of her.

"Hey, babe!" Maris yells from the kitchen. "I got us dinner."

In the shadowy living room, Jason swirls his now-empty glass. Still saying nothing, he still listens. There's the sound of bags being emptied, containers being set on the counter, keys being dropped in the dish.

"Elsa loaded me up with vow-renewal leftovers," Maris goes on. "Lasagna and chicken parm today. All I have to do is heat everything up."

He hears the refrigerator door being opened.

"I even have salad," Maris' muffled voice calls out as she finds space in the fridge for the food. There's a pause then. Quite a long one before she talks again. "Jason?"

All day he managed to keep Shane's words out of his head: *What are you doing marrying my fiancée?* Jason had two choices as the hours wore on. Either stop by Maris' writing nook at the inn to get to the bottom of this, or say nothing. Just stay so incredibly busy with clients; and working at the Fenwick cottage; and checking out a vintage viewfinder; and designing; and returning CT-TV phone calls, that there was no room in his head for that stinging question. No space for it to sneak in and pester him—just like Shane knew it would, damn it.

And being busy helped.

The question didn't really fester until the work stopped. Until Jason got home and dropped the day's gear on the kitchen table, thumbed through the mail and poured himself a shot of whiskey.

"Jason?" Maris asks again after closing the refrigerator door.

"In here."

21

She pokes her head into the living room. "What are you doing sitting there by your lonesome?"

He still sits and simply watches her waiting for his answer. She's leaning into the room, her brown hair falling forward. Her smile is genuine. She's wearing a sleeveless chambray button-down over shredded black-denim skinnies.

And his wife is as beautiful as ever.

Which is why Jason still can't believe she was ever engaged to that asshole.

"Are you even listening to me?" Maris asks, her voice playful.

"Yes, I'm listening."

"Good." That said, she rushes across the room and kisses him first, then runs her fingers through his hair. "One positive thing about the weekend? The drama."

"Seriously, Maris?"

She nods. "Yes, *seriously*. Because I actually channeled all of that angst right into Neil's story. Got so much written today, I was burning up the keyboard." As she heads back to the kitchen, she calls over her shoulder, "Can you go light the tiki torches? I'll heat up some food and bring dinner outside to the deck."

Still sitting, Jason doesn't get up until she's done opening and closing cabinets, taking out their dishes, fussing. "It's such a nice night," she's saying as he approaches the kitchen. "Maybe we can walk on the beach later."

Jason stops in the doorway while Maris lifts a scoop of lasagna to a pan. He can't help but notice how absolutely upbeat she is. And he supposes that if what Shane said earlier *is* true—that Maris had been engaged to him—she damn well *would* be happy thinking he left. Her secret would be safe that way.

"It's such a relief to get back to normal here, don't you think?" Maris asks as she samples a bite of the cold lasagna at the counter.

"Normal?"

"Sure. Our normal routine. You know. With Shane gone."

Jason walks into the kitchen. Walks in, lifts the foil from another of Elsa's covered plates, then looks at Maris beside him. "He's not."

~

There's a hidden path somewhere down here, along the far end of the beach. Shane looked for it earlier in the day, but couldn't spot it from the water's edge. If he's not mistaken, the path cuts through the dune grasses—which must be keeping its location nicely cloaked. The evening lighting doesn't help, either. It's the twilight hour now. Shadows are long, the breeze light—enough to get those sweeping grasses to whisper softly.

Shane still walks the beach, looking for an opening in the grasses that might give away that secret sandy path. Back in the day, how many times did the gang traipse from the beach, through those tall grasses, to the old Foley's hangout? They probably were the ones who *made* that path.

23

So he knows it leads straight to Elsa's inn now.

More than anyone, Elsa had been most gracious to him these past few days. And he'd like to explain some things to her, especially since Celia probably let on that he's sticking around.

Up ahead, the last-standing cottage on the beach rises on stilts. A few lights are on inside, the windows glowing. After being gone for fifteen years, Shane's glad to see that cottage is still here. It's nothing less than imposing, the way it stands there on the sand after defying every hurricane that's barreled up the Connecticut coast. Though plenty of other beach homes were destroyed, no storm could take this lone structure down. None could send waves to claim it and bring it into the sea. So there's always been something reassuring about the sight of that one cottage. Something awe-inspiring. Maybe even a little badass.

As small waves lap at shore, Shane passes that lone cottage as he keeps an eye out for that darn path that's eluding him this evening.

"Kyle?"

Shane looks up at the cottage's elevated deck to see a woman … probably in her early thirties. She's watching him from where she leans on the deck railing.

"Kyle! It's good to see you."

"Not Kyle," Shane casually answers.

"Oh! Oh, I'm sorry. You look so much like somebody I know."

"I know him, too. Kyle's my older brother."

"You're kidding." This woman walks to the deck stairs

and looks down at him. "Damn. You must be Shane, then."

"Guilty as charged," he admits as she comes down the stairs. She wears a fitted midriff top with frayed denim shorts, all over loosely laced ankle boots. Her hair is sun-bleached, and long bangs sweep her eyes. "Pleased to meet you," Shane tells her as he reaches out for a handshake. "Shane Bradford."

"I'm Carol. Carol Fenwick."

"And how do you know my brother, Carol?"

"Through my architect, Jason Barlow. He's renovating our cottage for his TV show."

"Really now …"

"Yeah. Kyle's a good friend of Jason's, and was kind enough to help out on a personal segment we already filmed." Carol sits on a low step and hangs her hands over her knees. "It'll air later in the season."

"So this is your place?" Shane motions to the grand cottage.

"My family's."

"I always thought of this cottage as king of the beach."

"Lots of people do."

Shane backs up a step and takes in the sight of it. "And now it'll be on a television show?"

"*Castaway Cottage*, on CT-TV. Public TV?"

Shane nods.

"Jason renovated the beach inn here, for the pilot episode," Carol explains.

"Elsa's place?"

"Sure is. That first show was a pretty big deal around

these parts. Did you see it?"

"Carol." Shane looks at her for a moment, then walks closer to the lapping waves and picks up a stone. He joggles it in his hand before skimming it out across the water. "I spend my days at sea, anywhere from a few miles to a hundred miles offshore. TV's not really a part of my life."

"Oh. So you must be in the Navy, then?"

"No. I'm a lobsterman. Work out of Rockport, Maine."

"No kidding." In the dusky light, Carol squints up at him. "Not sure I've ever met a lobsterman before."

"First time for everything," Shane says, picking up another skimming stone from the sand.

"You mentioned going a hundred miles offshore. So you're, like, hard-core into lobstering. I mean, big time."

"Absolutely. It's what I do," he says, turning up his hands. "For many years now."

"That sounds very idealistic, being out on the ocean. Nothing but the wind in your hair, leaving your worries behind." She tips her head, still sizing him up apparently. "But I'm sure you'd tell me otherwise?"

"Well you'd be right, sometimes. Me and lobstering have kind of a love-hate relationship."

"I hear you. Such is life. The good with the bad, it's always the way."

"You say that with a certain conviction?"

Carol nods, then glances down the beach as the sun sets further. "Listen, if you're looking for Kyle, I don't want to keep you. But I haven't seen him around."

"Wasn't looking for Kyle, actually. Was trying to find

the hidden path to Elsa's inn. I stayed there this weekend, and saw it from a window in my room."

"It's back thataway." Carol points over to dune grasses up behind her cottage.

After a glance in that direction, Shane checks his watch. "It's probably a little late for a visit. Think I'll catch her tomorrow." Tossing up his skimming stone and catching it in one clasp, he starts walking back down the beach. "Thanks, Carol. Nice meeting you."

"Same here." Giving an easy wave, she stands and climbs the stairs up to her deck.

A few things catch Shane's eye as he continues toward the boardwalk on the other end of the beach. The cottages up on the hill are illuminated now that the sun's setting. Tall trees in the yards are silhouettes against a darkening sky. Twinkle lights wrap around some of those cottage porches; someone's firing up their grill; decorative solar lights glow in summer gardens.

But something else catches his eye, too. Shane's surprised when he looks back toward the Fenwick cottage, just once. Throwing a glance over his shoulder, he can't miss seeing Carol standing on her deck, her arms leaning on the railing as she watches him still from the shadows.

~

Beneath the twilight-blue sky, Jason pours Lambrusco into both their wine goblets. Surrounding tiki torches cast flickering light on the patio table, where a low candle glimmers. Napkins and silverware are set out. Salt and pepper shakers, too. Across from him, Maris is putting down platters of their heated dinner. The lasagna and chicken parm, a side of meatballs in sauce, rolls and butter—all won't taste as good as they otherwise would have. The meal's tainted, already, by the mere mention of Shane.

"Why didn't you tell me earlier that he was still here?" Maris asks as she sits.

"I was too busy."

"You couldn't make one phone call?"

"Maris." Jason drops a meatball and sauce onto his roll and makes a mini sandwich appetizer. "My day started at the crack of dawn. Remember, I took last Friday off for the vow renewal, so I'm backed up to kingdom come. A design consultation at White Sands. Filming at the Fenwick cottage. Reviewing plans with the contractor there. Off with one of my camera guys to Rick's salvage yard to get footage of a vintage viewfinder. It was too bulky for me to load in my truck, so Rick's delivering it to the Fenwicks some time this week, stacking it on top of my already toppling schedule. And the list goes on. Emails, catching up with Trent at the station … I barely had time to eat a ham sandwich for lunch, never mind talk on the phone."

"Okay, I get it. I'm sorry." Maris sips her wine. "Things are so crazy busy around here these days."

"You know what they say … No rest for the weary."

"Isn't that the truth." Maris scoops up a piece of lasagna. "So where's Shane staying? I was writing at the inn all day and definitely didn't see him there."

"He's not at the inn, sweetheart," Jason tells her as he finishes off his small sandwich. "He's staying at a place here on Sea View Road."

"On *our* street?"

"At the other end. One of those cottages looking right out at Long Island Sound. The one that's kind of run-down."

"You mean," Maris says, "the yellow ranch?"

Jason sips his wine, then reaches for the lasagna. "No, before that one. It's shingled, and pretty weather-beaten."

"Not too many cottages are for rent down there. I can't place it."

"It's got that old walkway made from boardwalk planks, running through some scrubby grasses." He watches her try to picture it as he tastes a mouthful of lasagna. "It's that … that little beach bungalow," he says around the food.

"Oh, the one with the big open porch around back?"

"That's it. And there's a small private beach area just behind it."

"But how do you know Shane's there?" Maris asks while buttering a roll.

"I was driving by this morning on my way to work. Saw him unload his duffel from his truck, then throw it right up onto that porch. Just like Elsa said about how he tosses his duffel onto the lobster boats."

Maris sets down her knife and holds her roll aloft. "Wait. Are you telling me that Eva rented him a cottage without telling me? Because my sister would—"

"Break every realty code in the book before doing that, I know," Jason says, nodding. "So you can relax, I doubt it was her. There's a big *For Rent* sign in the front window. Shane must've seen it and called the owners. Probably rented directly through them."

"Oh, shit," Maris whispers before nibbling at her roll. "Well, this is bad news."

Jason, slicing his fork through a cheese-and-sauce-covered chicken cutlet, glances up at her. As he spears a hunk of the chicken, something nags at him. Maris seems a little *too* bothered by this Shane news. After all, what difference should it make to her if Kyle's estranged brother is in town? None—unless she has something to hide.

"I wonder what he's doing here," Maris says then, setting down her roll and picking up her fork instead. She pokes at the lasagna and takes a small mouthful.

"Don't know. We did have a nice chat, though."

Okay, so there it is. It's why Jason was sure to keep a wary eye on her as he dropped *that* bomb. Because as soon as he did, Maris nearly gagged on her lasagna.

"You talked?" she manages to ask, then clears her throat and reaches for her wine. "I thought you just drove by."

"I did drive by. And I kept driving straight around the block and went back for a second look. Which is when I got out and had a few words with Shane."

"Jesus, Jason," she says, swatting his arm with a napkin. "What'd he say?"

"Not too much. But from the looks of his duffels and

some cardboard boxes, I'd guess he's settling in for a while."

"Oh my God. Did you tell Kyle?"

"No. And you're not telling him, either." Jason scoops up another mouthful of chicken parm. "No one is," he says around the food. "Because Lauren and Kyle are on shaky-enough ground as it is and need time away from here."

When he sits back, Jason looks past Maris. The air is still, and he hears waves sloshing against the bluff. Closer, just past the deck, solar landscape lights illuminate their barn studio off to the side. In the dim lighting, faded red and yellow and blue lobster buoys hang on the dark barnboard walls. Just down the stone steps leading from their deck, a plastic kiddie pool is filled with fresh water. Madison lies in it, her muzzle resting on the edge of the pool. Occasionally the dog snaps at a passing moth, or laps at the water.

Jason can't imagine needing what Kyle and Lauren need: time away from here.

Away from the dewy night lawn; from the old framed seascape paintings inside; from the photographs of Neil, and Neil's leather journals; from the stone bench overlooking the Sound—the bench his father built when he came home from the Vietnam War.

Away from here? Jason thinks that in his life, every answer, every comfort he might ever need, is right on this one patch of coastal land, at his gabled house by the sea.

"Anyway, for all we know," he goes on, reaching for his wineglass, "Shane could be gone by Wednesday. Which is when Kyle and Lauren will be back from their cabin."

Maris dips a hunk of her roll into tomato sauce and drags it around her plate. "I just can't believe this," she says.

Jason sips his wine, saying nothing more. But he's not *noticing* nothing. In the low candlelight and evening shadows, he's noticing that pretty much? Maris is just moving around her food, with little to none actually being eaten. Knowing Shane's back, she's lost her appetite.

"Well," she continues, setting her bread aside. "What did you and Shane even talk about?"

"I was only there for a few minutes. Like I said, we just had some words."

"But about what? Because, I mean, Kyle's not even around."

"We didn't talk about Kyle," Jason lets on as he lifts the bottle of Lambrusco and pours more wine into his glass. "We talked about you."

# *five*

DIDN'T SHE ALWAYS KNOW IT. Something about a certain December night would always come back to haunt Maris. It was the day after Christmas, fifteen years ago. What started as a road trip to Maine turned into so much more. On that cold winter's night, Maris saw how fast and efficiently Shane Bradford actually lived—on the boat and off.

Now all it takes are Jason's four words—*We talked about you*—to bring it all back.

~

*"Don't look." Shane glanced at her from the driver's seat of his pickup as he said it.*

*"I won't." With her mittened hands pressed over her eyes that cold evening, Maris thought of what she'd seen last. That would be barely*

33

*a red glimmer of the setting sun on the horizon.* "How much longer?" she asked Shane.

"A little bit."

*Sitting quietly in the passenger seat, Maris still saw nothing from behind her soft mittens. But she heard. There was the sound of snowflakes tap-tapping the truck's windows. And wind whistled outside, blowing the northern cold right past the pickup. When she suddenly felt the truck slow, and turn, curiosity nearly got the best of her.*

"Now?" she asked.

"No."

"Well, I know we're in Maine. Rockport. I saw the road signs before." *She didn't dare peek and spoil Shane's surprise, though.* "Why can't I look?"

"Shh."

*In the darkness, she heard him lean over, then felt his kiss on the side of her head.*

"Not yet," *he whispered near her ear.* "Any guesses?"

*Well. Being that it was the twenty-sixth of December, all Maris could think of was Christmas. And winter. And snow.* "Taking me on a sleigh ride?" *she asked, keeping her eyes covered.*

"No. Guess again."

"Hmm. I saw that lighthouse earlier, the one with Christmas lights on it. Touring the lighthouse on the bluff?"

*Shane hesitated for a long moment. In that pause, Maris heard the truck's tires humming over the pavement. But still, she didn't look.*

"Nice try," *Shane finally said, his voice low.* "But no lighthouse tours tonight."

*As far as Maris was concerned, it didn't matter. Nothing*

34

mattered. Nothing except being with Shane at Christmastime. She could sit in his old beat-up truck all night and just drive. Cruise the roads, and talk, and be together. Even behind her mitten-covered eyes, she felt the magic in that pickup. Yes, after spending a quiet Christmas with her father in Addison the day before, everything— every minute about this day with Shane—felt magical. The snow. The warmth in the truck. The miles passing beneath the tires. The stop at a roadside diner for a hot supper.

But their surprise destination? Nothing prepared her for the sight she saw next.

"Welcome home." Shane stopped the truck, then leaned over and lifted her mittened hands from her face.

It took a second for her vision to adjust. To make out what she was actually seeing outside the windshield, behind swirling snowflakes, and silhouetted against the night. Shane had parked in front of a small, shingled house, his truck headlights shining on the property. The house was so small, some might mistake it for a shack. But it wasn't. It was a home, with a balsam wreath on the door. In the wind, a red velvet ribbon fluttered from that wreath. Curtains hung in the paned windows. And tiny white lights outlined the house against the cold, dark sky.

"Shane! It's so beautiful."

"Not as beautiful as you."

Maris looked over at him, then back to the house. It was difficult to tear her eyes from it. Something about it, and Shane, left her suddenly cautious. She got out of the truck, slowly, and the first thing she noticed was the pungent salt air.

Shane got out, too, pulled on a wool newsboy cap and held her mittened hand in his. They leaned against his truck and took in the simple sight of a silver-shingled house on a snowy night.

"It's so charming," Maris said as she huddled close to him. "Are we staying here overnight? Is that your surprise, that you rented it for a getaway?"

"Not exactly."

"Oh, look! The docks are just past it. I see lobster traps stacked there."

"That's right. Close to work. And it's a nice place for your denim sketching, the way you like, on the docks. The house is near MaineStay, too, where you'll be working."

"Might be working, Shane. Might be. I didn't get the job yet."

"You will. I know you will. You'll be a fashion designer for an up-and-coming outdoor clothing store, and I'll get a lobstering job right here, on these docks. Noah said he knows a few skippers looking for good help." Silently, Shane leaned over and kissed her cold cheek. "So I got us the house." He hitched his head toward the For Sale sign she'd missed before.

"What are you saying?"

Shane nodded to the small, utterly coastal shingled house. "It's ours, Maris."

"What do you mean, ours?"

"Well, it will be. I booked us a room in town because I'm making an offer on it tomorrow. On one condition." He pulled a velvet box from his coat pocket, and in the cold wind, opened it. "If you'll marry me."

Maris reached out and cupped his hand holding the ring box. The ring itself was a sailor's knot. A white-gold sailor's knot, with a diamond in the center. She looked up at him, then back at the ring. And she was crying, too, just like that.

"Start the New Year married to me. We'll elope in January, before you head back to campus."

"That soon?"

He nodded.

"But how would we ever be ready?" she asked, then swiped away a tear with her mittened hand.

"Listen. I love you, Mare. And I've been thinking about this for a long time. Been saving up, too. For the house, the ring." Shane reached out his hand and tipped up her chin. "We can do this."

"Get married? Where? And how?"

"In Connecticut. We'll elope back at home, then move here slowly. A little at a time while you finish up school."

Shane didn't wait for her answer. He took the ring, gently pulled off her mitten and slipped the glimmering sailor's knot on her finger. Of course, it fit perfectly.

But he didn't stop there. He cradled her face, stepped closer, and beneath those swirling snowflakes, beside a frosty harbor, he kissed her. His hands, they pulled her close, cupping her face as he deepened his kiss so that her whole life felt like a swirling snow globe—magical and wondrous and exciting. And oh so familiar, and comforting, in his touch, his words.

"Shane," she managed to whisper into that kiss as she felt she was spinning, too, beneath the swirl of snowflakes and Christmastime and love.

Shane pulled away, lifted the newsboy cap from his head and set it at a jaunty angle on hers. Then, and only then, he stepped back and watched her.

"Yes." Maris looked at the sailor's knot ring on her finger, then at him. "Yes, I'll marry you," she heard herself whisper. Behind him, *snowflakes dusted the shingled house on the harbor. It all seemed like a dream, soft around the edges, easy, good. "And the ring, I love it." She kissed him then. Looped her hands around his waist, stretched up and kissed Shane right there, in front of what would be their new home, their new life in Maine. When she pulled back, then kissed him again, she said it once more between their kisses. "Yes."*

～

"So Shane was telling me the truth?" Jason's asking now.

"Yes," Maris says.

And oh, she feels the heavy weight of that word. It's an entirely different type of *yes* this time. "Yes, Shane and I were engaged. A long, long time ago."

Jason tosses his hands, starts to say something. But then he stops.

"I was a kid, Jason! Young, naïve, and totally caught up in the moment. Shane surprised me—not just with a proposal, but with a little harbor house in Maine." She reaches across the deck table and takes one of Jason's hands in hers. Behind him, tiki torches flicker in the darkness. "But it was a long time ago. And it was nothing."

"Nothing? You were going to marry him."

Maris lets go of his hand and sits back in her chair. "But I didn't."

"Why not?"

Her thoughts swirl, just like on the snowy night Shane proposed. *Why not?* What it came down to was this: Shane was fast. Fast and efficient on the lobster boats, and in life.

38

Fall in love, get engaged, get married, buy a house, settle in, go, go, go. She wasn't ready.

"My father's why not, mostly," Maris says instead. "He convinced me I should wait."

"Your father did? Louis?"

Maris nods.

"Well, I'm sure he had his reasons. Maybe didn't want you isolated out there in Maine."

"Yes and no … I mean, there was a job offer spearheading a new fashion line at MaineStay. They were recruiting designers on campus and tried to bring me on board. But Dad wanted more for me. Though I didn't know it at the time, we *all* know now that my father had given Eva up for adoption. So he wanted the very best for me—the only child he had left. He thought I would be throwing everything away, marrying Shane and working at some start-up in Maine."

Maris stops then, sips her wine and looks at Jason in the night's shadows. His own face is shadowed, his eyes serious, his jaw unshaven. During her pause, though, he says nothing. Not a word. And his silence unnerves her, so she keeps talking. "I didn't see it then, but my father did. My college education, a promising career ahead of me? It would all be lost, living at the docks up north."

"It's lost now, isn't it? With me?"

"What?"

"You quit your denim design career, while married to me."

"Jason, please. Can we not go there tonight? You know

how I feel about finishing Neil's book."

"I do. But it took giving up your fashion design to take that book on. And you know it's always bothered me, the way you just walked away from your denim work—without even talking things over with me first."

"Really, Jason? That was last fall. It's history now. And I thought you understood why I quit. To be closer to family, to be connected. Here."

"Still. You were at the *top*. Director of Women's Denim. Saybrooks gave you their full support. And then you quit."

Maris only nods.

"Didn't quitting seem a little extreme?" Jason presses her. "There was *no* other way to keep close to family, Maris?"

"Maybe there was … I don't know."

"*And* … And you have no real *plans* for the book, once it's done. So aren't things essentially the same now as they might've been with Shane? You threw away your denim design career, living here at the beach."

"No. Yes. I don't know, Jason! You're confusing me." She stands then and leans on the deck railing, her arms crossed in front of her as she faces him. "It was different back then. It felt like I'd lose a career I hadn't even started yet. So I broke up with Shane in college. My senior year."

"Senior year? You were together that long?"

"You knew we were going out, Jason. Back in the day."

"But I didn't realize it was for years." He lifts his fork and spears half a meatball. "And this wasn't some made-up bullshit out of Shane today? You *were* actually, legitimately, engaged?" Jason asks, fork hovering midair.

With regret, Maris closes her eyes. "Yes. Very briefly. One Christmas."

"So you loved him."

"I suppose." She walks to the patio table, turns her chair and sits again. "But do we really know what love is at that age? Come on, I was in my early twenties."

"I danced with you that summer right after you graduated college," Jason says around a mouthful of food. "On Foley's deck, remember? At that last party before the place closed down for good. So that would've been around when you broke up with Shane."

"Kind of." Maris looks out over the yard, toward the bluff. "Shane and I split up right before New Year's," she lets on.

"New Year's? So this engagement, it lasted only a few days?"

Maris stares at him, then nods.

"Okay, fine." Jason drags a roll through the sauce on his plate. "But one question is really gnawing at me, Maris."

"What is it?" she asks.

With the roll in one hand, he watches her closely.

Problem is, Maris knows that look. Nothing, but nothing, will get by it. Not a glimpse away, not a hesitation, not a reluctant hint of a smile, not a quick breath. Nothing. So she holds his gaze. It's the only way he'll believe her answer.

Jason takes his time with the delivery of his question, too. He bites into that sauced roll, and washes it down with a good swig of red wine. Then, and only then, does he ask the words. Quietly, but directly.

"Why didn't you ever tell me?"

And she does it. Does nothing. Doing nothing gives away nothing. So she just looks at him through the night's shadows. Crickets chirp in the yard. There's a slosh of waves breaking out on the bluff. A neighbor's screen door slams. But from her, she simply holds his gaze in hers. The strain of doing so brings hot tears to her eyes.

"No mention?" Jason practically whispers across the patio table. "After all these years you and I are together, it never occurred to you to tell me, even in passing. You know … *There was this time, Jason, when Shane and I*, whatever. I would've understood, Maris."

"Jason," she says right away now. "I was young." She gets up right away, too. Gets up and sneaks a finger to swipe an escaped tear as she walks to the deck railing. She collects herself the best she can in one long moment before turning to him. "And then there was that pact we all made with Kyle. Around that bonfire one night, remember? We all swore not to say Shane's name again. And it just … didn't even matter anymore."

"Didn't matter?" Jason walks to her, and when he does, when he stands, Maddy climbs out of her kiddie pool in the yard. The dog gives a shake that gets the water droplets flying, then lopes up the stone stairs to the deck. But Jason ignores her. Instead, he stands beside Maris. "Listen," he says. "If some ex comes into town, I don't care. We're all adults with pasts here. I've had girlfriends. You were

42

engaged to Scott when you arrived here three years ago. Life happens, I get it." He hooks a finger beneath her chin. "But Shane? *Shane?*" Jason squints through the shadows at her. "He's one of *us*, Maris. And you never told me?"

"Was one of us, Jason." Maris swipes his hand away and returns to her seat. Once there, she looks over at him still standing at the deck railing. "*Was.*"

~

Ever since the motorcycle accident when he felt the impact of his brother's body against him, Jason's been keenly aware of body language. Ten years ago, on a hot summer day, it happened beneath the glare of white sunlight. As a car drove straight into them—and right before the motorcycle spun out from under him—Jason took the force of his brother's weight fully on his back. It was the last he knew of Neil, alive. In that one moment, Neil's heart was still beating, his lungs breathing, his eyes seeing, his ears hearing. His body fully with his brother right before death.

So Jason knows. You can communicate through more than words, after all.

Like right now. On this summer evening, with the salt air warm, and the sea damp settling on the grass and the deck railings, he doesn't need Maris' words. Not on this still night.

Surrounding cottages have their windows open. Every now and then, scraps of neighbors' voices carry. They're friendly in tone, sometimes laughing, familiar with one another. Dinner dishes clatter; silverware clinks on plates. Other decks are illuminated, too, because it's that type of night. Summer's turned by mid-August, and these warm nights don't go to waste around here. Instead, they're held onto as folks linger outdoors beneath the misty starlight.

But right now, in all of that, Jason pays attention to only one thing: his wife's body language. It's telling him more than her words now that her engagement secret's out. The way she gets up from the patio table and sits again, then goes to the deck railing and looks out into the night. Then sits, picks at the food on her plate without actually eating *any* of it. Lifts her wineglass and sets it down. The way she turns her body sideways in her chair, away from him. Tucks her hair behind an ear. Her glances out toward the bluff, right as she says certain phrases.

The problem is, her words counter what her tense, withdrawing body is saying.

Though Maris insists her engagement to Shane was merely a too-young, too-fast story, Jason's not liking what he's seeing.

Hell, even her nightmare the other night was odd, the way she bolted up in bed from a sound sleep, perspiring and winded.

So despite his wife's assurances that her prior engagement to Shane Bradford was nothing, no, Jason's not liking what he's seeing at all.

Not liking some other secret story he's reading between the lines.

# six

---

## Early Tuesday Morning

ONE THING SHANE BRADFORD NEVER counted on was this idle time getting under his skin. No, he'd thought that the *people* here would do that, just fine—if he could ever find them.

But after driving past his brother's house for the second time Tuesday morning, checking to see if Kyle's around, Shane's back at his rented cottage. And still idle, which makes him fidget. So he does what any hardworking lobsterman might do in idle moments. He cleans the deck.

That's right. Grabbing rags and brooms and mops from a small utility closet, Shane works his way through this tired old beach cottage. Grains of sand are swept from the kitchen and living room floors. Sofa pillows are fluffed. Furniture and lamps are dusted, cobwebs brushed out of corners, walls sponge-washed. While wiping out the tacky windowsills, he notices that the windows facing the back porch are foggy with salt. Wind and waves must carry sea spray right up to the glass panes.

Minutes later, though he's standing on the open back porch, he might as well be on a lobster boat. Long Island Sound spreads out just beyond a private beach behind the cottage. The salt air is sharp here, being so close to the seawater. And dragging a soapy squeegee over the cottage's rear windows, it feels like he's cleaning the salty wheelhouse windows aboard ship. Even the glass casings of the few lanterns set on the porch are salt coated, so he polishes those, too.

Because he knows. Those lanterns, which he lit last night and plans to again every night he's here, are beacons for anyone who might show up once the sun sets. Like Lauren, maybe, after reading his letter. Or even Kyle, should he walk by to say a word or two.

Finally, Shane gets the broom and sweeps the porch's painted wood floor. The furniture out here is sparse: a faded white table with mismatched chairs; a couple of weathered crates used as accent tables; a rusted milk can filled with dried beach grasses; a basket of patchwork quilts on an old whitewashed bench. Carefully, he reaches the broom around and beneath it all to clear away any sand windblown from the tiny beach beyond.

But he does something else, too. With each bristled sweep, Shane looks over his shoulder. Let's face it, there's always a chance—however slim—that someone might mosey on by. He scans the sunny beach road, the cottage driveway, the planked walkway. Listens for a footstep there, gritty on the grains of sand. Looks for any sign of a familiar face. Or any shadow of someone walking beside the dune grasses lining the cottage. His brother. An old friend, maybe. Anyone who might sit and talk for a minute or two. Who might make his trip to Stony Point worthwhile.

～～

"After spending the past fifteen years lobstering offshore, I'm not used to this much downtime," Shane tells Elsa when he's pacing her kitchen an hour later.

Once his cottage was shipshape, he'd taken a quick shower, first. Finally, when it seemed a civil enough hour, he walked to the Ocean Star Inn.

"On the boat with the boys, it's go, go, go," Shane says. "The hauler starts up, and we work one string of buoys after the other. Done hauling up and rebaiting one string, on to the next, checking hundreds of traps a day. Lobsters measured, kept, tossed, bait bags filled, traps set, more traps lifted." He stops pacing only to take a fresh cup of coffee Elsa hands him. "So I'm not used to having nothing to do." Sipping the hot brew, he glances out her large garden window surrounded by tiny red herb pots. "At the very least," he says, turning to Elsa as she brings her own coffee to the marble kitchen island, "I thought I might've talked to my brother by now. Or maybe Lauren."

"Well I'm glad you stopped by, Shane," Elsa tells him as she sits and sets down her coffee cup. A few copper pots and a bottle of Worcestershire sauce are arranged on a towel on the island, too. "Celia mentioned you were still here, and I must say I was surprised."

"I knew you would be." Shane takes a long breath and brings his coffee over. "Elsa, you've been nothing but gracious and accepting of my being here. So I wanted to return the courtesy and explain why I'm sticking around. Especially after all you've done for me."

Elsa says nothing while picking up a damp cloth and pouring some of the Worcestershire sauce on it.

"Cooking something there?" Shane asks.

"Oh, no. Cleaning my copper pots." She holds up a tarnished pot. "Worcestershire sauce restores their shine." As she resumes rubbing the damp rag on the pot, she adds, "It's something your brother told me. Another of his trivia facts."

"Huh," Shane says, standing and sipping his coffee. "Sounds like something Kyle'd pull out of his hat."

Elsa nods and, while polishing, manages to nudge a plate of sliced cake Shane's way.

So Shane finally does it. He just sits. Pulls out a stool next to Elsa and sits his anxious bones down. "I'm renting a cottage over on Sea View," he quietly explains.

"Oh! Close by."

"It is," Shane says while eyeing that slice of cake. And he's no fool; he knows exactly what that cake is: wedding cake. It must be left over from his brother's tanked vow renewal ceremony. Shane forks off a frosted hunk and digs in. "I like the cottage," he says around the cake. "Being on its open porch, beneath an overhang, it's like standing in a boat's wheelhouse."

"Wheelhouse?" she asks, rubbing the dark sauce onto one of her tarnished pots.

"It's an enclosure housing the steering wheel on the boat's deck. A sheltered space, protecting whoever's navigating from the wind, sea spray. Waves, even. So when I stand on that back porch and look out on Long Island Sound right there, that's what it feels like. Looking out the big wheelhouse windows to the sea."

"Wait." Elsa sets down the copper pot and squints at him. "I think I know which cottage you're staying at. It has a sandy yard, right? With lots of dune grass around it?"

"It does."

"Yes! It's that … that little beach bungalow, isn't it? The one with a narrow boardwalk going around the side? That leads to a small private beach?"

"That's the one."

"So you're hoping to see your brother, then."

"I am."

"Even after everything that's happened?" Elsa asks, picking up her coffee cup this time. "Not only this weekend, but between you and Kyle in the past, too? Which I'm really in the dark about, so, well …" She sips her coffee, watching him and giving a slight shrug.

"No one's told you the story?" Shane asks. "Nothing about what's kept me and my big brother estranged all these years?"

"No." She lifts her copper pot again and dabs on more sauce. "They've talked circles around it, that's for sure, and then tell me it's a long story for another time."

Shane looks at Elsa beside him.

Elsa, who stopped her busy day to pour him a coffee and chat some.

Elsa, wearing a tie-front blouse with denim capris and sneakers. Her brown hair is pulled back with a rolled bandana as she shines her tarnished copper pots. Shane also can't miss the cleaning gloves and even more rags on the counter. He glances over at them, at the chores she set aside because of his arrival. *Important* chores to prep for a beach inn's grand opening. One unexpected knock at her door, and Elsa dropped everything to welcome him instead.

Elsa, a rare friend from the very get-go.

Shane raises his coffee cup to her in a toast. "After all you've done, Elsa, the least I can do is fill you in somewhat."

"If you're sure," she says, turning a pot and applying Worcestershire sauce to its finish. "I don't want to put my nose where it doesn't belong—"

"You're not. But tell me. What *do* you know?"

"Only that you and your brother had a serious falling-out, fifteen years ago now."

"That's right. It all started after a bad breakup I'd gone through."

"That would be you and Maris?" Elsa asks, looking up from scrubbing a tarnished spot of copper. "Your broken engagement?"

Shane sits back, shaking his head. "Seriously? You know about that, too?"

Elsa sets down the copper pot and raises her coffee cup to his earlier toast. "No secrets at Stony Point, Shane."

"So I've heard." He eats another mouthful of white-frosted cake, then talks more. "It was a terrible year for me, back then. After the breakup, I uprooted my whole life to Maine. Lock, stock, and barrel. Didn't leave a trace of myself behind. Including my attitude, which probably could have been handcuffed and thrown behind bars, the way it was spoiling for a fight." He pauses to fork off another piece of cake. "Because as heartbroken as I was, I buried that beneath my anger. I wanted to get even with something—anything—after Maris and I split. Fortunately, my father actually came to Maine with me."

"Your father?"

"He did. Dad was a widower in his sixties, and I'd been living with him here in Connecticut. You know, while I was seriously saving up to buy a house—*and* a wedding ring. So he witnessed how devastated I was to lose Maris. Still, I was totally surprised that he came with me up north. Was clueless he even *intended* to until the day I packed my pickup to leave, looked back at my old man's house and saw him standing there on the front stoop with a suitcase of his own. Oh, we argued about it the whole way to Maine, but he said he wanted to get me settled. Keep me on the straight and narrow went *unsaid*."

"Your father was worried about you, then." Elsa reaches over and briefly squeezes Shane's hand. "Maybe was afraid you'd get into trouble, carrying all that heartbreak and looking to get even with life."

"I'm sure he was. Like I've told you before, I had a rough time growing up. Maris was my saving grace, and my father damn well knew it. Once she left me, Dad must've thought I'd backpedal to bar brawls, and rowdy trouble, and run-ins with the law. So he got in my truck and came north with me. Ended up staying on in Maine, too. Permanently."

"You mean he never returned home?"

"Only to sell the place, which was already in disrepair. He'd hit hard times after my mother died, and I think he was actually relieved to get rid of the old house, which sold quickly. So yeah, *he* lived with *me* then, in a little shingled house by the harbor that I'd scrimped and saved for, thinking I'd be a newlywed living in it—not a bitter, lonely fisherman."

"Hmm. Life had other plans for you?"

"It did," Shane says. When a seashell wind chime outside clatters in a salty breeze, he gets up and looks out the kitchen window toward the distant beach. The warm air drifting in feels good on his skin. "Dad took care of that harbor house while I was out on one lobster boat or another, for weeks at a time. I got down and dirty on the Atlantic, throwing myself into my work. Which was fine by Dad—it kept me out of jail, right? And he *always* loved the sea, so he'd sweep up around the house, cook a little, and sit on the docks with a few other old salts repairing lobster pots, coiling rope. Even got a part-time job at the local doughnut shop a few mornings a week."

"He stayed busy." As she says it, she raises her Worcestershire-sauce-covered pot and damp rag.

"He did. It was something he'd only dreamt about,

living simple like that, by the sea. So for a little while, he actually had a sweet life, Elsa."

"A little while?"

Shane watches her from the window. "He died—it was very sudden—when I was out on the Atlantic." He tosses up his hands, still feeling the weight of that regret, that sadness. "From then on, everything spiraled in my life."

"Oh, Shane. I'm sorry to hear this. It pains me, because it reminds me of the way my son died."

"Sal."

"Yes. He died suddenly, in surgery."

"Yeah, and you're left reeling. It was a pretty dark time when we lost Dad," Shane continues. "That's when my brother and I fought. Oh, Kyle had his own issues back then, mostly with job insecurity as a union steelworker, building ships. So it was a tense time for him, too. We just couldn't see eye to eye on things, and he ended up blaming me for our father's death. Which is another story."

"That doesn't sound good," Elsa says, picking up a second pot and dabbing sauce on its tarnished surface.

"It wasn't. There's more, but I'm not going to drag you into the muck. Words were said, Elsa, that can never be taken back. So in the heat of an emotional moment, our relationship ended. We both walked away and never looked back."

"In the heat of the moment," Elsa repeats. "Isn't that the worst? No thought, no consideration. Just gut emotions controlling our words."

53

"Absolutely." Shane tips up his coffee cup for the last few drops, then walks to her coffeemaker on the counter. As he's pouring another half cup, he tells her, "Now, fifteen years later, I get an invitation from Lauren. *Completely* out of the blue." He sets down the coffeepot and walks back to the island, where he sits on his stool again. "So here I am, fifteen years older and wiser. But I'm *here*, for God's sake. Be a damn shame not to try and fix things, Elsa." He shakes his head, knowing that after this brief stay, he'll be gone, unreachable, out to sea. "When will I ever get a chance again?"

"Except Kyle's not here."

"What?"

"He and Lauren are trying to keep their marriage together." Elsa shrugs, slightly, with a sad smile. "They unplugged and went to a cabin they'd rented for their second honeymoon."

"I didn't know." Shane drags a finger around the neck of his T-shirt. "And days are going by, wasted."

"How long will you be here?"

"Length of the next lobster outing. Two weeks."

"Oh, don't worry then," Elsa says while pouring more sauce onto her damp rag. "Kyle said he'd be back to work Wednesday."

"Wednesday." Shane looks at his watch. "You mean, *tomorrow*?"

There's a knock at the inn's front door just then. "Mrs. DeLuca?" Cliff Raines' voice calls out from down the hallway.

Elsa stands and sets down her copper pot and rag. "Be right back," she whispers to Shane.

~

Sitting alone in the old Foley's cottage—apparently gutted and renovated by the esteemed Jason Barlow himself—Shane looks around. He takes in the large kitchen with custom cabinetry, that garden window surrounded by mini red herb pots, the professional stainless steel appliances.

But there's more than Jason's touch in here. There's evidence of Elsa. While she's in the hallway talking to Cliff, Shane sees pieces of *her* life. There's a baby's bouncy seat on top of Elsa's grand marble island. Of course, always a seat in the kitchen for her much-loved granddaughter. And there's an old vintage wall clock wrapped in fishing rope. Tomato sauce, from the scent of it, simmers in another copper pot on that substantial stove, and a wooden spoon is on the counter beside it. Shane leans back on his stool and glances into the living room. Over the weekend, he never noticed the lobster buoys in there. Taking his coffee, he walks closer. Several faded and nicked buoys hang on the wall on either side of the fireplace. And above the driftwood mantel? Two old rowboat oars are mounted with decorative ropes.

"How beautiful! What gorgeous hydrangeas," Elsa is saying, still in the hallway with Cliff.

Shane touches one of the fireplace buoys while listening to the talk of some flowers the commissioner brought for Elsa.

"And fresh cut from the best garden around," Cliff says. "Yours."

Footsteps then, as Elsa hurries into the kitchen. Shane turns from the living room mantel and sees her peering out her kitchen window toward her hydrangea bushes.

"Cliff!" Elsa calls out. "You cut *my* flowers? But they were spilling over like, like … well, like an ocean wave!"

"I know." Cliff, sounding distracted, comes into the kitchen behind her. "I thought I was killing two birds with one stone. Wooing you while helping you prune."

"But … but …" Elsa bends to a low cabinet and pulls out a large vase. "But now there's a big *hole* in that bush," she scolds while running the tap water. In a moment, Shane sees her look over her shoulder. "Cliff? What are you doing over there?"

Well, Shane would like to know, too. So he brings his coffee back into the kitchen and sits at the island again.

"I'm looking for that confounded domino of mine," Cliff is saying while bent over a kitchen drawer. "I can't seem to find it, and my luck's all out of sorts now." He rummages through one drawer, then another. His hands shuffle papers, pens, loose cooking utensils.

"That old beat-up thing? Don't you have another?" Elsa asks while filling her vase with water. "Dominoes usually come in sets."

"Not mine. That one lucky domino was my *only* one, and I remember having it when I was here this weekend." Cliff closes one drawer and opens another beside it. "Have you seen it around? It's black, and a little scuffed. Some of the white dots are faded."

"Believe me, I wouldn't have missed it if it were here." Elsa brings her vase to the marble-top island, where she'd set Cliff's cut hydrangeas beside her tarnished pots. "Have you seen it, Shane?" she asks while tucking an escaped strand of hair behind her rolled bandana.

"Shane?" Cliff straightens and whips around. "I thought you left."

"Commissioner," Shane says, nodding to Cliff.

"Oh, Cliff. Haven't you heard?" Elsa asks as she lifts a small branch heavy with blue blossoms. "Shane's staying on longer."

"Is that right?" Cliff looks from Elsa, to Shane sitting at the island.

"Have some unfinished business to tend to," Shane explains.

"Here? You're staying here? At the inn?" Cliff asks while closing the kitchen drawer.

"No," Elsa assures him. "Over on Sea View. He rented a cottage."

"Sea View Road?" Cliff walks over to the island now. He wears khaki pants and a black short-sleeve button-down with a COMMISSIONER patch stitched on the pocket.

"Down on the far end," Elsa says right as Shane hands her another twig of flowers. "That cottage with the pretty open porch on the back."

Cliff looks from Elsa to Shane. "That, that … that little beach bungalow?"

"That's the one." Shane stands then and brings his coffee cup to the sink. "Headed back there now, actually.

Don't want to keep you from your copper-polishing, Elsa. I know you've got an inn to open."

"And I know you've got a relationship to mend."

"Well, not much I can do until my brother's back. Think I'll grab an umbrella I saw at my cottage," Shane tells her. "Sit on the beach this morning and stir up some memories. Been practically two decades since I've done that."

"Elsa." Cliff nudges her shoulder. "Don't you have something for Shane?"

"Oh, that's *right*. I was going to package it up and mail it. Shane, wait just a second." She tucks one last flowered branch into the vase before going into the dining room. When she returns, it's with a Mason jar. "It's your happiness jar."

"That's okay, Elsa." Shane holds up a hand. "Maybe you can use it here."

"No, I have plenty." She sets it on the island top. "And it's Ocean Star Inn policy. *Every* guest—you included—leaves with a happiness jar filled with memories of their stay."

"Wait a sec." Shane takes the jar, then lifts it closer while looking at the sand inside it. "Did you put something in here?" he asks.

"Mm-hmm. Your skipping stone from the other day. The one you said brought back memories of your brother. It was a nice thought. I put a tea-light candle in there, too. Oh, and one more thing," she says, grabbing a paper bag from the counter. "I'm not sure what supplies are in your little beach bungalow, so you might need this."

Shane takes the bag. "What is it?"

"A box of spaghetti. To light the candlewick," Elsa says while nodding to his happiness jar. "And some leftover Italian cookies from the vow renewal. You take them, for a snack."

Shane looks from the jar to Elsa, and gives a quick wink. "Commissioner," he says then, nodding to Cliff before heading down the hallway and leaving the inn. He steps out into the morning sunshine, bag and happiness jar in hand, and walks the quiet beach roads back to his cottage.

# *seven*

MARIS NOTICES THE LAST GRAINS of sand dropping through the pewter hourglass. They get her to quickly wrap up her writing session, typing the final words in the scene …

*Ever since he woke up in this big old cottage today, it's felt like it does when a storm is coming—but it's more than the storm. There's the air, pressing so close that you feel it on your skin, in your breathing. There's the sky darkening, and gray clouds silently building. And that calm before the storm hits. That dead calm.*

*Now, even though gale-force winds coat the windows with sea spray outside, inside that's what it is. Dead calm, tensions close. He stands at the bedroom doorway and looks out toward the staircase. An eerie silence builds among the friends. The mood is dark. The rooms, still.*

"Perfect," Maris says as she saves the file on her laptop. She sits in the tiny fisherman's shack in their backyard. Neil's secret shack that Jason had towed off that desolate beach and brought here on a barge. The shack looks much the same here as it did there. Lobster buoys hang from its weathered shingles. Strips of white paint peel from the window trim. She and Jason even planted ornamental grasses around it, much like the dune grasses on that wild beach.

Inside the shack, hurricane lanterns and Neil's half-burned candles line the shelves. Dusty jars of shells and sea glass are nestled among the lanterns. And sitting by Neil's things this morning, her hands seemed out of control. Words poured from her fingers and onto the computer screen. This new passage will be inserted earlier in the story. It's just what was needed at a pivotal plot twist.

Maris sits back and rereads the pages of new words. Beside the computer, all the sand grains have fallen out of the top bulb in the hourglass. One hour has passed. She's not sure when she's written this many words in a mere sixty minutes. But oh, she knows damn well *what* did it. What brought all those words and thoughts to the story. A pile of Neil's leather journals is stacked on a nearby shelf. A few seagull feathers mark salty pages Maris has been referencing.

But she knows. Neil would, too. It's *not* his notes that inspired her writing—not after the hellish weekend she just had.

No. It's her own worry, and tension, and twisted-up gut that all made it onto the page. If they say to write what you know, Maris just nailed it. Because everything she's feeling matches the characters' torment in the manuscript's boarded-up cottage. So much so that Maris actually jumps when the shack door bangs open, as if a hurricane wind suddenly loosened it on its hinges.

Far from it—but with just as much intensity—her sister sweeps in, all summer-casual in her striped top over cuffed denim shorts and strappy sandals. A leather-wrap bracelet is on her wrist; her star pendant hangs from her neck.

"Yoo-hoo!" Eva calls out, raising a white bag. "Did you forget about me?"

"What?" Maris asks, turning in her seat. "Forget what?"

"Our weekly coffee?" Eva's already set down her bag and is pulling two take-out coffees from a tray.

"Yes, actually." Maris stands and stretches, then joins Eva at the small table near the door. "I've been on such a writing roll, I really did forget."

"Well," Eva says as she lifts a massive, icing-covered cinnamon roll from the bag, "as long as it's because you're writing."

"I am." Maris glances back at her work area surrounded by seaside trinkets. Not much sunlight is making its way through the paned windows, so she props open the shack door with a large piece of driftwood. "I had a really good session just now."

"Excellent. So you're ready for a break then," Eva tells her while peeling the lids off their coffees. "And hey, this might be the last coffee we'll have together before I leave next week. Matt, Taylor and I are off to my parents' condo on Martha's Vineyard."

"That's so nice that Theresa and Ned do that, giving you guys a mini-getaway before Tay begins school." Maris sips from her steaming coffee. "She'll start out well rested."

Eva is dragging a plastic knife through that gooey cinnamon roll, but glances up at Maris, too. "And how about you?" she asks. "*You* look tired today."

"Had a rough night." Maris takes her half of the roll and bites in.

"A rough night? How come?"

"Believe it or not," Maris lets on, plucking a sweet iced finger from her mouth, "Shane Bradford is *still* here."

"What? No way! I thought he left."

"Me, too. Everyone thought so."

"You saw him?" Eva asks as she's sinking her teeth into her pastry.

"No. Jason did. He told me last night that Shane's still around."

"Seriously? *Here?*" Eva lifts her coffee, then sets it back down. "Where?"

"Oh, you'll know the place. It's a cottage further down on Sea View."

"On *your* street?"

"Afraid so. The cottage with its own tiny beach around back, below the retaining wall."

"You mean, the one with that walkway made from boardwalk planks? It goes through some dune grasses?"

Maris nods.

"I can just picture it," Eva says. "That … that … little beach bungalow?"

"Yes! With the open back porch."

"That one's super charming. I always wish the owners

63

would list the cottage with me. I'd have the place rented in a jiffy."

"It's rented, all right. By Shane."

"Wait."

And oh, Maris hears it. She hears exactly where her sister is taking this conversation as Eva leans back in a rickety shack chair and squints at her.

"*Wait*," Eva says again. Her voice drops low now. "You knew this last night and didn't tell me? No text message even? *Nothing?* Maris, Shane is still here. This is big."

"It is," Maris agrees.

"And you didn't let me know yesterday? Okay, sis. What's going on?"

Maris takes a breath while eyeing her sister. Eva's bobbed-and-layered auburn hair has a fresh blonde streak on her long, sideswept bangs. Oh, but they're not swept enough to cover her eyes. Piercing eyes seeing right through Maris' hesitation.

"Fine," Maris relents. "I didn't say anything last night because Jason and I got in a little fight. It seems that he and Shane talked. Apparently, Shane told Jason that I was engaged to him. *And* planned to marry him at one time."

"No."

It's the way Eva says it—drawn out, with dread—that leaves Maris slowly nodding. "And it's not good timing for Jason to learn *that*," Maris tells her. "Between the horrible weekend with Kyle and Lauren's fiasco leaving him exhausted, along with the ten-year anniversary of the accident coming up fast and furious, not to mention his TV show—"

"*Castaway Cottage.*"

"Mm-hmm. Production is going into high gear." Maris shrugs. "And now this?"

Eva leans forward, her voice still low. "What'd Jason say?"

"He was *really* upset, Eva. Not so much about the engagement. But you know, more that I never, ever told him. I kept it secret. So things were tense, and it wasn't a good night for us."

Eva grabs up her coffee and walks to the shack door. She looks out across the yard to Maris and Jason's rambling cottage on the bluff.

From where Maris sits, she can see some of the cottage, too. Sees the stone steps that could use a powerwash. Gritty steps leading to the deck needing some railings replaced. And though Eva's sipping her coffee and looking outside, Maris knows that's not what her sister's *really* doing. No, no, no. Eva's fuming, is what she's doing. She's stacking up her words like ammunition, ready to propel them Jason's way—if only he were here. Instead, Maris gets the full brunt of them.

"Well," Eva finally begins while turning and shoving her now-empty coffee cup into a bag. "Jason Barlow is a grown man and just better handle this and not bother you. The past is the past, and we all have histories. No, he should be *supporting* you because you have so much on *your* shoulders, too. With Neil's book, I mean."

And as they eat the last sweet crumbs of that gooey cinnamon roll; as they wipe off the tabletop and put their crumpled napkins into the take-out bag; as Eva hugs Maris goodbye, she never stops defending her sister. Not for one second.

Even as she leaves. Driving her golf cart down the twig-and-leaf strewn driveway, Eva waggles a finger back at Maris in the yard. "If that Jason doesn't watch it," she warns, "he'll be hearing from his sister-in-law!"

Which only leaves Maris smiling. It feels good knowing that someone always has your back like that. When Maris grabs a tote and her straw cowboy hat, then closes up the little shack door, something else strikes her, though. It's uncanny how Neil's old shack actually resembles Shane's house near the docks in Maine. Neil's shack is much smaller, but the rest of it—the silver shingles and hanging buoys and planked door—has always felt familiar to Maris. Maybe that's why she's so fond of this tiny nautical hideaway.

Standing back and eyeing the shack in her yard, she wonders if Shane was right all those years ago. His harbor home would've made a perfect spot to design clothing lines for MaineStay—an outdoor lifestyle store that has since turned into a huge household name.

For now, though, it's *this* shack that's custom-made for Maris' work. Neil's novel, DRIFTLINE, is absolutely coming together at her hands. Setting her straw hat on her head, she decides to take a walk on the beach. The passage she wrote this morning needs a few visual details. It's obvious Neil based his novel's setting on the last-standing cottage on the sand. So walking the beach, Maris can better gauge the views her characters might've seen from it, right as the storm hits.

# eight

## *That Same Morning*

FOR ONCE, HAVING A JAM-PACKED schedule got Jason *out* of a jam. When Rick called from his architectural salvage yard at the crack of dawn to say he could squeeze in the vintage viewfinder delivery—mission accomplished. That early delivery got Jason out of the house, and out of any more Shane talk with Maris. Quite honestly, enough was said last night to last all day.

"It's a beauty," Rick says now as he adjusts the coin-operated binocular-viewer.

Jason has to agree. From the silver lens-housing-unit to the black pedestal base, the old viewer is in fine condition. It's a small miracle that one of CT-TV's camera guys was available yesterday. He went with Jason to film the find, lost among dusty antiques' and rusted iron fencing and a salvaged marble fireplace outside Rick's warehouse. Nothing like capturing the scene raw on film. The binocular-viewer stood among tarnished-green garden statues, and near a cast stone pediment. Even then, they had to maneuver around a tottering pile of aged bricks, and move aside a stack of wooden shutters—their paint chipped and peeling—just to get to the silver-topped viewer. The footage will be for an early segment of this *Castaway Cottage* reno.

And now the viewer's here, *at* the cottage. What surprised Jason was the viewer's weight: three hundred pounds. He and Rick carried it in pieces to the Fenwicks' deck and reassembled it there. After temporarily mounting it with the installation hardware, they're ready to give it a whirl.

Rick digs a quarter out of his pocket and drops it in the coin slot. "I'll take a quick look before hitting the road. Busy day today."

"Same here," Jason tells him as Rick leans into the eyepiece and swivels the silver top. Jason looks out at Long Island Sound as Rick scans the water. It's a good day for viewing, all sunshine and blue skies, with no mist or fog rolling in this morning.

Rick eventually steps back from the viewer and motions for Jason to have a look, which he does. Quickly. Rick needs to get going and is waiting for the all-clear.

"Awesome," Jason tells him. "What a view."

"Good thing I found it, guy," Rick says while packing up his tools. Jason helps him carry them to the salvage yard delivery truck. "When I stumbled across it with the old garden statues, I knew it had your name on it, Barlow."

It's those kinds of connections that make Jason's job a hell of a lot easier. All it took was one phone call last week to get Rick scouring his treasures in that salvage yard. Now, after waving off Rick and his loaded-up truck, Jason returns to the Fenwicks' deck. Carol's fussing with the vintage viewfinder there.

"Mr. Barlow, this is *so* much fun," she says while panning the beach. Wearing layered tank tops over cropped acid-wash jeans, she slowly swings the viewer around while bending close to the eyepiece.

"Glad you like it. They're hard to come by."

"Really cool," Carol tells him, still looking out. "Could've used this last night," she says then as she steps back from the viewer. "Because get this … I said hi to this guy, thinking it was Kyle on the beach. It really looked like him, but it was Shane. Did you know he was still here?"

"Yes, unfortunately." Jason sits in the shade beneath the patio umbrella. Carol had brought out a few bottled waters for him and Rick, and he cracks one open.

"I thought Shane would've left by now. You know, with the vow renewal called off and all," she says while leaning on the deck railing. "So I was kind of surprised, especially for Kyle."

"Who isn't even aware of the situation."

"Oh, boy." Carol lifts her round, green-tinted sunglasses to the top of her head. "How *is* Kyle? Did he ever make it to the cabin?"

"He did. Thanks for asking." Jason tips up his water for a long swig. "His wife's with him there."

"Well that's good to hear. Hope they work things out."

"Me, too."

Carol gives another brief look through the beach binoculars. "So what's Kyle's brother still doing here, do you know?"

"Raising hell, pretty much," Jason says from his shaded seat. He worked up a sweat assembling that viewfinder and takes another drink of the cold water. "What'd he say to you?"

"Not much." Carol turns and, facing the Sound, rests her arms on the deck railing. "I was right here, like this, and saw him walking by on the beach," she explains over her shoulder. "Said he was looking for the hidden path to the Ocean Star Inn."

"Elsa's place."

"Right. The same lady you told my dad to call."

"She's the one. Elsa survived her inn's reno for the *Castaway Cottage* pilot. So she can give you guys some filming pointers."

"Okay, we'll get on that … Anyway, Shane and I talked for a few minutes, but then he changed his mind about Elsa and went back the way he came." Carol still leans on the railing and vaguely points toward the distant boardwalk.

*Good*, Jason thinks as he downs the rest of his water. *Maybe he'll go back to where he came from, too. Back to Rockport, Maine.* While walking to the viewfinder then, he hears the slider screen scrape open behind him.

"Wasn't expecting you this early, Jason. Just got out of the shower," Mitch Fenwick says as he steps into the sunlight. "What've you got there?"

"Hope you like it." Jason motions to the vintage binocular-viewer. "An authentic coin-operated viewfinder."

"No shit," Mitch says, standing there in wrinkled khakis and a loose, short-sleeve button-down. He drops a beat-up safari-style hat on over his damp hair. "Now that's one damn blast from the past if I ever saw one."

"Also known as beach binoculars." Jason steps aside. "Try it out."

"Don't mind if I do." Mitch tips his safari hat back, inserts a quarter in the viewfinder and leans close, panning Long Island Sound.

"Look. Over there." Jason points to the right, where a few sailboats bob. Further out, the Gull Island Lighthouse rises over the Sound. Mitch lets out a low whistle before giving his daughter, Carol, another turn at the viewer.

"Now that brings back memories." Mitch draws his hand along his scruffy goatee. "After I got tenure as English professor at the college here, I took Kate to meet my family and celebrate in South Carolina. Kate and I? We spent a night or two at Myrtle Beach, and she loved looking out at the sea through one of these." He steps back while considering the vintage viewfinder. "Wouldn't my Kate be smiling now?"

"Yeah, Dad," Carol says, still scanning the beach. "Mom would've got such a kick out of this."

Mitch nods. "I love it, Jason. Where'd you come up with the idea?"

"From a picture in one of my brother's old scrapbooks,

71

actually." Jason thinks of that photograph now. The canvas-bound scrapbook is still on his studio worktable. He'd sat there days ago, beneath the light of his swing-arm lamp, and looked long at the photo. In it, someone he didn't recognize stood beside another coin-operated viewfinder. Jason wondered where, and when, Neil had taken the picture. "Neil had a snapshot of one," he tells Mitch now. "And I liked it."

"No kidding. Nice to have Neil's influence here."

"I always try, Mitch. And these beach binoculars date back to the thirties. They're historical, like your cottage is. So the viewer suits it," Jason explains. "I also have the right connections."

"I like your thinking—and your people," Mitch says, clasping Jason's shoulder before heading to the viewer again. "Hey, I meant to ask you. Have you heard from your friend? Kyle?"

"I did. Carol and I were just talking about him." Jason takes another swig of his bottled water. "I actually brought Kyle's wife to the cabin Saturday night."

"Is that right …" Mitch turns to Jason.

"Yeah. They're unplugging and are together there now."

"*Excellent.*" Mitch gives a last look through the beach binoculars. "Hopefully that cabin will give them clarity, like it did for—"

"Thoreau," Jason finishes. "Yeah, yeah. Heard all about that."

"Please tell Kyle and Lauren that our offer still stands," Carol says from the deck railing. "If they ever reschedule their vow renewal, they're welcome to take pictures right here on our deck."

"You've sure got the perfect backdrop." Jason motions to the Sound glistening behind her. "So will do."

"Kyle's all right, man. My heart just about broke in two for him on Saturday. Really glad he and his wife are at that cabin." Mitch draws a hand along his goateed chin. "All that quiet. The birds singing. Have some downtime together, no one around. Best thing for them."

"Couldn't agree more, Mitch. Maris and I are doing the same thing this weekend, actually," Jason adds while checking his watch. "Going to a chalet in Vermont for a couple of days."

"Really? Special occasion?" Mitch asks.

"Wedding anniversary. Been married two years now."

"Congratulations!" Carol chimes in. "Sounds like a nice trip."

"Tell your wife we're sending our best wishes," Mitch says, tipping his safari hat.

"You bet." Jason checks his dinging cell phone, then drops it back in his pocket. "So I'm busy wrapping up some things this week and wanted to run an idea by you."

Mitch crosses his arms and leans against the deck railing. "Lay it on me."

"Okay. When the Hammer Law lifts after Labor Day, we'll be starting up on your reno, including the expanded deck." Jason turns and takes in the sight of the now-aging deck. "Thought I'd design a custom notch to place that vintage viewer in."

"I like that," Carol says. "Nice for looking out at the water, stargazing at night. No?"

"Absolutely. I approve," Mitch agrees, nodding to Jason. "But how about all the sand from the beach? Will it damage the lenses?"

"No." Jason points out the top part of the viewer. "The binocular component is fully enclosed and protected. And I've got a cover for the entire unit, too. Sand won't be a problem."

"Can we bring it inside before demo begins, though?" Carol asks. "I'd hate to expose it to all the construction mess."

"Definitely." Jason eyes the cottage. "The crew will pack it up and keep it protected." But Jason wouldn't mind a better look himself, now. He checks his pockets, then turns to Mitch. "Got another quarter?"

"Sure. Have at it." Mitch hands him a quarter, then sits with Carol at the table beneath the umbrella.

Just off the deck, small waves lap at the sand, and a crying seagull swoops low as it heads toward the nearby rocky ledge. The sun's rising bright, beating down on the sand. It's definitely going to be a hot one, and the beach is already getting crowded. Jason inserts the quarter into the viewfinder and pans the sand at the water's edge. He's surprised to actually spot Maris walking along the shore. She's barefoot, with her sandals dangling from her fingers. Through the lens, he doesn't miss a detail: the wide leather belt looped around her olive shorts; the black fitted tank top; even her star pendant glimmering on its braided chain.

But he especially can't miss that straw cowboy hat she wears.

Jason looks away for a second and swipes some perspiration from his face before looking again. The thing is, he loves Maris to pieces and hates it when something's wrong between them. Maybe tonight they'll go out for an easy dinner. Hit up a local seafood joint for fried clams, French fries, slaw. And they'll talk more, smooth out yesterday's argument.

When he pans the viewer back to his wife, he sees that she's stopped and is talking to someone beneath a beach umbrella. Someone Jason can't make out. He shifts the viewer left, then a little right, but still can't see who's sitting in the shade of that big umbrella staked in the sand.

Not until that person stands and Jason sees that it's actually Shane Bradford.

Shane, who steps closer to Maris.

Shane, smiling and shaking Maris' hand, before taking *both* her hands in his and turning the whole thing into a close hug.

"See anything interesting?" Mitch calls out from the deck table.

"No." Jason glances back at him, then looks through the lens once more. "Quiet on the beach today."

It's the hat that does it. The straw cowboy hat that gives her away. It's the first thing Shane notices, remembering how Maris wore one just like it years ago. So, sitting in the shade of his beach umbrella, small waves breaking close by, he knows exactly who it is walking down the beach. Exactly who is headed his way.

But he has a minute or two to study her, unnoticed. And the thing is? After nearly marrying Maris—and not laying eyes on her in the fifteen years since she broke off their engagement—he's riveted. She wears olive-green shorts with a leather belt and black tank top. That hat shades her eyes; her brown hair is long and loose. Yes, Maris is as casual and beautiful as ever. The mere sight of her still captivates him, maybe even more so now. Now, there's the mystery of time between them. All those days, and years, are like a curtain that came down and kept them apart, well hidden from the other.

It's odd, too, seeing her like this—right on the beach where they first got together. First fell in love. Because it's hard to believe that now she's someone else. *Somebody* else's, too.

"Maris Carrington," Shane says, standing when she gets closer. "Now there's a sight for sore eyes."

Maris slows her step and gives a small smile. "Shane?" she asks, still walking closer. "Shane Bradford. What's it been, fifteen years?" She sets down her sandals and extends her hand for a shake.

"At least. Wow." He takes her hand, but doesn't stop there. After clasping both her hands in his, he pulls her into a close, but quick, hug. Holding her at arm's length then, he touches the tip of her hat. "And you are still the same."

It's enough, those few words, to set her at ease. To get a light laugh out of her. "Shane," she begins.

"No," he insists, looking her up and down. "You haven't changed." He raises his sunglasses to the top of his head. "And it really threw me, seeing you *here*. At Stony Point."

"I know! It's good to see you too, Shane." She hesitates, adjusting a canvas tote slung over her shoulder. "Really."

"I came for my brother's vow renewal. Too bad it never happened. Would've been nice catching up with you, and the whole gang."

"It's tough," Maris says. "Unfortunately, things kind of fell apart with the ceremony when word got out that you were here."

Her smile this time—a sympathetic smile with a slight shrug—doesn't sit right with him. "You *know* I was asked here, Maris, right?"

Her nod comes quick as she stands there facing him at the water's edge. But there's an awkwardness to their talk now. "I know," she nearly whispers.

"Completely out of the blue, Lauren's invitation was. Surprised the hell out of me. But after reading it," Shane explains, "I came here thinking the weekend would be something else. That folks were good with things. Maybe letting bygones be bygones."

"It's just that … well, there was some missed communication, and …" Maris tips up her straw hat. "But hey, you're here now," she says, touching his arm.

"That I am. And you, too," he says. "So what's the

elusive Maris Carrington been up to for fifteen years?"

"Well, for starters," Maris says with a glance over her shoulder, "it's not Maris Carrington anymore. It's Maris Barlow."

"So I've heard." Shane crosses his arms and slightly leans back. "But I assumed you kept your maiden name for your denim design career?"

"Shane."

When she just stops talking, Shane hesitates. He motions for her to sit on a beach towel set up beside his chair.

"I should probably get …" Maris stops, watching him for a long second before sitting on the towel. She draws her knees up in front of her and looks at him sitting in his sand chair now. "Shane," she says again.

"Thanks," he tells her. "You know. For staying a bit. And talking."

Maris nods. "About my denim work … Well. You'd have no way of knowing, but I left all that behind."

"What?"

"I walked away from it almost a year ago now."

"Jesus, Maris. I'm floored to hear this," he says. And he is. Because though Elsa mentioned *something* about Maris living here, he assumed she still had her hands in the fashion industry. Somehow. It was her first love, denim design. She lived and breathed denim. "You walked away from *all* of it?" he asks.

"My whole fashion career."

"You mean, like, for maternity leave? Did you have a baby?"

"No. No children."

"Wow. Elsa, well … I asked her about you being here, and she was vague." Shane looks out at the Sound, at its waves lapping along the shore. "Back in the day, you were all about fashion design, Maris. You had such plans for your denim work."

"I did, you're right." Maris, sitting in the sun, adjusts her straw hat. "And I did very well. Made it to Director of Women's Denim for Saybrooks, in their Manhattan office. So I lived that dream for many years."

Shane blows out a long breath, because what can he say? Maris' life took some unforeseen turn, obviously. He pauses, shaking his head. "Well … I'm still at it, anyway. Lobstering, you know? Funny, we were going to make it work together, remember? You designing clothing lines for MaineStay, me a lobsterman … But it wasn't enough for you, life on the water." As he says it, he motions to Long Island Sound at their feet. A few vacationers stand knee-deep, drizzling cool water down their arms, or diving in for a quick dip. "You thought I was going to hold you back," he says, turning to her. "And now? Instead of living in New York City, or L.A., you're living *here*?"

"Oh, Shane." Maris sets her cowboy hat on the towel and runs her fingers back through her hair. "How can I explain all those years to you?"

"Not all those years. Just this," he says. "You gave it all up for Jason Barlow?"

With a quick breath, Maris grabs her hat and stands. Her hands fuss with that straw hat, then she tucks her long hair back and sets the hat on her head. "You've been gone a long time, Shane. There's a lot you don't know about us."

"I'm listening."

He says it, but doesn't move. Sitting in the shade of the umbrella, he's still—except for watching Maris come undone. She looks again back in the direction she came from, toward the winding footpath just off the beach.

"Maybe this isn't a good idea," she's saying. "I really can't talk, and have to leave now."

"Married to Jason Barlow and kept on a short leash, too?"

"*What?* No. No way, Shane! It's not like that at all. It's that I'm actually *working*. Here, now. I'm doing research for a book I'm writing." She lifts that cloth tote and slides out a journal halfway.

"Let me see it." Shane holds out his hand. "What are you writing?"

Maris shakes her head and quickly swipes at her face as though she's brushing aside a strand of hair, not brushing aside a sudden tear. "It's not a good time."

Watching her closely, Shane has his doubts about Maris, and the state of her life. Gone is her quick, easy laugh. She's rattled now. Fidgeting. Tucking that hair back. He's not sure what's gotten to her, but something hit a nerve.

"I have to go," Maris says while scooping up her sandals from the sand, then walking back in the direction she came from. Just like that.

So Shane sees it all.

Sees that Maris is so flustered, their talk brought her to

tears. Surprising tears, or she wouldn't hurry off so suddenly. Not only suddenly, but in the wrong direction, too, back the way she came instead of down the length of the beach.

Still sitting in the shade beneath the umbrella, he watches her go. Maris turns then, briefly. Turns and gives a little wave before hurrying off the beach.

# *nine*

---

## *Tuesday Night*

No TRUER WORDS WERE EVER spoken, Kyle thinks, than there's no place like home. Or home, sweet home. Or home is where the heart is. Or heck, maybe the best? Welcome home.

By Tuesday afternoon, he'd seriously felt all of those. He and Lauren had lunch earlier at their cabin in the woods, took a hike around the little lake there, then finally drove home to Stony Point.

Home. Home, sweet home.

Walking through the front door, it felt like months—not three days—had gone by since Saturday. Since their vow renewal fiasco.

But the beauty of it? Their screened front porch facing the bay, and their comfortable living room—all of it felt just plain … normal. Felt like where they were supposed to be again. So it worked. The best thing they did was unplug,

82

from everything, and reconnect. Just the two of them, alone. No phone calls, no text messages or emails. No news flashes, no gossip, no concerned questions.

Just quiet, in a cabin in the woods. Just the sounds of cicadas, and the hoot of a barred owl in the trees. The squeak of the cabin's back door. It all made the hours pass slowly as they sat outside near the firepit; as they heated the food Lauren brought along. As they talked and agreed to get back to their old selves—the couple they were before his brother, Shane, rolled into town.

They talked about Shane, too, during these past few days. Considered the what-ifs and how-abouts. The would've's and could've's. *What if* Shane stayed in Stony Point longer? *How about* if Kyle talked with him? They *could've* had a beer together, at least. *Would've* maybe come to some truce.

But it wasn't to be.

Shane left early Sunday morning, and that was that. For all Kyle knows, his brother is somewhere out on the Atlantic Ocean right now, hauling up lobster traps from the bottom of the sea. Another fifteen years could pass before they cross paths again.

Still, a painful regret lingers from the weekend … from the derailed vow renewal ceremony, to hurting Lauren, to Kyle's embarrassment in front of his friends, to the missed opportunity of talking to his brother. So to clear his head of all that damn regret, Kyle knows just what to do.

Yes, that evening, Kyle has a solution he wants to try, one he read about in a men's health magazine.

He's taking a hot bath.

It's the perfect time. The kids are with Lauren's parents for a few more days, so the house is quiet. His and Lauren's bags are unpacked, they had dinner, and Lauren's busy going through the mail before starting a load of laundry. And they agreed to stay unplugged until tomorrow. It's still just the two of them, resuming their regular life in Stony Point.

So Kyle does it.

In the bathroom Tuesday evening, first he lights an apple-scented candle he found in the linen closet, then runs hot water into the tub. Leaving the light off, he opens the window, too, onto the twilight outside. The sky is dusky, the air only slightly cooler at day's end. While the tub's filling, he takes off his clothes, neatly sets them aside and hangs a soft towel nearby before stepping into the tub. Steam rises around him as he sinks down into the water. The warmth covers first his legs, then his stomach, chest. Slowly he settles in until only his shoulders and head are out. He even brought a tub pillow with him, and now he leans his head back on it, closes his eyes and breathes.

Already he feels his mind unwinding. The steam lifts away his worries. His body relaxes, too. It's so peaceful soaking in the deep tub, he could almost doze off. What a sensation. One so long gone, he'd forgotten what pure relaxation could feel like.

As he relishes his liquid therapy, there's a soft knock on the door.

"Kyle?" Lauren asks from the other side.

"In here," he answers without moving. Without even opening his eyes.

"Are you coming downstairs soon?"

"No."

"But I put on the TV. You wanted to see the weather for tomorrow, when you go back to the diner."

"No. I'm decompressing."

"What?" Lauren slowly opens the bathroom door and peeks inside.

"I read that soaking in a hot bath is good for you," Kyle says with his head resting on the tub pillow. His arms are raised on the sides of the tub, his eyes blissfully closed. "The steam rises around you, and you can feel your stress melting right off into the bathwater."

"But isn't it too hot in there? You're sweating."

"That's the point." Kyle touches his wet fingers to his perspiring forehead. "According to the article I read, that's how you destress. Imagine every tense muscle and thought washing right out with the steam and sweat."

"Oh. Are you eating something, too?" Quiet, then, "An ... *apple*, maybe?"

"That's my scented candle," Kyle calmly answers, still without moving. "The apple aroma is proven to slow heart rates. Ease muscle tension."

Another quiet moment passes before Lauren asks, "Is it working?"

"Absolutely."

"Really?"

From behind his closed eyes, Kyle can tell she hasn't

stepped into the room as she scrutinizes the situation. As she takes in the sight of steam rising around his naked body; inhales the apple scent; hears the tap dripping into the tub water. It's all in her silence, some disbelief of Kyle's hot summer bath.

So he opens his eyes and looks at his wife. The wife he didn't know if he'd even still have after this godawful weekend. Lauren stands in the doorway, barefoot, wearing black frayed shorts and only a sleeveless buttoned denim vest for a top. The vest is short, exposing her midriff. Wire bracelets hang on her wrist. A lone robin chirrups outside the window. Steam covers the mirror on the wall.

"So you're telling me soaking like that lowers your blood pressure," she says, still in the doorway.

"Want to try for yourself?" Kyle asks.

"Now?"

"If you're feeling a little tense, works wonders." Kyle lifts his hand then, motioning her closer.

"You mean …"

"There's room for two in this big old tub." He hitches his head. "Come on, Ell."

Lauren only looks at him. Well, at first. Then? Then she smiles, slowly.

Smiles as she steps into the bathroom and starts unbuttoning that vest while softly closing the door behind her.

# *ten*

Nothing.

Maris said nothing about talking to Shane. Jason can't get that thought out of his head. She said nothing to him all last night. Not during their dinner out, over fried clams, coleslaw and onion rings. Not when they sat on their deck afterward with a glass of wine, waves breaking on the bluff. Not when they watched some TV program or another.

His wife said not one word about her encounter with Shane Bradford on the beach. That silence serves a purpose, Jason supposes. By saying nothing, she's got nothing to deny. No words to trip up on. No lies to tell. No questions to answer.

And he has plenty of those. Hell, after watching through the coin-operated viewfinder as his wife talked with Shane, that's all that's on Jason's mind. Questions.

But from Maris' mouth? Nothing. Lord knows, Jason

gave her every opportunity last night, every lead-in. He asked about her day. About her writing. If there were any story parallels to their real lives in whatever passage she worked on.

God damn it, he'd asked her if she took a walk on the beach.

And … nothing.

Even after his shower today, when he stood in the bedroom and buttoned his checked short-sleeve shirt, Maris was quiet at her dresser. She fussed with her earrings, threw him a quick smile when she caught his eye in the mirror reflection. When she crossed the room then, Jason thought, *Maybe*. Maybe she's about to tell him. But, no. Instead she crouched and rolled a narrow cuff on his khaki pants. That's it. Stood then, kissed his cheek and told him to have a nice day.

It all still bothers him when he sits at the Dockside Diner counter before work, waiting for Kyle. Most of the red-cushioned stools around him are filled. Some customers are texting while eating; the guy beside him scoops his buttered toast through a sunny-side-up egg; a woman on the other side reads a folded newspaper page while dragging a pancake through maple syrup.

But no Kyle in sight. It's obvious he knew Jason was coming, though. Jason's regular counter spot near the glass pastry case was reserved with a cinnamon cruller and hot coffee set there.

Still, Jason doesn't take a bite, or a sip. Sitting with his chin on his clasped hands, his thumb runs across his jawline, over the faded scar there. Even two days of unshaven whiskers can't hide it. He's sure that if Kyle sauntered out right about now, he'd tell Jason it looks like he's stewing.

Well, he is. He's stewing, *and* mad at how clueless he is. Of *course* Maris kept herself holed up in the shack last night. After their glass of wine, she said she wanted to finish writing a page or two before going to sleep. But now Jason realizes it was something else.

She was hiding out the rest of the evening.

Maris hid from him. Jason's damn sure of it. If she knew he was still up watching TV when she finally rolled into the kitchen, she'd no doubt have holed up in the shack even longer. Anything to avoid talking about Shane.

Still waiting for Kyle, Jason leans over for a glimpse into the kitchen. His friend must be busy cooking up breakfasts at the big stove. Jason drags a knuckle down his jaw again, then glances back at the diner tables and red-padded booths, most of them full. Weathered buoys—red, yellow and blue—hang from the ceiling like pendant lights. A fishing net laced with starfish and seashells is draped on the wall near Lauren's painted driftwood display.

All the while, Jason knows one thing for certain. Whatever went down between Maris and Shane on the beach yesterday morning, it was bad enough for Maris to act like it never happened.

So it's working. Shane's getting under all their skin.

And now? Now Shane's about to get under Kyle's.

Jason stands, takes his coffee and cruller and walks

around the crowded counter toward the kitchen. He stops in the doorway and sees Kyle at the stoves. He's a big guy, wearing black pants and a black tee beneath his neatly pressed white apron. Shelves over his stove are stacked with gleaming white dishes. Eggs and flapjacks and hash browns cover his griddle. The few days away with Lauren must've gone well because Kyle's also whistling. So he's feeling all right about his life today.

But his whistling also means Kyle has no idea that his brother is still in town. How could he? Kyle's been unplugged and oblivious at that cabin in the woods.

Damn it. From where Jason stands, all six-feet-two-inches of Kyle is happily working—spatula in hand, flipping and scraping, lifting those eggs and pancakes and sausages, snatching and buttering whole-wheat toast, loading up plates for the waitresses. And yep, whistling the entire time. Distractedly, but still. He's whistling.

Which is about to stop.

Standing there, Jason dunks a piece of cruller in his coffee and dreads what's coming. With his next few sentences, there's no way around it. He's about to totally ruin Kyle's first day back.

Kyle's glad to be back. Back to nonstop orders delivered by his waitresses. He's got a half-dozen eggs sizzling to the left on his griddle; four slices of bread toasting beside them; bacon cooking beneath the cast-iron grill press. He just finished adding scallions and pepper to grated potatoes, and has a mountain of those cooking on the right. With his spatula, he divvies up a few servings of the hash browns. And the orders keep coming.

So does his whistling. Busy is good. Routine is good. Especially now that things are chill again with him and Lauren.

"Hey, Bradford," a familiar voice calls out behind him.

Managing a quick glance over his shoulder, Kyle spots Jason leaning in the doorway.

"You coming out?" Jason asks. "Take five? Bullshit for a minute?"

"Can't. Shorthanded." Kyle slides his spatula beneath a couple of eggs and flips them. "Just me and Rob cooking today. Jerry's got the rest of the week off."

"Fine. I'll have my coffee right here."

In a quiet moment when Jason must be sipping that hot coffee, Kyle manages to fill two plates with breakfast orders, set them on the shelf and ring the bell for pickup.

"So how you doing?" Jason asks from behind him. "Weekend go okay?"

"I made it, let's put it that way." Kyle talks while never taking his eyes off the stove. Eggs, bacon, pancake batter poured into flapjacks along the top. "Hell, did the weekend even happen? Because being back here working my ass off, it feels like nothing ever went down."

"Oh, it did," Jason assures him around a hunk of dripping cruller he must've just stuffed into his mouth.

"Yeah. What a bitchin' piece of shit Saturday was," Kyle

tells him over his shoulder.

"You and Lauren all right now?" A second of coffee-sipping, then, "Staying put in that marriage of yours?"

"So long as she'll have me. Christ, Barlow, you know she had my best interests at heart with that invite to my bro, right?"

"Of course she did."

Kyle presses his arm to his forehead, then grabs the wooden handle of the grill press and uncovers the bacon. "Good to go," he whispers, sliding the spatula beneath the bacon slices and dropping them on two waiting plates. "So," he says, spatula in hand as he half turns to Jason. "Ell's stocking up on groceries today, picking up the kids Friday." Kyle checks his watch. "Poor kids, man."

"Why's that? Aren't they with your in-laws?"

"Yeah, but *damn*. They wanted to have a good time last Saturday." Kyle drags his spatula across the stovetop. After wiping away some grease, he cracks open two eggs on the hot griddle. "They practiced old-school dance moves with me for the past month. Little bit of the Batusi," he says, setting down the spatula and turning. His fingers on both hands form a horizontal V. Then he gives a jivin' sway while pulling his V'd fingers over his eyes.

"Oh, man. You're killing me, Bradford," Jason tells him.

"That's not the half of it." Kyle checks the eggs and flips the pancakes. "You should've seen my kids do the Twist, the Swim. Hailey-copter *loved* that one." In full chef apron, Kyle holds his nose and shimmies down in a cannonball move—waving his other arm as he does. When he comes up for air, he tells Jason, "And ... the dancing was detonated." Kyle turns back to his eggs and pancakes and hash browns, leaving the dancing for another life, maybe. "Ev and Hay just wanted to party with the 'rents, you know? Groove to that jukebox in the old Foley's back room," he calls over his shoulder. "Too bad," he says, more to himself now as the whole thought of his let-down kids saddens him. He scoops the pancakes onto a dish and adds a couple of sausage links.

"So what are you saying?" Jason asks. He moves aside to let a waitress pass by. "You should've *had* the ceremony?"

"No. Not with my brother showing up. Wasn't prepared for that," Kyle says while turning the order carousel. He quickly whisks a few eggs and pours the mixture on his griddle, then scoops it into a low mound once the eggs begin to set. "Had a tough time dealing with the surprise and all. Didn't handle it too well."

"You think maybe you *should've* talked to Shane?"

Kyle glances over at Jason just as he dunks a piece of cruller into his coffee mug. "Maybe," Kyle tells him, then grabs a rag and swipes spattered grease off the front of his stove. "After listening to Lauren's reasoning, what the hell. Would it have killed me to hear what he had to say?" Kyle asks, pressing the scrambled eggs with the spatula. "But Shane's gone now, and I'm not about to make a five-hour drive to Maine to hear him out."

Grabbing a half-dozen bacon slices and dropping them onto the griddle, Kyle can't miss that Jason's silent behind him. Not saying a word. Not until Kyle scoops a serving of warmed hash browns onto a plate and adds an over-easy egg.

"You don't have to drive five hours. It'd be more like a five-*minute* trip," Jason says, his voice low behind him. "Shane's still here."

"What?" Kyle turns around, spatula in hand.

Jason presses the last of his cruller into his mouth before moving aside for a waitress again. "Your brother's staying at a cottage," he tells Kyle. "At Stony Point."

When Kyle catches the scent of burning food, he spins back to the stove, scrapes off a scorched serving of scrambled eggs and dumps it in the trash. "You shitting me?" he calls over his shoulder, then presses his arm to his damp forehead again.

"No, I'm not. I saw him Monday morning and we talked. I even asked him to leave, Kyle. But … no go. Obstinate as ever."

And just like that, it's all too much.

The food sizzling. And burning.

The dishes clattering.

The waitresses carrying platters high on their shoulders while calling out *Heads up* and *Coming through*.

The hum of customers' voices in the diner.

Rob scraping the other stovetop, and mixing some concoction in a small pot—his spoon banging against the pot sides.

The dish that slips from Kyle's hand and shatters on the floor at his feet. He grabs the kitchen broom, quickly sweeps up the mess, clears the burning and smoking eggs from his stove, and finally turns to Jason.

And just stops. Starts to say a few words, then stops and takes a breath while dragging a hand through his hair. "I got to grab something," Kyle says while wiping his hands on his apron front and hurrying off. "From the freezer."

~

Which is exactly where Jason finds him two minutes later—standing in the walk-in freezer. Catches Kyle bent in half, hands on his knees, inhaling as though the air can't get in and he's about to drop of a heart attack.

"Shit," Kyle says, hands still on his knees as he looks up at Jason. "Shit, shit, shit."

"I know, man." Jason steps into the frosty space. "You okay?"

"Overheating, big time." Kyle straightens and drags a finger around the collar of his sweaty black tee. Hell, all that decompressing in the tub last night? Undone in a minute, flat. "Just need to cool down."

"In your freezer?"

"It works," Kyle says, moving past Jason and heading toward the rear delivery door. "Yo, Rob! Cover for me," he calls out. "Going outside for a minute. I need a smoke."

"No, man." Jason catches up and grabs Kyle's arm. "You've got to quit those things. And I have to leave, anyway."

Kyle peels off his apron and stops near the rear exit. He tosses his apron on a wall hook before pushing the metal door open. "Either you're having a smoke with me or I'll smoke alone."

"I'm really busy," Jason says when he walks outside behind Kyle. "Got a full schedule and have to hit the road. I just wanted to let you know Shane's around. Break it to you easy."

Kyle walks to the side of the diner to check on the patio area, which is also standing room only. Each table's umbrella is opened against the summer sun, and each chair is filled. On every table, wire jam racks are stuffed with foil packages of strawberry and raspberry jellies. Maple syrup dispensers are also set out. A waitress carries a loaded tray. Copper and bamboo tiki torches are unlit until late afternoon, when their flames draw patrons for outdoor diner cuisine.

For now, the only thing lit is the cigarette Kyle places between his lips. He returns to the shady rear of the building and leans against it. "So what's my brother want this time?" he asks through a cloud of smoke.

"Don't know," Jason admits. "If he wants to see you, guess he knows where to find you."

Kyle hands Jason the cigarette pack. "Take one. For the road," he says as Jason grabs the pack. He watches Jason pull out a smoke and slip it in his shirt pocket. That's when Kyle also notices how casual Barlow's dressed in this heat: short-sleeve checked oxford loose over canvas khakis, rolled at the hem. Old leather boat shoes finish the look. "Nice threads, dude. Where you headed, anyway?"

"New project at White Sands."

"Oh." Kyle takes a drag of his cigarette, thinking of nothing but Shane, but not letting on to Jason. "Close by, so that's good. Keep you around home."

Jason nods, then crumples Kyle's pack of cigarettes and tosses them in a dumpster.

"Hey, *hey*." Kyle turns up his hands at him.

"Come on, man. We quit these two times already. One last smoke in my truck and I'm done. Not going down that rabbit hole with you again."

"Suit yourself." Kyle glances up at the glaring sun, then fans his damp T-shirt fabric over his chest. Squinting through the cigarette smoke, he takes another long drag. "Hey," he says, flicking Jason's shoulder. "So what's the job you're doing? For your TV show?"

"No." Jason pulls his keys from his pocket. "This one's my own. A full reno. Total gut in a shotgun-style cottage."

"A what? Shotgun? What's that?"

"You never heard of a shotgun cottage?" Jason jangles his keys and takes a step toward the parking lot. "Shotgun. They're narrow cottages, and the rooms are all lined up one behind the other. In a row. Legend has it if you stand at the front door and shoot a gun into the cottage, the bullet has a clean shot. It'll go straight through each room's doorway, then right out the back door, no problem."

"Shotgun. I get it."

"Yeah. Bullet blows through the house, front to back."

Kyle drops his burning cigarette butt on the pavement and stamps it out. "Just let me get Shane to stand in the backyard before you pull the trigger."

# *eleven*

## Wednesday Morning

IF A MOVIE PRODUCTION COMPANY were to film a day in the life of Celia Gray, she'd want these noises to comprise the opening soundtrack. Celia pushes Aria's stroller onto Bayside Road and listens to the first sound— stroller tires gritty on the sandy pavement. And there are the bees, buzzing lazily over marigolds and potted geraniums. And her flip-flops, yes. Flipping and flopping softly, keeping beat with stroller tires rolling along. The sounds set her so at ease. The director could call, *And … Action!* about a block before her destination. Wearing her long sundress, Celia would take several steps before turning into Lauren's yard, so that you'd get the full sound effect.

The problem, Celia knows, is that her day is about to change once Lauren catches sight of her. So on second thought, this *isn't* the day-in-the-life Celia would want filmed. Not a day when she's about to deliver really bad news to her beach friend.

"Hey, Cee," Lauren calls out. The front porch screen door flies open and Lauren, wearing a fitted black tee and distressed Bermuda shorts, runs barefoot across the lawn. "I *thought* that was you. I saw you through the window."

"Lauren." Celia wheels the stroller over the dried-out grass. "I'm so glad you're home!"

"Me, too," Lauren tells her as she sweeps her up in a hug, then steps back, all smiles.

"It's nice to see you happy again," Celia says before she unstraps the baby from the stroller. "How are you? Things are okay?" she asks over her shoulder.

"Better, anyway. I'm doing better." Lauren picks up the stroller and walks toward the house. "I'm also unpacking a week's worth of groceries in the kitchen. Come on in and keep me company," she tells Celia behind her, then stops suddenly. "And hi there, my sweet little godchild!" she says, leaning close to kiss the baby's cheek.

"Your kids aren't around?" Celia asks.

"No. Not yet." Motioning for Celia to follow her, Lauren carries the empty stroller inside onto the porch and through the living room. "I'm picking them up Friday." In the kitchen, assorted paper and plastic bags cover the table, the counters, and are stacked on the floor. After setting the stroller to the side, Lauren pulls margarine from one of those bags and puts it in the fridge. "My parents are taking them berry picking today."

"You're lucky your mom and dad could watch Evan and

Hailey this week," Celia tells her as she sits at the table with Aria in her lap.

"They've been *so* helpful, taking the kids mini-golfing. And to a museum." Lauren looks back at Celia from the refrigerator. "Effectively keeping them distracted from *everything* that went wrong."

"Speaking of which … How'd it go in Addison? Is Kyle feeling better now, too?"

"He's all right. Decompressed a little and is back at the diner today."

"So you worked things out at the cabin, then?"

Lauren nods while reaching into a brown bag. "We're getting there. It was awkward, at first. After all that intense buildup to the vow renewal, it felt like hitting a brick wall when it didn't happen." She opens a high cabinet and lines a few cans on the shelf. "But we talked it out," she's saying as she pulls more cans from the bag, then stretches up to that shelf again. "Hiked in the woods. Sat by that pretty little lake."

"Well," Celia says while stroking a strand of Aria's hair. "I'm just glad you're still together."

"So am I." Lauren folds the empty bag, sets it aside and pulls two yogurt containers out of another. "Did we miss anything here?" she asks.

"Miss anything?" Celia bounces the baby on her lap and hesitates. "That's actually why I stopped by …"

"Oh, no." Lauren glances over her shoulder. "This doesn't sound good."

"Wait. Because it *could* be good. But … brace yourself."
"What now?"

"Shane's still here," Celia says.

"*What?* At the inn?"

Celia shakes her head. "At a cottage over on Sea View."

"You mean, *Eva* rented him a cottage?" Lauren asks, slowly taking the two yogurts to the refrigerator.

"No. No, I think the owners had a sign in the window. You know. *For Rent*, with their phone number. Shane must've called them directly and made arrangements." Celia lifts Aria to her shoulder. "I just walked by the cottage. It's that one in the dune grasses overlooking the Sound. Silver shingles? Pretty cream trim?"

"You mean the cottage with the open porch facing the water?" Lauren squints over at her. "That … that little beach bungalow?"

"That's the one."

"No way! But why's he here?" Lauren closes the refrigerator. "Everything's done. And I thought he left to get on the next lobster boat."

There's more Celia can say. Like how she bumped into Shane on the beach Monday morning. In those few minutes at the water's edge—in those few words, few looks—she learned a lot. But before she can begin to explain, a loud knock at the front door interrupts them. Reaching into a bag, Lauren looks over at Celia.

"Do you think that could be *Shane*?" Celia whispers.

"Hang on," Lauren says while hurrying out of the room. "I'll go find out."

"Well?" Celia asks several minutes later. She's circling the kitchen while lightly bouncing Aria on her shoulder. "I heard voices. Was it Shane?"

"No." A few blonde wisps escape from Lauren's topknot as she walks back into the kitchen and drops into a chair. "It was Cliff, believe it or not."

"Cliff? What did he want?" As she asks, Celia walks her drowsy baby to the open window. She can tell by Aria's relaxed weight that she's falling asleep in the summer warmth.

"Cliff was actually delivering a letter. *From* Shane."

"You're kidding!"

Lauren fans herself with the envelope for a moment before tearing it open. "I'm afraid to read this," she says while pulling out a sheet of neatly creased stationery. "Kyle and I worked through so much these past few days. And now a letter? It feels like it can undo it all." She holds the paper out to Celia. "Here. You read it."

Celia pauses, then gently sets her sleeping baby in the stroller before taking the letter. After unfolding it, she slowly sits while silently reading Shane's words.

*Dear Lauren,*

*It's Shane. I really wanted to reach out to you in person, but hope you'll accept this for the time being.*

*First of all, let me just say thank you. Hear me out. I know your vow renewal day didn't come together with Kyle,*

102

*and you're probably getting a lot of flak for inviting me. But do know that I'm grateful you did, because my brother's been on my mind lately. And now that I'm here, it would be a shame not to get the chance to talk …*

*I'll be sticking around Stony Point for the next two weeks. So when you get this, could you stop by my place? It's the shingled bungalow over on Sea View. Cottage named This Will Do.*

*Would like to speak with you alone first. Whenever it's good for you, I'm here.*

*Shane*

"Well?" Lauren asks.

Celia only looks at her across the kitchen table, past several still-stuffed grocery bags.

"What does he want, Cee?"

"Looks like this isn't done yet." Celia folds the note—which she recognizes as vintage stationery from the Ocean Star Inn—and hands it to Lauren. "He wants to see you."

Lauren takes the letter, saying nothing. And Celia can figure why. What can Lauren say when she suspects whatever words Shane penned will change everything? So Celia watches as Lauren's eyes drop to the folded piece of paper. Watches as her fingers turn it over once, then again, before opening it. Watches as Lauren skims the words, reading so fast she has to backtrack and whisper random

103

lines aloud. *I'm grateful … chance to talk … stop by my place … whenever it's good for you.*

"Right," Lauren says. "As if there'd ever be a good time."

"Now is."

"What?"

"You have to talk to him, Lauren. You *invited* Shane here, and the poor guy needs to hear your story."

"Wait. What do you mean, *poor guy*?"

"Come on. Shane made the trip to Stony Point, *invited*, and everyone turned on him. In my book, that's pretty lousy."

"Okay, fine. I get that." Lauren holds up the letter. "But I'm not sure about *this*. I thought everything was all done, and we moved on when Elsa said Shane left."

"She didn't know he left the inn to stay at a cottage."

"Still. Life got easy again, even just *thinking* Shane headed back to Maine and the Atlantic Ocean." Lauren looks at the letter. "Kyle and I worked things out. Oh, he would kill me if I went behind his back—*again!*—and talked to his brother. And anyway, when would I ever—"

"I told you. *Now.*"

"Get real, Celia," Lauren says, sweeping a hand to the bags covering every surface of her kitchen.

"No, wait. Listen." Celia takes a quick breath. "I talked to Shane this weekend."

"Kyle mentioned that you did, when he came back to the cabin after Elsa's dinner. He said you and Shane talked when you cleared the flowers out of the rowboat?"

"It's true, we did. Shane was walking by, and stopped when he saw me there."

"And how'd he seem?" Lauren cautiously asks. "Because I was surprised to hear you went *out* in that rowboat afterward."

Celia looks long at Lauren. Everyone here has been circling around the topic of Shane in a way Celia just doesn't get. "You know," she finally says, "someone had to give the guy a chance, Lauren. So I did. And he was fine. I mean, let's put it this way. I talked to Shane enough to know if I got a bad vibe. Which I *didn't*. And now I'm telling you as your friend that I really think you should go and clear the air with him."

"But I have three hundred dollars' worth of groceries to put away."

"No. *I* have three hundred dollars' worth of groceries to put away." When Lauren opens her mouth, Celia abruptly raises her hand, saying, "Listen. Shane's there *right now*. I walked by and saw his truck." What she doesn't say is that she also heard his harmonica. The sound of it drifted on the summer air, a slow and melancholy tune. "You set this all in motion with your invitation, and *have* to see it through. Go now, and I'll put away your food so it doesn't spoil."

Lauren stands, fills a glass with cold tap water and takes a long drink. When she's done, she checks her watch, glances at her utterly casual black V-neck tee and ripped denim shorts, fiddles with her sterling-silver spoon bracelet, and finally, *finally* meets Celia's eye again.

"Come on," Celia quietly says. "Kyle's at work. Your

kids are at your parents'. Aria's asleep. So *go*. Take an hour." Standing, Celia gently wheels the stroller holding sleeping Aria to the hushed living room. "I'll put your food away and lock up when I leave."

"You're sure, Cee?"

"I'm positive," Celia insists, returning to the kitchen. She gives Lauren a quick hug, whispers "*Go!*" and shoos her dear friend out the back door.

# twelve

*Later Wednesday Morning*

Yesterday, Shane had aired out a few dusty rag rugs on the porch. The rugs are beach colors. One, slate blue and cream. The other? Olive, ivory and sand. Now he's got them hung over a small clothesline in the side yard. The best way to get the dust out of the rugs is to beat them. So beat he does, using the straw bristle broom. With each *thwack* onto the old rugs, a cloud of dust rises. Over and over again. It feels good, swinging that broom at the rugs. With the sun on his back, each swing also gets some anxiety out of his muscles.

"I'll bet you'd like to turn that broom on some of us," a woman's voice calls out.

He recognizes the voice. You wouldn't know fifteen years have passed since he last heard it. But heck, a familiar voice is like a sweet song we never forget. So Shane turns, sets down the broom and brushes off his dusty hands.

107

"Lauren," he says, walking toward her as he wipes rug dust off his jeans. "Good to see you."

Though he's not sure if Lauren feels the same, not with the way she holds back. Her step slows. Her gaze takes in the shingled cottage, the wood-planked walkway, and finally, him. Which is when, hands open, he walks right to her. They try to hug, but get a little tangled up first, both reaching the same way, then bumping and getting flustered. They manage, though, stepping back with an uneasy laugh before trying again, their arms tentative, the hug light.

Tentative or not, he hears what he needs to. Hears *Shane*, whispered into their embrace.

"It's been a long time," he says, backing up while holding Lauren's shoulders at arm's length. But his eyes? They take in the sight of his old beach friend. Wisps of blonde hair fall from her topknot. A spoon bracelet is cuffed on her wrist. She's ever casual in a black fitted tee and distressed denim shorts. Ever casual, ever Lauren. "Life's treating you okay?" he asks.

She nods, just nods, as she steps back with a quick smile.

"I'm glad. You have a family? You and Kyle?"

Again she nods. "Two children. Evan and Hailey. Hailey, she's seven. And Evan's nine."

Standing there, Shane draws a hand down his jaw while shaking his head. Two kids. A son and daughter he's never heard of. Never laid eyes on. This reunion of sorts won't be easy. His heart already breaks with not knowing those kids.

"I can't stay too long," Lauren is saying. "Kyle and I just

got back yesterday, and I'm busy catching up with things." She looks from Shane, to the Sound behind his cottage, then to him again.

"You came alone?" Shane looks past her to the empty street. No car idles in the sunshine there; no golf cart is parked at the curb. No six-foot-two brother waits in the yard, shielding the sun from his eyes as he watches Shane from a distance. "Not with my brother?"

"No. I mean … Well, your letter asked that I come alone." She holds up her hand, showing him the envelope with his note in it.

"Okay, good. You got it, then. And we can talk a little?"

"That's why I'm here. I have some time right now. Kyle's actually at the diner."

"The diner. Really …" Shane feels Lauren's scrutiny. He runs a hand up and down his arm as her gaze moves from his face, to the several tattoos inked from his wrists to his shoulders. "So Kyle's still doing that part-time gig with Jerry?"

Lauren shakes her head and looks him straight on now. When she speaks, her words are quiet. Serious, too. She's not here for small talk; it's in her tone. "Kyle owns the place, Shane."

"No shit. Elsa mentioned he was at the diner, but I didn't know he *bought* it."

"You've been gone a long time. So much has happened over the years."

"I guess so. But to be frank? It's the last month that I want to know about. Come on, let's talk." Shane turns and heads to the open porch. When he looks back, Lauren hasn't moved. She stands stock-still, that envelope clutched in her hand. When Cliff delivered the letter, Lauren must have read it and rushed right out, her fingers never even setting down the note.

Which means she's got something to say. So Shane stops and faces her, waiting. She waits, too. Tears fill her grey eyes. Not much, but he can't miss the glisten. Watching her, he feels the sting of those tears. The sting of regret. Of sadness at time that's passed. The sting of missed birthdays and holidays. The sting of the phone not ringing. Of the ribbing and bullshitting and shoving and stone-skimming and beers and laughs that stopped happening with him and Kyle.

The sting of two brothers lost to each other.

And from the looks of Lauren standing there—seeming tired and hot in the midmorning sun, *and* uncertain—he can't tell if she's about to turn on her heels and leave. Change her mind and let well enough alone.

But she doesn't.

Between them is the weathered boardwalk-planked walkway. Sweeping dune grasses brush alongside it. Shane stands near the cottage now; Lauren stands further back, near the driveway. They're uncomfortably silent as she gives another reluctant smile, then throws a glance to the street before turning up her hands.

So Shane does the same. Wordlessly, he turns up *his* hands. In a moment, Lauren gives in and takes a few slow steps on that walkway winding beside the cottage. She looks up at the silver-shingled bungalow, then out to the water beyond the back porch. When she stops again, she winces with that damn uncertainty—until Shane motions for her to follow him.

And he doesn't look back again as he crosses the sandy wood planks and quickly takes the seven olive-painted steps up to the little beach bungalow's open back porch.

A certain formality is bred from distance—even the distance of time. Years and months, weeks and days. Endless hours and minutes mount into a sea of emptiness when you've been away from a place, from people you know. Such that you act a little like you *don't* know them, when that sea is bridged.

Now that feeling of formality has Shane panic. Especially when Lauren said she'd wait outside, maybe take a walk on the little beach behind his bungalow. So she's finding it hard to talk, too. To broach *any* subject with him, painful or not.

"*Shit. Shit,*" Shane whispers in the cottage kitchen. At the very least, he needs to put some food together to bring out on the back porch. Having something to fuss with, to move around on a plate, to bite into, might help ease the uncomfortable distance between them.

He scans some of the shelves near the sink; opens the refrigerator; checks a cabinet for any snack. Surprisingly, it's Elsa to the rescue. There, on the kitchen counter, is the plastic container she sent home with him yesterday. A container filled with delicious Italian cookies, good for picking at as he and Lauren talk. Again Shane opens one cabinet door, then another, looking this time for a dish or platter. Something to present the food on. He turns to the tall aqua-painted cupboard. A wood grain shows through the distressed paint, and its door sticks. But inside it? A hodgepodge of dishes and bowls; glasses and pitchers; mugs and saucers. All of it is perfectly chipped, or faded, or mismatched—custom-made for back porch use. He grabs a simple white ironstone platter and quickly arranges a half-dozen cookies on it.

"Okay, okay." Pressing his arm to his sweating forehead, he looks around. "Drinks." There's a carton of store-bought lemonade in the fridge. Good enough, when it's poured into a ceramic pitcher. The problem is, he can't figure what has him so tense. What has his hand tremble as he pours the lemonade into the pitcher. Hell, this is what he wanted. To talk. To finally learn what moved Lauren to invite him here.

Lauren. He glances out the kitchen window. She took a quick walk on the tiny beach behind his cottage. He sees her there, idling along the shore, stopping and bending to maybe pick up a shell or beach stone. A sea breeze loosened more of her hair, and she fusses with wisps blowing across her face. He watches as she turns and walks back to the porch. While climbing the painted steps, her eyes take in the large open space beneath the overhang. She paces for a moment; holds her sandals before lightly dropping them on the porch floor; walks barefoot to the happiness jar he left on the pale white table; picks up the jar; sets it back down.

But it's the view that does it. That gets her to stop and lean on the porch half-wall and just look out at the sea.

With little time to spare, Shane tucks napkins into two glasses before he stops, too. Stops and looks down at his damp T-shirt. When he lifts the fabric, it sticks to his chest. After one uncertain second, he peels it off, balls up the sweaty tee and blots his face with it before giving the tee a hook shot straight into the trash can.

Because this is it. It's do or die. He either has a family, or doesn't. This talk with Lauren will clue him in.

In no time, he's in his small bedroom and ripping open a package of new navy tees. After pulling one over his head and straightening it, he bends to his reflection in the dresser's tarnished mirror. There's a shadow of whiskers on his face, but he'd stopped at a barber's on the way here last week, so his hair is short. He brushes his hands through it now, spiking it some, and finally hurries back to the kitchen.

While putting the lemonade pitcher and cookie platter on a tray, something on the countertop catches his eye. It's just what he needs, actually. He scoops up the domino there and joggles it in his hand. He'd swiped it from Cliff Saturday night when they jump-started Cliff's car battery. Giving the scuffed domino a good flip now, Shane catches it and drops it in his pocket. These days, he needs all the luck he can get.

# *thirteen*

---

## *Moments Later*

W HAT A VIEW," LAUREN SAYS. "All that water."

Shane's shouldering open the squeaking screen door. He carries the food tray out to that old wooden table off to the side. By the time he returns with their glasses, Lauren's sat herself on the porch half-wall. Leaning against a tall post, her arms around her bent knees, she keeps her gaze on Long Island Sound glistening beneath the late-morning sun. He can see that she'd pulled her cell phone from her pocket; the phone and his letter are on a weathered crate beside her.

"Closest I can get to the sea," Shane says from the table. "I get claustrophobic when I'm not near it."

Lauren looks from him, to the seawater, obviously taken by the view of blue from his sparse porch. But she says nothing.

"I brought us something to eat," he says then. "You

know, a snack." He pulls out one of the distressed painted chairs. "The chairs are wobbly, but they work."

"I'm good here," Lauren says from her half-wall seat and its panoramic view.

Shane gets it. It's where he always sits, too. So he puts a couple of sprinkled and sugar-dusted cookies on a napkin and brings them to her.

"I recognize these cookies," Lauren says after taking them and tasting one.

"Elsa pawned them off on me," Shane tells her while pouring lemonade into a tall glass. "I guess her kitchen is full of leftovers after the vow renewal didn't happen."

There's a silence, then. He's not surprised, because what can anyone say to that disappointment? To that bomb that went off in all their lives.

The thing is, his coming here *shouldn't* have been some detonating bomb. So as much as he wants answers from Lauren, he also wants to confront her. To argue, *Why didn't you tell Kyle you invited me? Give him time to process that? Hell, why didn't you ask him if inviting me was okay?* But if he starts up with all that, she'll probably book it and just leave. So instead, he sets Lauren's lemonade glass on the crate near her perch. Neither one of them is comfortable. The quiet between their words stretches on. It's not until Shane's gotten a napkin of cookies for himself and sits on the half-wall, leaning on another roof post and facing her, that Lauren talks again.

"Elsa give you that happiness jar, too?"

"Yeah. She insisted." Shane looks over at the painted

table where the jar sits beside the cookies and lemonade. "Every guest at her inn leaves with one, I guess. Sweet gesture."

"Kyle actually proposed to me, this time around, using one of those happiness jars. On the beach. Put my diamond ring right in the jar."

Lauren's voice is low when she talks. And on an even keel. None of those words will be minced, it's very clear. Every one will be used to accomplish something. What that might be, Shane's not sure yet. Not sure if they can get past the breach between two brothers. Not sure if any of this is even worthwhile—judging by his and Lauren's awkwardness.

He looks over at her as she gives a slight smile. That's it, just a silent smile. So biting one of his cookies, he looks across the porch to his happiness jar again. "You put something in that jar of mine?" he asks. Standing, he walks over and picks it up.

"Seaweed. From your beach here. Some sea lettuce, a little kelp."

Shane looks at the damp green seaweed tucked on top of the fine sand. There are sprigs of red, too. "Irish moss?" he asks.

Lauren nods. "It's symbolic, all that seaweed. You know. Because we're all about as tangled up as the seaweed is."

Shane sets the jar down and returns to his seat, facing Lauren on the porch half-wall. "And that's happiness? Being tangled up like that?"

"What do you mean?"

Shane picks up the cookie he'd started. "You put the seaweed in my *happiness* jar."

"Well, it *could* be happiness. Lives being tangled together, blended and mixed." Still sitting on the porch half-wall, Lauren sets her napkin of cookies on the nearby crate. "Listen. I got your letter. Cliff brought it to me. And I'm guessing you want to know why the heck I invited you to Stony Point." She reaches for her cell phone and flicks through some photographs on it. Finally, she holds out the phone. "This is why."

Still eating, Shane puts the cookie half in his mouth, brushes off his fingers and takes the phone. On it, there's a picture of a man, mid-thirties maybe, waiting tables in Kyle's diner. "Wait. Isn't that Elsa's son?"

"Sal. Sal DeLuca. How did you …"

"Had a long talk with Elsa Saturday night. She filled me in on some things." Shane looks at the picture again, then at Lauren. "Sal was a waiter?"

"No. Sal was a Wall Street hotshot kicking back for the summer. And hiding from everyone that he was living on borrowed time. He wasn't well, but we never knew it."

Shane scrutinizes the photo of Sal. He's got dark hair and serious eyes, but a wide smile for the camera. "So what was he doing working at your husband's diner?"

"That's the way Sal was. I'm not sure how to explain it, but he'd meld right in." Lauren looks out at the blue waters of the Sound. "It was something he did, tagging along with Jason on reno jobs. Riding shotgun in the security cruiser."

"With Nick?"

"Yes. You know Nick?"

Shane nods, but looks back to Sal on the phone. "And he waited tables for Kyle?"

"He did. But it was *more* than that. Or … not really *about* that."

"Sorry, Lauren. But I don't see what this has to do with me—pretty much living on a lobster boat off the coast of Maine."

"It has everything to do with you," she insists. "You *and* Kyle." She leans forward and takes her phone back. "Here's why. There's a credo Sal lived by." She scrolls through more photographs while talking. "It's that second chances are God-given. *Molto speciale*, Sal would say in his Italian way."

"Very special?"

"Right. Here are a few more pictures. I made an album on my phone."

Shane takes the phone again. Sitting on the half-wall, he leans back on the post behind him and first flicks through more pictures of Sal waiting tables. Then? Sal and Celia standing at the water's edge, the sun on their faces, a breeze blowing. Another snapshot is of Celia, happy, and wearing a fedora as Sal kisses the side of her face. A flick to the next picture and there's Kyle, Jason and Sal sitting out on the rocks. Shane studies that one, particularly the face of the brother he hasn't yet seen. Kyle's wearing a *Gone Fishing* cap while digging in a tackle box. Shane looks at Jason next, and his prosthetic leg, and the fishing pole in his hand. Sal's fishing, too. Finally, he holds up the picture to Lauren. "What's going on in this shot?"

Lauren stands and walks over to Shane. She looks closer at the shadowy image taken at twilight. "Friday night fishing. It's something the guys do, every week. Like *religion*."

Shane nods and looks at it again, then the next picture. It's of Sal tasting pasta sauce in Elsa's kitchen. Elsa hovers nearby, wooden spoon in hand.

"I snapped that when I was painting the inn's stair mural."

"Wait, I saw that mural. That was *your* work?"

Lauren nods.

"Wow. It's beautiful, Lauren. Had no idea you'd taken your art that far …"

"Thanks. Anyway," she says, hitching her head toward the photo, "Sal loved to sample his mother's recipes. Would drive Elsa nuts sometimes. But you see, that's all he was after—a simple life by the sea. And all he wanted was a second chance *at* that life. He'd hoped, with his valve-replacement surgery, to get that chance. But … we don't always get our wishes."

"Isn't that the truth."

"Sal died in surgery almost a year ago. He didn't get that second chance to live."

"Died in surgery." Shane gives Lauren her phone back before standing, leaning against the post and looking out at the sea. "Elsa told me a little about it. Damn, that's a tough one."

"The thing is? Everyone here was affected by his death.

We *all* reacted in some way," Lauren's saying while setting her cell phone back on the distressed crate, then sitting on the half-wall again. "We ended up making some rash decisions, some life changes."

"Everybody did?" Shane asks.

In a moment, she nods.

"Maris?" he asks.

"You know she's here?"

"And that she's married to Jason."

Lauren barely raises an eyebrow, as if surprised he knows this. But she says nothing.

"Saw a big framed photo of everyone this weekend," Shane explains. "On the wall in the old Foley's back room. Elsa filled in some of the blanks for me."

"Got it."

"So Maris … What rash decision could she have made after this Sal died?"

"Here's the thing, Shane. Sal was her cousin, who she just met last year. *Family.*" Lauren hesitates then, as if uncertain of how much to reveal. "Maris quit a very demanding denim design career. To be more present with people she loves."

Shane can't help it, the way regret has him briefly close his eyes. He was too hard on Maris on the beach yesterday. "How about Elsa?" he asks Lauren. "She do something rash?"

"Elsa put her beautiful cottage up for sale. She didn't want to open the inn without her son. This happened all before the inn's renovations, so her decision put the brakes on many lives. Jason's, with his architecture work. Celia's, as assistant innkeeper."

"Celia. I met her over the weekend, too. She was going to marry Sal, right?"

"She was."

"So how did she react?"

"Celia left here. Packed her bags, drove under that train trestle and hit the road. She went home to Addison, leaving us all behind for good … until … Well, it's complicated."

They're quiet. Shane feels why, feels the realization of one man's life. Whoever this Sal DeLuca was, his death somehow made them all change their own lives. So much so that a year later, his impact is still rippling through them. Shane takes a deep breath of the salt air—the air that's supposed to cure what ails you. Sitting on the half-wall again, he looks at Lauren. "Kyle?" he asks. "And you?"

"Kyle made changes to his diner, but mostly? Mostly he kept everyone in check with *their* rash decisions. And me? I was a little late to the game. But my reaction to Sal's death actually was to send you an invitation to the vow renewal, Shane."

"So the invitation was for a second chance?"

"After what happened with you and Kyle fifteen years ago? Yes. It was time. We're all different now."

"You think people change?"

"I *know* they change."

"You say that with some conviction, Lauren."

"Listen. You and Kyle were two hotheads in your twenties."

"Fair enough."

"But seriously?" Lauren asks. A light breeze lifts off the water, and she inhales a breath of the salt air. "Kyle is actually unbelievably strong, Shane. He's a different man now. Don't judge him by his reaction to your being here. I gave him no warning. So learning you were suddenly here after a difficult fifteen-year absence?"

"Wait." On the porch wall, Shane pulls a knee up and wraps his arms around it. "You didn't even *mention* that I might show up? Or even that you invited me?"

Lauren shakes her head.

"Why not?"

"You never responded to my invitation. I assumed you either didn't get it, or *did* get it and blew me off. So I let it all go and kept my mouth shut, thinking it was probably for the best."

"I got your invitation right before I went out to sea." Shane looks out at the Sound, thinking of the day he boarded that boat. He'd opened the emailed invitation at home that morning. "Didn't know if the boat would be back in time to make it here. And where me and the boys were lobstering, there was no Internet, spotty phone service. Pretty much cut off from the world. So when that trip *was* done, I barely had a day to clean up, throw some gear into my truck and get my ass here for the ceremony. There wasn't even time to get into it with you. To let you know that I'd make it."

"You have time now. And the second chance is still on the table."

There it is again. Lauren's way of not mincing words. Everything that's happened in these past few days all boils down to this. A second chance on the table. Take it or leave it.

"You're amenable to this?" Shane asks. "After what went down between me and my brother fifteen years ago?"

"That's up to *you* two to hash out." She sweeps a windblown strand of blonde hair from her face. "Not me."

"And Kyle?"

Lauren looks long at him. Her grey eyes don't waver. She wants this; it's obvious.

"Kyle's amenable?" Shane asks again.

"I'll work on him, let's put it that way. He's really busy now that he's back at the diner." Lauren rests her head on the post she's leaning on. "But we're going to open-mic night at The Sand Bar tomorrow."

"That dive's still around?"

"Sure is. Celia's got a gig there, and I promised we'd give her some moral support."

"Celia?"

Lauren nods slightly. "She plays guitar, does some singing. It's her thing, stopping in for open mic every now and then. So I can talk to Kyle there, over a drink. Then, *hopefully*, he'll have some downtime this weekend and … I don't know. Maybe you and him can talk."

"Okay, that's decent. And you'll let me know?"

"Well." She stands, checks her watch and picks up her cell phone from the crate.

"Hey, hold on there." He motions for her phone. "Let

me give you my number."

"Guess that'd help," Lauren tells him as she passes it over.

"You can call me, text me. Anytime, Lauren," he tells her while typing.

"Don't expect anything earth-shattering, though. But maybe over a drink I can convince Kyle to meet you and just … *begin*. Whether it works or not in resolving your issues, who knows?" She hesitates before walking closer to where Shane still sits. "But you have to try, Shane," she says, taking back her phone.

He hears what's left unsaid. *Before it's too late. Like it was for Sal.* Shane only nods. Because he sees it, too. He sees his sister-in-law hurrying to get out of here now. Sees that Kyle hasn't read that letter she's also picking up from the rickety crate. If it was just delivered, Kyle would have no way of knowing about it. So Lauren is here behind his back. On the sly.

Here—on Shane's porch—trying to move mountains.

"I'll talk to Kyle. Tell him you're around," Lauren says, folding the envelope in half and sliding it in her pocket. "So long as you're good with all this."

"I'm here, aren't I? Seriously, though? When I got your invite, I thought my brother was sick, maybe needed something."

"No. Kyle's fine. He just needs a second chance." She heads to the porch steps, but stops at the top to look back at him. "And if you can talk, maybe at our place, well … Like I said, it could be a start."

When she silently waves and hurries down the steps, Shane waves back but doesn't get up.

～

For the rest of the day, Shane wonders. *It could be a start*, Lauren had said.

As Shane sets the beaten rag rugs back on the cottage floor; as he makes a sandwich for lunch; as he drives to town to pick up some groceries; as he returns, driving his pickup beneath the stone railroad trestle, he can't *stop* wondering.

*It could be a start.*

A start of what? Monthly meet-ups with his brother when he gets off the docks? Going to an occasional baseball game with Kyle? Birthday cards? A Friday night fishing thing whenever he's here? Thanksgiving in Maine?

Shane can't get the questions out of his head the rest of the day.

Finally, late afternoon, he takes a pail of rocks from the porch, cuffs his jeans and walks barefoot to the private stretch of sand beyond the cottage's dune grasses. At the water's edge, small waves lap at shore. Standing there alone, Shane reaches into the pail, picks out a stone and skims it. He goes through half the pail, skimming each stone, one at a time, pausing between each side-armed throw.

And each stone's skim over the water—each skip and spray beneath each smooth pebble—is a question in his mind, rippling with no answers.

125

# *fourteen*

## *Wednesday Evening*

HELLO!" MARIS CALLS OUT FROM the Ocean Star Inn's front hallway. "Elsa?"

"In the kitchen!" Elsa answers.

Turning into the room, Maris spots her aunt sitting at the massive marble-top island.

"And where's Jason?" Elsa asks.

Maris can't help it, the way she glances over her shoulder. It's the same way Elsa just did, looking for her nephew-in-law. "He's still working," Maris says. "Can't make it for dinner tonight."

"Too bad. Because I still have so many leftovers from the vow renewal. But I'm glad *you* came, dear."

"Me, too." Maris sets her shoulder bag on the counter. "This way, I can tell you more about my engagement story. You know, to Shane."

"*Shh*, Cliff's in the other room. We'll talk later."

"Oh, okay." Maris walks around the island to where her aunt sits. Elsa's thick brown hair is down, and she wears a long black V-neck tee over flower-print capri leggings. A copper pot and bottle of Worcestershire sauce are off to the side, but Elsa's fussing with some tan fabric folded on the island. "What are you doing there?" Maris asks, sitting on the stool beside her.

"Sewing." Elsa looks at Maris over the rim of her leopard-print reading glasses while holding up khaki pants. "Cliff had a hole in his pocket and wondered if that's how he lost his domino. So I took a break from some pot-polishing to stitch his pants."

"He lost his good-luck charm?"

"Table's set," Cliff says before Elsa can answer. He walks into the kitchen from the dining room. "No Jason tonight?"

"He's working late," Maris tells him. "I'll bring him home a dish."

Cliff nods. "And that's right, Maris," he continues while opening a cabinet and getting out drinking glasses. "I seem to have lost my domino these past few days, and look what's happened since. Everything's gone downhill."

When Maris leans over to see Cliff on the other side of the kitchen, she does a double take. "Oh my gosh!" she says, watching him standing there in a polo shirt over blue-striped *boxers*. Quickly she looks … anywhere! To Elsa's red-pail herb pots, to the seashell wind chime clicking and clacking outside the garden window. But she can't help herself. Her gaze drifts back to Cliff and his blue-on-blue striped boxers before she claps a hand over her eyes. "Elsa! You should've warned me."

Elsa turns and lowers her reading glasses, taking a long gander at Cliff at the cabinet before getting back to her pocket-stitching.

"Heck," Cliff's saying. "We're all practically family. That is," he adds while picking up the three drinking glasses and crossing the kitchen, "*if* your aunt might someday say *Yes* to me."

"Wait. Has there been a formal proposal I don't know about?" Maris asks.

Elsa simply shakes her head, then waves off the beach commissioner and his love talk.

With her hands still partially over her eyes, Maris keeps at Cliff. "Don't you think it might *help* your wooing if you left some things to the imagination? Be more, I don't know," she says, stealing a glimpse at him from beneath her split fingers, "*mysterious?*"

"Well, sure. Maybe." Still holding the glasses, Cliff stops on the other side of the marble island. "But Elsa did *offer* to stitch my pocket."

"Just about done," Elsa tells him while looking over her leopard-print glasses again. "Go wait in the other room!"

"And I'll keep an eye out for that good-luck charm," Maris says, watching Cliff leave the kitchen. "But isn't it a little odd, pinning your hopes on an old domino like that? Especially some scuffed-up thing you picked up in the Maritime Market parking lot?"

At first Cliff is quiet. There's only the sound of glasses being set out on the dining room table for their dinner.

"Don't you have a lucky writing journal?" his voice eventually carries through the doorway. "Or write with a particular candle flickering? Some creative talisman?"

Maris pictures her writing shack ... and the shelves of Neil's leather and canvas journals, all filled with his thoughts, and grains of sand, and seagull feathers. Or his old candles, the melted wax hardened in dribbles along the candle sides. And of course, there's Jason's pewter hourglass that she flips at the beginning of each writing session. The hourglass that was once his father's after he finished his tour in Vietnam.

But none of those are really writing *charms*. Maris' hand instantly goes to her gold star pendant then. "Yes! Yes. Okay, fine. My star necklace *always* brings me luck."

"That's right. Mine, too." Elsa waves the khaki pants in the air. "Cliff, here! All done. Get dressed now. You can put these on in the bathroom."

When Cliff comes into the kitchen, still boxer-clad, Maris suppresses a laugh and covers her eyes again.

"Imagine if you lost your necklace, Maris, and how you'd feel," he's saying. "My life was *good* when that domino was close by." With that, he takes his pants and walks down the hallway, calling over his shoulder, "And dagnabbit, I'm going to find it!"

Maris, still at the island, sneaks another peek at Cliff before looking at Elsa.

Elsa, who simply shrugs beside her, then clasps Maris' arm. "Everything okay at home?" she whispers.

"Oh, Aunt Elsa. I hope so. I have so much to tell you."

129

# *fifteen*

## *Wednesday Night*

ONCE HE'S HOME, JASON MAKES two trips from his SUV. First he heads through the backyard and opens the barn's double doors. Inside, like always, he stops and inhales the scent of aged wood—the planked floors, the walls. It's a scent that conjures images of his father's old masonry workshop inside these very walls. In the dusty space, can't he just see his father hanging his mortar-stained trowels, scratched and dinged chisels, a wooden level on the cluttered pegboard? Even though the pegboards are long gone—and the barn renovated to house Jason's architecture studio now—that sense of his father still remains.

When Jason deposits several tubed cottage blueprints into the rack near his work desk, he spots one of Neil's canvas-bound journals. It's still open on the desk beneath the swing-arm lamp—open to the photograph he mentioned to Mitch. Jason snaps on the lamp and gives the misty picture a long look. He'd been meaning to show it to Maris. Maybe she'd recognize where it was taken, and who was standing beside the old beach binoculars.

Shaking his head, Jason finally closes the weathered scrapbook, wraps some fishing line around it and returns it to the bookshelf where many of Neil's journals are kept— stacked and propped and leaning against each other. "Another time," Jason says before locking up the studio and heading back to the house.

After stopping at his SUV for trip two, he barely makes it inside. His arms are filled with his duffel, leather messenger bag, lunch tote, envelopes and fliers from the mailbox. All of which he finagles up the stone stairs to the deck and through the slider, where he finally drops everything on the kitchen counter. The whole time, Maddy is impatient at his feet, so he goes into the pantry and fills her bowl with kibble. Once the dog digs in, Jason reads the note he'd noticed further down on the counter. It's from Maris.

"*Dinner at Elsa's,*" he whispers. "*Will bring home a plate.*"

So that's why the house is so quiet. She took off to her aunt's, where he's sure she can at least relax and enjoy the meal. Won't be any arguing there. No quibbling over a baked potato. No silence with some decadent dessert. He reads the rest of her note. *P.S. Fire detector upstairs is chirping. Replace battery?*

He figures he'll get to that later and instead sorts through the mail. Until he hears that warning *chirp*. It's just enough, that one little sound, to get under his skin—along with everything else under there annoying him. So after digging through a kitchen drawer for a new battery, he heads down the dark paneled hallway to the stairs.

Again, a warning chirp. "*Aargh*," he says under his breath. Once upstairs, he gets a stepstool from the hall closet, unclips the smoke alarm and removes the bad battery. Dropping it in his pocket, he puts in the new battery, clips the alarm back onto the ceiling mount and tests it. With all good and quiet, the stepstool goes back into the closet.

Before returning downstairs to the mail and his workbags, Jason stops in his bedroom. It's been a helluva long day, and the thought of winding down has him emptying his pockets at his dresser: coins in brass dish, keys and wallet in valet. He takes off his checked button-down shirt, tosses it on the bed and finds an old concert tee in his bureau drawer.

"Much better," he says, pulling it over his head. Standing in front of Maris' dresser mirror then, he bends close and runs a hand along his jaw. From the looks of the darkening shadow on his face, he's definitely overdue for a shave. Turning, he picks up a pair of boat shoes and puts them in the closet. Grabs Maris' cowboy hat off the bed and puts that on a hook in the closet, too. Straightening a window curtain on the way out, he notices one of Maris' silver chain bracelets on the floor near the nightstand. She takes them off when she's jotting notes on her manuscript in bed, so he picks up the bracelet and walks to her jewelry box.

Which is where he finally stops. The house is quiet, the room warm. The window is open and no breeze moves the curtains. Before putting her bracelet back in the jewelry box, Jason looks over his shoulder to the door, then back at the jewelry box. Heck, if Maris was engaged to Shane, there had to be an engagement ring. Certainly she wouldn't still have it.

As much as he doesn't want to look, he can't seem to turn away. Can't stop himself from brushing through a few pieces. There are more chain bracelets, stacked, so he adds the one from the floor. Her earrings—hoops and studs—are neatly organized. A few necklaces are coiled off to the side.

And then there are the rings. He picks up a silver dome ring, then sets it down. A solitaire citrine in gold. A silver initial ring.

And a sailor's knot ring. Jason looks closely at it. He remembers Maris wearing it once or twice, but never gave it a thought.

Until today.

Because a sailor's knot ring is one thing. But a white-gold sailor's knot ring with an embedded diamond is another. Still. It's the sailor's knot itself—looped over and under, twisted together—that matters most.

That unnerves him as he rubs his thumb over the knot.

Because he knows the significance of a sailor's knot—to hold something close. To create an unbreakable bond.

He and Neil became expert on those knots when they were barely teenagers. And all because of their father.

Knowing the nautical knots was a critical aspect of boating. That was made clear the day their new little Boston Whaler was docked in the boat basin. But his and Neil's moment of uncontained joy was short-lived, because their father wouldn't let them board it. He caught Neil by the collar of his tee while barricading Jason with an extended arm. They couldn't step one *foot* on that boat.

Not until they mastered their first rule of the sea.

～

*"You're not going out in that boat until you know how to take care of it,"* Jason remembers their father telling them that day. *They stood on the concrete walkway around the boat basin, right in front of their shiny new Boston Whaler. The boat gently bobbed, and pulled against the docklines. The creaking noise it made, the boat talk, was a siren song—begging them to get in and take a ride out on Long Island Sound.*

*And it was torture, not being able to board that sweet boat. The sun beat down on them as Jason and Neil stood there in shorts and striped tees, sneakers on their feet. The summer morning was hot, and they suddenly felt like they were in school, learning lessons, instead of cruising the open seas, free, the salty breeze blowing.*

*"The first sea rule you'll learn before stepping foot on this here vessel?" their father continued. "How to tie a knot. A cleat hitch, to be exact. It's the knot that will secure your boat to a cleat when docking the vessel. Use the wrong knot and your boat can go adrift. Tie a cleat hitch improperly? You'll never unknot it to leave the dock, and what good's that? So today, you'll learn to tie a knot."*

*And learn they did. But not at the little marina behind the Stony Point boardwalk. No, their father led them to their home on the bluff, straight to the barn out back. Inside, in his dusty masonry workshop, he'd attached two dock cleats to a slab of wood mounted on the wall. He handed them each several pieces of rope.*

*"There'll be no going out on that boat until you've mastered the knot," their father warned them.*

*He wasn't kidding. Oh, it was the worst agony for Jason and Neil, working their young fingers raw to learn the knot their father demonstrated. Complete turn around the cleat base, cross over and under the horn, flip a loop, over and under again.*

*Turn, cross, over and under, flip. Over and over again.*

*Eyes open; eyes closed. Again and again.*

*They practiced for two days, for hours on end, until finally their father issued the true test. He brought them to their Boston Whaler in the boat basin, then upped the ante. They couldn't just tie the sailor's knot with the boat's dockline. No. Their father blindfolded them to be sure they could make that knot without even looking.*

*"Okay, boys. One attempt each," he warned them while tying the bandanas snugly behind their heads. "So get it right. Because sometimes in life, you only get one shot."*

⌒

And now again, like when he was a kid, Jason's turning something, crossing it over, under, flipping it this way and that.

Just like he did with his blistered fingers so many years ago on those cleats mounted in his father's barn workshop.

135

These past few days, how many times has Jason turned over in his mind the question of Maris' engagement to Shane? Turned it, crossed over it, under it, flipped it, to get to the truth.

Alone in his bedroom, he holds the sailor's knot engagement ring. It feels like Maris and Shane's past entanglement is slowly wrapping around his life.

# sixteen

*Early Thursday Morning*

EVERY MORNING, SHANE FINDS HIMSELF on the hunt.

Once the sun's up, he slips off his boat shoes and walks Stony Point's main beach just below the high tide line. There, he searches for smooth, flat stones washed ashore overnight. Any worthwhile ones get dropped into the old bucket he brings along from the cottage. Today, he needs to replenish his supply after skimming stones well into last evening.

Something else happens on these early walks, too. The ghosts come out. When no one else is on the beach this early, Shane sees those spirits in the shadows. In the fog. Mostly they show up near his and Kyle's old haunts: the movie frame on the sand; the swim raft they'd race to, growing up summers here; the boat basin where they'd head out in Jason and Neil's Whaler, then get lit on the Sound.

137

Every long-ago memory crystallizes on Shane's morning walks while looking for perfect skimming stones. The rising sun plays tricks on his eyes, bringing the low mist to life in ethereal shapes running on the beach, or swimming and splashing. Until Shane looks again, squinting through that mist. The wind, too, carries distant voices that get him to turn and listen. The way the dune grasses whisper in the sea breeze, it sounds just like two adolescent boys, maybe, plotting some summer day adventure.

This morning, the ghosts and memories suddenly evaporate, though. When Shane walks further down the beach, he tips up his cap for a better look—to be sure *this* person is real. She is, and she's alone. Like he is. It's a woman struggling to assemble a small pop-up tent on the sand. Still holding his bucket, he keeps walking until he recognizes Celia. She wears a long tank dress and straw fedora, and she appears to be reading paper directions.

"Need a hand?" Shane calls out.

Celia looks, then looks again. "Every time I see you, I think you're your brother."

"Not Kyle." Shane walks up to Celia and takes the instructions from her. "You don't need these. They're just confusing."

"But I've been here ten minutes and all I've done is make a mess." She motions to the mesh screening and nylon panels and loose tent pegs. "Oh, why'd I even buy it?"

"I could figure why. A little shade tent? To keep your daughter safe from the sun's hot rays." Shane sets down his skimming-stone pail. "Aria, right?"

Celia nods, pressing back a wisp of auburn hair blowing in the sea breeze. "She's at Elsa's while I set this up." Halfheartedly, she picks up a piece of the tent frame.

All the while, as she explains and fusses with her shade tent, Shane looks at Celia. She's tall and willowy in her ankle-length sundress. Her skin is lightly tanned, her expression a bit defeated. In his mind, though, he thinks of the framed photograph in Elsa's back room, the picture of all the friends together. Celia's in that picture, too. With Sal. And she was undeniably happy. So now Shane sees what he didn't notice before—her sadness. It's there, in her eyes. She's haunted by ghosts of her own on this beach.

"Here." After folding his cap into his back pocket, Shane takes a piece of tent from her. "Let me get that for you."

Celia tips up her fedora. "I don't need some man to come over and rescue me, you know. Assemble my tent for me as if I'm … I'm … helpless!"

Shane glances up at the rising August sun. "If you want to use your tent today, you might need rescuing," he says. With a wink thrown in. Something, *anything*, to get her to smile.

Instead she sighs. "All I wanted was a nice beach day before the inn opens, when I'll be too busy with Elsa to do this."

And there's that defeat again, in her voice. A tone suggesting, *As if that's too much to ask*. As though, after Sal's death, she really doesn't expect much anymore. Shane turns the tent piece in his hand.

"I told you so," Celia tells him. "It's complicated, isn't it?"

"Get me a rock." Shane hitches his head toward the dune grasses at the top of the beach.

"A rock?"

"A good-sized one, to hammer the pegs in the sand. There. On the berm."

"The what? Berm?"

"The embankment," Shane explains, pointing to where the beach slopes. "In the dune grasses there. The berm."

"*The berm*," Celia whispers, heading in its direction.

Meanwhile, Shane snaps together pieces of the baby's tent, finally kneeling down and zipping on a flat mat beneath it. When Celia returns with a hefty rock, he takes it from her.

"See? I didn't swoop in to rescue you," he tells her while pressing the mat smooth. "This is teamwork."

At last, Celia relaxes and lightly laughs. Shane stands then, and together they carry the assembled pop-up shade tent to find the right spot for it.

"Not too close to the water," Shane suggests. "Tide's coming in and the waves will hit it."

"Good point."

So they backtrack a few steps until Celia sets the shade tent down and gauges where the sun is in the sky. When Shane drops his hammer-rock and shifts the tent over with her, they get tangled up—both reaching at the same time, both sidestepping each other. She laughs again, and Shane watches her.

Watches the way she quiets, too.

Which is when he puts a hand on her face, tips up her fedora and gives a little kiss on her lips.

A kiss in which they surprisingly get caught up as Celia reaches a hand to her nudged-and-slipping hat. When both Shane's hands cradle her neck, she hesitates, pulls away … and a moment later? Slaps his face.

"Whoa! What was that for?" Shane asks, stepping quickly back. "A kiss?"

Celia leans close and lowers her voice. "A perfectly *timed* kiss for Maris to see!"

"What?" He looks back and spots Maris. She's carrying a big tote, and is far off in the distance—just leaving the footpath and stepping onto the beach.

"Your old flame? Maris walks along the beach to work at Elsa's some mornings. Because Elsa set up a writing nook in the inn's turret. And I'll bet you *knew* that, didn't you? Knew she'd walk by." Celia looks past Shane, shields the sun from her eyes, then looks back at him. "Trying to make her jealous, maybe?"

"*What?*" Shane wipes his sore jaw. "No! That kiss had nothing to do with Maris."

Celia glares at him before grabbing up her sand chair and opening it. "Everyone was right about you. You're *nothing* but trouble," she says under her breath.

"Celia." Shane walks around her to see her face and when he does, she turns away. But he persists, moving around her again, then holding her shoulder and looking her straight on. "I had no *idea* Maris was there. And she's so far down the beach, she wouldn't have even seen."

Celia looks past him again. There's a long, quiet second before she turns back to him still standing there. "Could you just leave? Maris is getting closer and I don't need her seeing us together." She picks up his pail of stones and holds it out to him. "And I *don't* need any more of your help."

"You misunderstood." Shane reaches over and lightly straightens Celia's crooked straw fedora. "I'm sorry," he says, taking his pail from her. "That kiss was *not* what you're thinking." He pulls his newsboy cap from his pocket and starts walking toward the granite steps to Champion Road—out of everyone's way. "You and your daughter have a nice beach day now," he calls over his shoulder.

Of course, there's no reply. He imagines Celia's fuming right about now. He also figures her fuming has nothing to do with Maris—who never would have noticed their brief kiss. No, Celia's agitation is more likely stemming from missing Sal, and being alone with their baby, and all the Stony Point drama, and bothersome ghosts hovering on quiet mornings on the beach.

Shane caught the brunt of it in one slap.

When he gets to the top granite step, he gives one look back at Celia. She's standing at the water's edge. The sea breeze flutters her sundress. Pressing a wisp of auburn hair off her face, she turns to greet Maris.

In his one glance back, though, something about Celia breaks his heart.

Actually, his heart broke for her the moment he saw her taking flowers off the old rowboat in the boat basin, late Saturday night.

# *seventeen*

## *Thursday Afternoon*

ONLY ONE NARROW LANE LEADS into Stony Point. It forks in an easy curve off the winding Shore Road. The lane is nearly hidden by the railroad trestle that runs over it, and by a market and secondhand bookshop that sit on the trestle's hill before it. If you didn't know that lane existed, you could drive right by it—unaware of an entire world unto itself.

A world that Kyle Bradford's now a part of. Ever since he and Lauren bought their bungalow by the bay, it's his favorite part of the ride home from work. Yes, he relishes that moment when he hits the blinker and steers his old pickup truck beneath the stone railroad trestle. The dark, damp tunnel is like a portal into a secret community.

One with a guard standing watch, too. Kyle drives beneath the stone trestle and stops at the guard shack on the other side.

"Nicholas," Kyle says through his open window.

"Kyle." Nick walks over, clipboard in hand. "What's happening, dude?"

"The commish still has you wearing those fancy threads?" Kyle asks, reaching out and flicking Nick's khaki button-down uniform shirt with black epaulets.

"Shit, yeah." Nick glances down at his black shorts and matching black sneakers, too. "Boss says you've got to spot the guards from the vacationers."

"That's Cliff for you. Right on things like that."

"Hey," Nick says. "Good to see you back from your getaway. You and Lauren doing all right?"

"Hanging in there." Kyle glances out the windshield to the cottages lining the street. "I miss anything here? What's up at this fine beach of ours today?"

"Other than clearing out a few kids crabbing in the creek, it's been quiet." Nick tips up his black security visor. "Just enjoying a nice sunny day before the rain comes."

"Rain?"

"Tomorrow. Downpours headed this way."

"Seriously? Damn."

"What's wrong, big guy?"

Kyle looks from Nick, to the perfectly blue sky that'll be dropping buckets of water this time tomorrow. "Listen. You coming to the driving range with us later?"

"Yeah, after my shift. Got Matt's text earlier. Why?"

"Hell if I even have time now," Kyle mumbles while checking his watch. "My grass is so high already, I've got to mow it before the rain gets here. Catch you later,

Nicholas." With that, Kyle puts his truck in gear and burns out down the sandy beach street.

"Hey!" Nick yells, raising his clipboard as he does. "Speed limit fifteen, Bradford!"

Kyle glances at his rearview mirror and leaves Nick in his dust. Driving along, he slows only to maneuver around a strategically placed speed barrier. And slows again when he notices Cliff. The commissioner's using a manual push-reel mower, cutting the nicely manicured patch of grass around the Stony Point Beach Association trailer. If Kyle wasn't in such a rush, he'd stop and chew the fat for a minute. Instead he simply waves and keeps driving.

Problem is, on his way home he sees the Gallagher house to the right, off the main road near the marsh. Can't miss Matt, actually. Because there he is on his oversized yard tractor, methodically cutting his grass. Yep, just like a state cop, too: precise, meticulous, mowing that lush green lawn in a perfect diamond pattern. You'd think his yard's the Yankee Stadium outfield, for crying out loud.

Kyle taps his horn and keeps driving. He passes several men in various stages of mowing: raking clippings; adding gasoline to mower engines; turning at the end of a row and quickly mowing the next. Hell, is everyone out to beat the rain? What it does—seeing every lawn mower fired up in this little beach community, hearing the snap of pull cords, the *putt-putter* of the engines, smelling the fresh-cut grass— is this: It makes Kyle really tense. He left the diner early to decompress … and now rain's coming?

Turning his pickup onto Bayside Road, he guns it and

flies into his driveway. The heck with going inside the house, getting a drink of water, checking in with Lauren. The damn grass has to be cut *today* or else the rain will make it too high for his pathetically inadequate push mower. And he doesn't want to miss his golf outing. So he jogs straight into the garage, drags out his old mower and pulls the cord three times before it sputters to life. Still in his black work pants and tee, Kyle begins walking the loud mower across his front yard. Lord knows there was no time to first clear any debris from the lawn, so right away he runs over a stick—which clatters in the blade.

In the next few minutes, he manages a couple of rows, back and forth—along the brick-edged petunia flowerbed near the front porch, around a tall oak tree, beside a cluster of orange tiger lilies. He swipes his sweating forehead as he goes.

"Kyle!" a voice calls.

He looks over to see Lauren at the porch door. She's wearing a short robe and her hair's wrapped in a towel.

"*Sheesh.* Slow down already! You didn't even come inside," she yells over the sputtering engine.

"No time," Kyle shouts, still pushing the mower.

Lauren walks down one step while holding the door open. "Shut it off! We have to talk, Kyle."

"*Can't* shut it off. It won't start up again. And it's going to rain tomorrow. *Buckets!*"

"Well, we'll talk when you're done then." As she says it, she holds her robe closed and turns to go inside the house.

"No. Hey, *hey!*" Kyle looks back while still pushing. He

gives a sharp whistle. "I'm hitting golf balls with the guys. At the driving range. Matt's treat."

"Today?"

"In an hour. They want to help me decompress after the weekend." *If I don't drop of a heart attack first*, he thinks as his heart palpitations kick in. Still pushing his crappy mower with one hand, he uses the other to lift his tee and dab at his sweating face.

"What about The Sand Bar?" Lauren asks, leaning out the open porch door while still holding her robe closed with one hand. "It's Celia's open-mic night. I just took a shower because I promised her we'd go."

Kyle motions for her to wait as he finishes mowing one row, turns and proceeds to the next row. "You go with Celia," he yells while approaching Lauren. "I'll grab a shower, golf, then meet you at the bar."

He doesn't hear what Lauren says next, or if she even says anything. Now, he's half bent over while walking, watching a tendril of smoke snake out of his mower. Which does a good job of getting him to walk faster—his arms pushing the machine, his heart pounding, perspiration beading on his face.

⁓

Everything's a blur. Beneath the brim of Jason's baseball cap, all of his property passes by unfocused: the gabled house, the stone steps to the deck and the maple tree beside it. Even the dog's plastic pool—which Jason emptied and

147

moved aside before firing up his riding tractor—is merely a splotch of blue.

That's how fast he's mowing his yard. The front's done, and he's driven the tractor up the sloping driveway to take care of the back. Row by row, he gets it all cut, every blade. When he rounds the corners around the barn studio and garage, sometimes he feels a tire lift off the ground. Okay, so maybe he's a little reckless with the riding mower today, driving it too fast. He could convince himself it's because he wants to finish up in time to get to the driving range. But that's not the reason.

No, it's because he's pissed, is why—which is making his foot heavy on the gas. He's mad at that damn engagement ring Maris kept. At this whole life she and Shane had that Jason knew nothing about. A life Maris still thinks of, if that hidden engagement ring is any indication.

So when he's done mowing, Jason just keeps moving to work off his anger. First he hoses off the riding tractor in the driveway. Madison hears the spray of water and lunges for it, snapping at the water like it's a writhing snake.

"Maddy! Stop that," Jason orders the dog. He's got no patience for the German shepherd's antics right now. When she sits, trembling with restraint, he finishes washing the mower.

And he keeps going, straight to the shed for his gas-powered weed whacker. Maddy follows closely behind him the entire time—as he gives the starter rope a few yanks, as he trims weeds around the house's stone foundation, along the driveway edge, around the barn. The dog is like a shadow, keeping right up with him. Finally Jason goes at the weeds around Neil's old fishing shack. He lowers the chugging trimmer, its string line spinning and slicing weeds, choking up on random fallen twigs. He repeatedly revs the machine along the front of the shack, where he missed some grass with his mowing. Setting the trimmer on high speed, the gas engine whirrs loud, quiet, then loud again with each rev as he moves it back and forth over a patch of thick overgrowth there.

"*Jason?*" Maris rushes out of the shack—the door flying open. "I'm *trying* to work. Can't you do this tomorrow?" she shouts over the sound of the weed whacker.

"Rain tomorrow," he shouts back over the revving engine. "Grass was getting too high."

Maris looks out at the now-manicured lawn. "Fine. But what about dinner?" She walks up to him and cups her hands near his ear. "How about The Sand Bar? When I saw Celia on the beach this morning, she mentioned she's playing there."

"Maybe later, yeah." He keeps moving back and forth, back and forth—idling and revving the motor with each sweep. "Hitting a bucket of golf balls with the guys first."

"*Today?*" she yells.

"When I'm done here. After a quick shower." Finally, he pauses with his weed trimming and shuts off the machine. Glancing at the yard, he swipes his damp forehead and resettles the cap on his head. "It was Matt's idea. To take Kyle golfing. You know, to lower his stress."

"Sure, I guess. I'll call my sister then, and see if she and

Matt want to have supper at the bar. Eva and I can meet you guys there?"

Jason simply nods while pulling the cord once, then again before the trimmer powers back on. "Let me get this done," he yells, glancing at Maris as she heads to the house, most likely to call her sister. "*Maris!*"

Maris stops halfway up the stairs to the deck and glances over her shoulder. He looks at her for a second—at her long brown hair twisted into a side braid; her white tank top over faded skinny jeans. Suddenly she impatiently turns up her hands. "*What do you want?*" she calls down.

He watches her for another second, the weed trimmer idling, before yelling, "Can you grab me a towel inside? I'll shower out in the cabana when I'm done."

After she goes in the house, Jason gets his leaf blower from the shed and fires that up next. He sets it at a steady high speed and blows every cut twig, every leaf, every blade of grass off his driveway, walkway and deck. Before putting the blower back in the shed, he sits at the patio table for a breather. Madison had scrambled up behind him and laps water from her bowl near the slider. It's hot, and Jason's perspiring, so he lifts the towel Maris dropped on the table and blots his sweaty face. When his cell phone dings, he pulls it from his cargo shorts pocket, reads the text message there and calls Kyle.

"You ready to hit the links?" he asks when Kyle answers.

"Not yet. I'm cutting the grass, before the rain comes."

"Just finished mine. You almost done?"

"I wish. Not everybody has a souped-up mega mower like yours, Barlow. My old push job stalls at every turn."

"Well, hurry up," Jason says while tossing his cap on the table. "It's getting late. And Cliff just texted me. He's done mowing, too."

"Of course he is. With that little wussie patch of grass he cuts, it's no wonder."

"No, man. But then he went and *fertilized* it."

"What? Is it really time for the weed and feed?"

Jason looks out at his now-tended lawn. "No pressure, guy."

# *eighteen*

### *Early Thursday Evening*

BRADFORD, THIS IS WHAT YOU need to do." Matt stands with his golf club propped against his leg while he tugs on a black mesh glove. In the four hitting bays next to him, the guys gauge the driving range's green lawn and practice-swing through the air. "Visualize this past weekend on your golf ball," Matt says.

"Oh yeah?" Kyle asks, stretching his arms to loosen up.

"Every minute of it. Because first you picture the weekend on a ball, and then?" Matt pauses as he swings his club, connecting with the ball and sending it zinging out onto the range. "You just whack the memory away."

"Not bad advice there," Cliff tells them from the adjoining bay. He shifts his stance and takes aim with his club, lifting and swinging it around. Shielding his eyes from the low setting sun, he looks out to see where the ball landed.

"Yo, boss." Nick points to Cliff's tee, where the golf ball still sits. "You missed."

"Dang." Cliff adjusts the width of his stance, flexes his knees and swings again. This time he clips the ball.

"Nice hit," Jason tells him. Standing in his cargo shorts and ratty college tee, Jason looks out at the green to size up the shot he wants. "But still, Commish. Two tries to connect? You might need glasses."

"Or those mean gloves Matt's got," Kyle adds. "How are they for your grip, guy?"

"Excellent." Matt lines up his club and cleanly hits another ball, sending it soaring. "The gloves are really lightweight, with a compression fit. Moisture wicking, too. Taylor gave them to me for Father's Day."

"Maybe you just need to work on your timing, boss," Nick tells Cliff. "In your swings."

"No. I'll tell you what I need." Using his club, Cliff nudges a golf ball into place. "I need that gosh-darn domino in my back pocket. Can't seem to find my good-luck charm anywhere."

"Come on." Jason motions through a practice swing, then rips a drive. "Do you hear yourself?" he asks while everyone pauses to watch his ball soar steadily out onto the range. "Lucky talismans and all that shit?"

"Don't knock it until you've tried it," Cliff tells him back.

"Could've used that lucky domino myself last weekend," Kyle adds. "Maybe it would've helped." When Jason looks over at him, Kyle simply shrugs.

153

And so it goes. Buckets of balls get emptied. Competitions ensue: closest to a target, or the farthest hit.

"To the white flag," Jason decides ten minutes later, when the range is covered with their balls. "Whoever gets closest, payoff is five dollars each." He goes through his whole routine: first moving a few feet behind his golf ball, shielding his eyes and studying the exact location of that distant flag. He walks to his tee then, holding his golf club pointed toward that flag as though measuring the distance and direction. Finally, he lowers the club, shifts his stance, focuses and takes his shot.

*And* opens his hand to collect twenty dollars in fives once the others swing and lose.

That's just the beginning, though. Arguments erupt later, trying to decipher whose ball landed near some designated distance marker. A few more bets are lost, money keeps changing hands. Golf clubs connect, and often clip the mats.

"Hey," Nick tells Kyle. "You're hitting the shot heavy, catching your mat first. I hear your club scraping."

"That's enough out of you, kid," Kyle says, reaching over and lifting the fabric of Nick's olive-green polo shirt. It's got sporty white stripes running down the sides and around the fitted short sleeves. "Where do you think you are, anyway? The PGA Championship?"

"Listen, dude." Nick gives a faux swing. "I stopped home after work just to change. Because if you dress the part, you become it."

"Eh. That's just psychobabble," Jason tosses over from his bay.

154

"No, man. It's true," Kyle insists. "To convey authority, studies say to dress the part, you know? Ever since I bought the diner, I iron my aprons, polish my shoes. For a crisp management look. And hell, it works." Pressing his arm to his forehead, Kyle squints out at the ball he just hit. *Damn, still off*, he thinks. "Looks like I need some new polo shirts now. Maybe then I'll whip your asses here."

But with all the golf talk, and ribbing, and competing, one thing's *plainly* obvious to Kyle. It's that even though he came undone last Saturday night, the guys don't hold it against him. They don't care that he blew the weekend to oblivion. It's business and bullshit as usual on this Thursday outing. Putting and driving. Swinging and missing. Laughing and boasting and paying up as the sun sets on the range.

Still, none of that changes one fact. One lousy, silent fact that's shadowing Kyle's every move, every grip on the club, every aim, every swing on this jewel-green driving range on a warm summer evening. And that would be this: Shane Bradford is sitting in some little beach bungalow, right in their community.

Kyle realizes something else, too. None of these guys are uttering Shane's name. It's just like after the pact they made so many years ago, when Kyle swore them all to silence around a roaring bonfire.

And Kyle gets it. He sets down a ball, shifts his stance, looks out at the green, then at his ball while lightly swinging his club. Finally he pulls back, swings and hits it. The guys just want him to decompress. To visualize the weekend-from-hell on his every golf ball and whack it away.

So he tries. Lord, does he try.

But the fact remains. Shit, it's always, always there. He feels it with every minute ticking by this August evening. Yes, every ball hit—every white ball sent flying high against the violet sunset sky—puts Kyle one minute closer to coming face-to-face with his brother.

He doesn't know how. Doesn't know when.

All he knows is that it's coming.

# nineteen

## Thursday Night

IT WAS WRONG ON SO many levels, the way Shane Bradford kissed her on the beach this morning.

Or was it?

Shane insisted Celia misread the whole thing. Did she? Was it just a spontaneous summer moment? Regardless, here she is now, sitting in The Sand Bar with everyone she loves—and everyone who despises the man. So she has her own Shane secret now, too. One so big, it might as well pull up a stool and take a seat beside her. Oh, if her friends only knew. Not so much that Shane kissed her, but that for a few seconds, she kissed him right back.

"A little nervous tonight, Cee?" Eva asks from where she sits with Matt, Maris and Jason in the booth behind her.

"What?" Celia feels it, the way she flushes with the question. Because it feels pretty darn much like Eva's reading her mind about that one illicit kiss.

"You know," Eva tells her, nudging Celia's shoulder over the booth back. "Playing in front of a crowd?"

"Oh. Kind of." Celia looks around. Beach umbrellas illuminated with twinkly lights stand at either end of the bar, where a few people nurse their drinks. Two of them spun their stools around and watch the second open-mic act about to perform. Most of the booths and tables are filled, too. Folks talk, laughing easy on this summer night. On the small dance floor, an amp and microphone stand are set up beside a tall stool … all of it centered beneath a ceiling spotlight.

Just then, a young couple takes the stage and chats with the audience—*How're you doin' tonight? Thanks for venturing out.* The woman moves aside the stool and stands in front of the mic. The man takes his place beside her as they settle in together, tap the microphone, then quietly sing a practice scale. They finally begin their a cappella performance with a verse of humming-in-unison before singing a familiar folk song. It's a song Celia knows well—one of questions, their answers blowing in the wind.

"You'll do great," Lauren is saying, squeezing Celia's hand and nodding toward the singing couple. She and Kyle sit in the booth with her.

"I thought it would be quiet tonight." Celia looks again at the crowded barroom. "You know. Mostly empty tables. You and Kyle giving me some moral support."

"You just have the jitters." From where he sits beside her, Nick tips his beer to Celia's glass of wine. "I've heard you sing, Celia. On the beach, at Sal's birthday party. You've got this."

"Anyway, everyone needed a night out after this past week," Maris admits from her booth seat behind her. "We came to cut loose. Eat, drink and get down with your tunes."

Celia looks over her shoulder. Maris and Jason sit facing her, and she gives them a weak smile. "Stage fright, you know? It's been so long." What she doesn't say is that one of the last times she *did* open-mic night, it was a week after Sal died—a year ago now. She'd downed several potent drinks before taking the stage, which was when Jason walked in, alone.

Alone, and missing Sal, too. Later that night, she and Jason ended up comforting each other in a very slow jukebox dance, leading to a lengthy kiss, leading to God damn trouble—if Jason hadn't stopped it cold. They'd since let bygones be bygones, but Celia never thought he'd show up at another of her open-mic nights again. "Probably doesn't help that it's so warm in here," she says now.

"Let me open the door and get a breeze in this joint." Jason slides out of his booth and crosses the room. After propping the door open, Kyle and Nick join him when he stops at the bar and talks with the bartender.

"You okay, Cee?" Lauren asks once Kyle leaves the booth. "Want to get some air outside? You look pale."

Celia feels the evening air that already makes its way through the open entrance door. Piecemeal traffic sounds come in, too: the roar of a passing motorcycle, a horn beeping. At that moment, Elsa and Cliff arrive, walking through the open door and stopping to talk with the guys at the bar. But in the breeze coming through that door? Unlike the song, no answers are blowing in on it. Nothing to allay a distracting kiss unnerving her tonight.

"Celia?" Lauren asks again.

Celia turns and looks at Lauren. But breeze and all, a glass of wine and all, Celia still feels … off. "Maybe I just need to freshen up," she tells Lauren. "Come with me to the ladies' room?"

~

The lighting is harsh in the bathroom; the tiled walls, dingy. When Celia and Lauren walk in, a woman is leaning close to the mirror over the sink and applying mascara. Celia pulls a hairbrush from her purse, and Lauren takes the brush from her just as the other woman leaves.

"Here, let me," Lauren says. She turns Celia toward that large mirror and begins brushing her hair.

There's nothing like having a beach friend, that's for sure. Sometimes Celia finds it hard to believe that she only met Lauren a year ago. So much happened last summer— a summer that changed Celia's life. Some might call it all fate, or destiny. Others would insist it was simply a seaside spell cast upon her as she drove beneath that darn stone railroad trestle.

Celia looks at her beach friend's reflection now. Lauren wears a sand-colored V-neck shirt with crisscross lacing, half tucked into fitted white skinnies. She looks a little tired, too. "Have you talked to Kyle yet?" Celia asks her. "After seeing Shane?"

"No." Lauren pulls the brush through Celia's hair. "Since we got home, Kyle's worked nonstop. I thought I'd mention things before coming here. But it's going to rain tomorrow, so he was in a cut-the-grass mania. Then the guys took him to hit some golf balls. To decompress?"

"Oh, jeez. He's going to have to decompress *again* after you tell him Shane wants to meet up."

"I know, right? So I figured I'd talk to Kyle privately here. Convince him with the music playing, and over a drink. Nice and easy."

"Sure. Then … let me guess. Everyone else showed up and nixed that?"

"You got it. And *tomorrow* I have to pick up the kids! There hasn't been a spare minute to talk since we got back, I swear."

"What will you do, then?"

"Try to pull Kyle outside later, away from the gang. If I can even talk for ten minutes about Shane—who *did* agree to meet with him—it'd help." Lauren finishes brushing Celia's hair. "Because believe me, Kyle can't deal with any more surprises."

"I don't blame him," Celia says, taking her hairbrush back. Surprise seems to be Shane's middle name these days; she had one herself earlier today on the beach.

"I can assure you, one more surprise would do Kyle in, so a talk with his brother needs to be *fully* planned." Lauren digs in her own purse, pressing aside her wallet, her keys.

"Here. I've got a new lip gloss," she says while handing it to Celia. "It's sparkly, so it'll look nice under the lights."

Celia leans close to the mirror, first adjusting her black tank-top strap. But when she applies the lip gloss, all she thinks of is that one surprising kiss from Shane. If it were a kiss from *any* other man, she'd tell Lauren about it. Hell, Lauren even put things together about her and Jason last fall. But … not Shane. Instead, Celia gives Lauren her lip gloss back, blots a tissue on her lips and adjusts a wide silver belt she wears low over her long black lace skirt. As she does, a woman enters the room and turns into a stall.

"Feeling better?" Lauren asks from behind Celia as they leave the ladies' room.

"Little bit," Celia says over her shoulder. "Just have a funny case of the butterflies tonight. That always happens before I go on stage. And of course, now I'm always thinking about Aria. Worrying about her."

"She'll be fine!" Lauren insists as she catches up and walks beside Celia. "Taylor loves babysitting Aria, so don't worry. And it's good to get out after the year you've had." They wind around crowded tables covered with food and drinks. "Too bad I didn't bring my tambourine, though. I could've played with you."

"That's all right." Once they get to their booth, Celia grabs her guitar. Grabs a deep breath, too, in case that might help. Oh, she could use a good dose of that sweet salt air that cures what ails you right about now. "Okay, guys," she says to the three of them—Lauren, Eva and Maris. "I'm going to set up."

"*Good luck,*" Lauren whispers, right as Eva punches the air, saying, "Knock 'em dead!"

Without looking back, Celia walks away, guitar in hand. Passing Cliff and Elsa with a wave, she heads to the shadows just beyond the stage area. Right then, the couple singing a cappella gives a quick bow to the crowded room.

~

A round of applause rises from the tables as the man and woman at the mic leave the stage.

"Jason, you next?" Patrick asks from behind the bar. "Got a story to tell? Song to sing?"

"You always ask me that," Jason says from his stool, where he's sipping a beer.

"Seems like you might be good for a joke or two." Patrick grabs a soda gun and fills a glass. "You could entertain the good folks in this establishment," he says to Jason.

Jason grabs a handful of pretzels and tosses a few in his mouth. "You're killing me, man. I don't have any hidden talents."

"Yo, Patrick," Matt says when the bartender slides him the soda. "You might want to ask *Maris* about Barlow's talents."

"Yeah," Kyle adds. He reaches for the pretzel bowl from his seat beside Jason. "Especially on a Sunday morning."

Jason gives Kyle a good shove, nearly knocking him off

his stool. "And what about that vow of *celibacy* you took, Bradford? How's that working out for you?"

"No vow renewal, no action?" Nick asks, drawing a hand over his goatee. "Pretty quiet in that countryside shanty you stayed at?"

Kyle gags on a pretzel, then gets Nick in a headlock and gives him a quick noogie, rubbing his knuckles roughly over Nick's head. "News flash," he manages, then downs a mouthful of beer. "Makeup sex ended that celibacy vow."

"Oh, man," Patrick says while tipping a glass and pulling a draft beer. "Makeup sex. Almost worth picking a little fight sometimes, no?"

Suddenly the ladies are all calling out good wishes as Celia takes her guitar over to the stage. When the guys turn with whistles and thumbs-up of their own, they see the food platters their waitress just piled onto their booth tables.

Kyle stands and reaches for his beer glass. "Time to chow down."

"From the looks of your monster dinners, you clowns are keeping me in business another night." As he says it, Patrick reaches for a wineglass hanging over the bar. "Enjoy yourselves."

~

And oh yeah, joy's the right word.

It begins right away as they gauge whose dishes were set at which booth and jockey for the closest seat. Maris slides

164

over for Jason to sit beside her; Kyle sits with Lauren across from them. The others—Eva and Matt, Cliff and Elsa—sit in the booth behind them, with Nick pulling up a chair and sitting at the end of that table. All the while, plates are shuffled, napkins unfolded, and the talking stops as everyone digs in.

"Oh my God," Kyle says after getting his mouth around some toppling deluxe burger.

"I always *said* paradise was a cheeseburger," Nick tells them, then bites into his own. While chewing, he leans back and nods to Jason. "Barlow. From the look on your face, this maybe tops Sunday morning paradise?"

As Jason swipes his mouth with his napkin, Maris shakes her head. "Jason, really?" she asks, giving a wink at the same time. "That's kind of personal?"

Right as Jason points a warning finger at Nick, Patrick's on the small dance floor where a microphone is set up. When he announces Celia's performance, they randomly clap and holler, Kyle calling out, *Rock it, Cee*, before turning back to their food.

From his booth seat, Jason's got a clear view of the bar's makeshift stage. Celia sits on a stool beneath the spotlight.

"Hi there. I'm Celia," she says, leaning close to the microphone. A silver thumb ring glimmers as her fingers draw a pick across the guitar strings. She taps the mic then, clears her throat and fusses with her long skirt. "I'd like to open with a new song for you tonight." Before starting, she adjusts the microphone again. At the same time, Patrick dims the bar lighting so that the mood becomes more

165

evocative, Celia more noticeable beneath that lone ceiling light. Her black lace skirt falls in folds down her crossed legs; her guitar rests on her lap. The spotlight shines on her straight auburn hair.

When Maris nudges Jason, whispering, "I can't see," he shifts in his seat. Sitting beside his wife in the dark booth, feeling her lean into him, watching her snag a few of his fries, the one thing Jason's thankful for is this: Maris is unaware that less than a year ago, he nearly blew his marriage to smithereens, right here. Shit, grief is a monster sometimes. And he was in the full throes of grief the night he walked into this bar alone for a quick sandwich after work. Coincidentally, it was Celia's first open-mic night since Sal's death the week before—a loss from which they both reeled. When a few drinks turned into a very physical slow dance and whispered words beside the jukebox, well, Jason's *still* relieved that they untangled from each other and wised up before crossing a dangerous line. Stinging regret has Jason briefly close his eyes at the memory. It never should have happened.

Lightly strumming her guitar now, Celia tunes a string. "I wrote this first song not too long ago," she softly says into the mic. "It's called *Beach Blues*." Another strum as she glides her pick over the guitar strings. "Take from it what you might … the blues of the sea." A sharp whistle cuts through the quieted bar, getting Celia to nod to the dimmed room before continuing. "Blue sea glass. The sky over the ocean." She tucks her hair back and looks to the side, as if listening to the sea itself. "Or maybe you'll feel a certain blue frame of mind you might have walking the water's edge."

When Celia begins her song, the music captivates. Her left hand moves along the guitar's neck; her other hand strums the tune. There are no lyrics, just her acoustic guitar playing. Jason, reaching for a few French fries, thinks the melody moves like waves. It recedes, advances. Changes course. Their two booths go quiet with everyone listening while digging into an abundance of food.

And if the dark barroom can go even quieter, a second later it actually does. At the other tables and booths, any random talking and laughter stops when a bluesy, low harmonica riff joins Celia's strumming.

"Oh, man," Jason whispers to Maris beside him. "Sounds good."

"Celia must've planned a surprise. Maybe that's why she was nervous."

"Who is it?" Lauren asks, twisting around to see the small stage illuminated by that lone ceiling spotlight.

Jason looks to where Celia sits with her guitar, the microphone stand close to her. The harmonica gets slightly louder, then fades, much like Celia's song. Just as Jason looks, Celia stops strumming and glances over her shoulder to see who's joined her performance. If Jason's not mistaken, everyone around him follows Celia's gaze, right at that moment.

Right at the moment when Shane Bradford, wearing jeans and a tee with the sleeves ripped off, walks out of the shadows.

Shane, with a braided leather cuff on his wrist, and tattoos covering those exposed arms.

Shane, with his devil-may-care attitude, walking straight across the small dance floor.

With his hands cupping a harmonica to his mouth, he plays on while stepping closer to Celia. His bluesy jam seems custom-made for her song as his fingers open and close around the instrument. He pauses when he bends into a particularly funky riff, his foot keeping time as he draws out the notes.

When Shane catches Celia's eye then, she nods. Slightly, but it's there. A true pro, she turns back and resumes her song—without missing much of a beat.

# *twenty*

## *Moments Later*

DECOMPRESS, LIKE SHIT. IT WAS all for nothing, hitting those golf balls. Hell, they might as well have ricocheted and flew right back at him. Because instead of relaxing with the gang in The Sand Bar—shooting the breeze, having a beer—Kyle's got a hard knot twisted up in his throat.

Here it is, the minute he knew was coming—he just didn't figure it would be this soon. Sitting in the dark bar, it felt as though Celia's bluesy guitar song pretty much unrolled the red carpet for Shane. Beneath that solo spotlight, he walked straight back into their lives.

Unable to stomach another bite, Kyle sets down the last of his burger and watches his brother approach Celia. Wearing jeans and a sleeveless tee, Shane's arms are obviously jacked from years of lobstering. He stands there, bent into his harmonica-playing—his hands folded over the instrument, his riffs weaving right through her song.

And Kyle's seen enough. Suddenly, he stands—toppling over the chair at the end of their booth as he slides out of his seat. He winds his way around several crowded tables, turning this way, veering that. Problem is, it's hard to get around with the barroom lights lowered. Several candles burn in globes on the tables, casting wavering light on the patrons there, but the place is in shadow. When Kyle trips on someone's chair, he turns and claps the dude's back. "Sorry, man," he manages to say, then heads straight out through the bar's side door. Heads straight out, drags a hand through his hair and looks around.

"Kyle!" he hears Lauren call behind him. "Wait!"

By the time she gets to the door, Kyle's standing at the railing beside a round table. His hands clench that railing; his chest rises with a difficult breath. And his beautiful wife, wearing a crisscross V-neck top over white jeans, stands beneath a flickering fluorescent light in the doorway. She walks to him on this ruined night.

"I've about had it," he tells Lauren. "My patience is worn so thin with that guy, I'm ready to put our house for sale and go back to Eastfield just to get away from him."

"Calm down." Lauren reaches for his hand and loosens its iron grip. She pulls him to a seat at a mesh table beneath a black umbrella strung with twinkly lights. "Now sit there. Just *sit*," she insists. "And I'm not going to even talk to you until you breathe."

"Lauren, if I—" Kyle stops when he sees Cliff standing in the doorway, then stepping outside once he spots them.

170

"Kyle." Cliff sets two strong-looking drinks on the table. "Maybe this'll help you two."

"Thanks, Judge," Kyle quietly says.

Cliff nods, pats Lauren's shoulder and goes back inside.

"Okay," Lauren begins, pulling her chair in close. She waits until the couple at a table beside them—obviously wanting to better hear the music—heads inside with their drinks. "Okay, listen," Lauren says then.

"Oh, no." Kyle takes a long swallow of the potent drink Cliff delivered. Because it's all there, in Lauren's tone, in her small smile. Yep, some trap's already been set and he's about to step right in it. "No, no, no," he says, shaking his head as he does.

"Wait. Just hear me out."

"What is it *this* time?" Kyle asks, his voice low.

As Lauren digs in her purse, she says nothing. In that silence, Shane's harmonica and Celia's guitar work their way outside to the still summer night. The harmonica is like the night's mist, wavering, rising. If it were anyone else on that harmonica, Kyle would've been so into the impromptu jamming going on in that bar. If it were *anyone* else.

"I got this from Shane." Lauren sets an envelope on the black mesh table.

Kyle looks at her, then wordlessly sits back—arms crossed over his chest.

"No!" Lauren harshly whispers. "Don't you *dare*, not with everyone here!" She leans close over the table, the crisscross ties of her blouse hanging loose, her grey eyes locked on his. "You *control* yourself this time."

Okay, so he knows she's right. The last thing they need is another fiasco like last weekend's. If that happens, he'll lose everything: Lauren; his friends; and yes, his house—because he'd seriously have to move from the shame of it all. So Kyle takes another sip of his drink and pulls himself together, best he can. "Go on. Just lay it on me."

"First? I absolutely did *not* know Shane would be here at the bar. And second, I tried to stop you at home. To talk. You *know* I did. I waved you down while you were running over all those twigs in your mowing mania."

"I had to get the grass cut. It's going to rain tomorrow."

"Yeah. And then you *had* to go hit a bucket of golf balls with the guys." In her pause, Shane's harmonica unleashes a low vibrato ending in a bluesy *wah-wah*, eliciting several whistles from the crowd inside. The remaining guys at a nearby table head into the bar for the show. Once they pass them, drinks in hand, Lauren continues. "I didn't even get a car ride here with you so we could talk about what's happened."

"What's *happened*? And what would that be, exactly?"

"After this was delivered to me yesterday …" Lauren picks up the letter and hands it to him. "I met with Shane at his cottage."

"*What?*"

Lauren nods. "I did."

"Why didn't you tell me, Lauren?"

"I planned to. Tonight. *Here.* Over a drink together."

"Tonight."

"Yes! But I had no idea Shane would show up like this.

172

And I especially didn't think *anyone* would be here except you and me, to watch Celia. So it seemed like a good time to talk."

"You ever hear of talking at home?" Kyle leans close, still holding the unopened letter. "You didn't think about filling me in on *what's happened* like, maybe, last night? When we *were* alone? In a quiet house?"

"And what then? You'd never have fallen asleep after what I'm going to tell you. You'd toss and turn and fret and be pacing the house all night."

Kyle's shaking his head. "But I already knew my brother was at Stony Point, so what's the big deal? Barlow filled me in yesterday. When I told you that last night, it didn't occur to you to—"

"No, Kyle. No. Because listen." She reaches over and lightly touches the skin beneath his eyes. "You're tired enough with all the stress of this week. And it *shows*," she whispers. "I wanted you to get a good night's sleep."

It's her touch—her soft fingers brushing his face—that finally does it. That gets Kyle to briefly close his eyes. That gets him to breathe a little easier, to unknot some muscles. After a second, he reaches up and loosens his shirt collar, then uses a paper napkin to pat his forehead.

"You *said*, when we were at the cabin," Lauren goes on, her hand stroking his arm now, "that you would talk to your brother. You *did*, Kyle."

"I know." He takes a long swallow of his tall, cool drink. "But then we got Elsa's text message saying Shane left. Done deal. I got out of it."

"Except guess what? Your brother stuck around. And he doesn't want to leave without talking to you." Beneath the glowing lights strung in the umbrella spokes, Lauren leans close. She touches Kyle's face again, and runs a few fingers through his hair, whispering, "Give him that much, okay?"

Kyle looks at her, dropping his voice. "What are you saying?"

"Here's your chance." She motions to the doorway, the same doorway where more harmonica strains float out into the night. "Your second chance, like Sal always talked about. So, I don't know … Maybe go in and have a beer with Shane. One beer."

When Kyle pulls back, his resistance is clear. "What would I even—"

"No. No, listen," Lauren interrupts. "You don't *have* to patch things up."

He looks at that damn doorway where, on the other side, the crowd is whistling and randomly applauding. Kyle's not sure he's ever seen The Sand Bar this electric. He picks up that letter and opens it. As he sees Shane's handwriting, and reads his words—*my brother's been on my mind … sticking around Stony Point for the next two weeks … speak with you alone first*—Shane's harmonica winds its way through the doorway. Inside the bar, there's a lot of rowdy foot-stomping going on.

Out here on the deck, it's different. The tables all emptied as folks went inside to watch that harmonica-guitar duet, leaving Kyle alone with Lauren. Hell, he could easily stand, pull his keys from his pocket and take off with her right now. Just go. Walk down the few steps to the parking lot, get in his pickup truck and split, leaving Shane and worry and an incredibly awkward reconciliation far, far behind.

Lauren leans close and squeezes Kyle's hand, getting him to look up from the letter. "Just break the ice," she says.

⌒

Maris wants to leave. Now. Right away. Ten minutes ago.

*Before* Shane started jamming with Celia on the bar's stage. Because now that he's here, it's happened again—her past keeps imposing itself on her life. Even worse, not only does Jason know she and Shane were once engaged, he also knows Maris kept it completely secret from him.

So the three of them in one room? It can't feel more uncomfortable. It might help things if someone were sitting in the booth *with* her and Jason. But Elsa and Cliff are sitting with Matt, Eva and Nick in the booth behind them. And Lauren hightailed it outside with Kyle. Without them sitting with her as a distraction, Maris knows damn well the night's headed downhill. The only way to salvage it is to leave.

She leans close, rubbing Jason's arm as he watches the scene unfold at the microphone. "Want to go, babe?" she asks.

"Why?" Jason looks from Shane onstage, to Maris. "I

want to see this play out. Need to be here for Kyle."

"Really …" She forces a small smile. "Kyle has to handle this himself, don't you think? We should actually give him some space. Let's go," Maris says while starting to stand.

"What's your rush?" Jason looks at her for a long moment. "What are you running from?"

Standing now, she looks down at him—still sitting and blocking her in the booth. "What?"

"I've seen you do this before, sweetheart."

"Do what?" Maris picks up her shoulder bag from the booth seat, all while hoping—*praying*—Jason takes her cue and stands to leave.

"You're running," he accuses her instead, leaning an elbow on the table.

"What are you talking about?" she loudly whispers, hitting his shoulder to get moving.

"I saw how you ran from Scott a few years ago." Jason takes a long swallow of his beer, then looks up at her again. "Ran from your past, too, the day I found you at the airport. Did it again, now that I think of it, at the Bushnell Park Carousel. The night before we were married."

With the music growing louder as Celia gets into the harmonica accompaniment, and with the crowd reacting with hoots and whistles, Maris glances to that elusive, distant, propped-open bar door and simply nudges Jason's arm.

"Maris?" a voice asks.

When she looks up to see Elsa standing in shadow at

their table, Maris slowly sits beside Jason again. Elsa, wearing a faded denim jacket over a black tee and black capris, bends low over the table.

"Maris, you look flushed." Elsa looks at Jason, too. "Jason, if she wants to leave …"

"Elsa." Jason nods at the booth seat across from them. "Have a seat."

Elsa does, but tentatively. "What's going on?" She leans forward, her hands clasped on the table. "If Maris want to leave, I mean … Cliff and I can take her home if she'd like."

"No, Elsa," Jason says over the music. He pauses when applause breaks out at a particularly raw riff. Finally, leaning forward too, Jason continues, his voice noticeably lower. "Now listen. And you listen good."

He moves aside his dinner plate to get even closer in the dark space. But that's not what tenses up Maris. No, it's the way Jason lowered his voice. She watches him closely, and silently.

"Elsa," he begins. "Nobody else saw Kyle last Saturday night. No one but me. And I witnessed all six-feet-two of the guy reduced to puddles, thinking his marriage was done. His life done. I saw how much Shane's presence upset my best man and good friend. No one else was there hauling Kyle out of the water when he was drunk and devastated. Just me." Jason stops and holds up his hand when Elsa tries to interrupt.

"*Jason!*" Maris whispers. "Let Elsa talk."

He doesn't. He merely drops his head until Maris is quiet again. When she is, he looks directly at Elsa—with no apology, no backing down. "I listened to Kyle say what a *mistake* it was moving to Stony Point. How if he didn't move there, he never would've unpacked his marriage certificate that got the whole vow renewal going, and Shane never would've shown up. I saw Kyle *undone*." He glances over at Celia as she begins a slower song that falls over the room like a hush. Shane's harmonica accompaniment fades to just a breath of vibrato. "So shoot me, okay?" Jason tells Elsa then. "But I'm staying here tonight, for Kyle. And so is Maris."

"Jason, I don't think—" Elsa argues, but just as quickly stops. She simply looks over at Shane on the bar's makeshift stage.

Jason does, too. Shane backs up a step, harmonica in hand while he listens to Celia sing before bringing in a mellow riff.

Problem is, Jason, Elsa, all of them … They're not even hearing the music. Maris knows it, feels it, tastes it. It's a moment thick with only tension as Elsa still watches the stage. Finally, she slightly shakes her head before standing when Cliff motions her back to her seat. As she goes, she leans over and squeezes Maris' arm—practically bringing Maris to tears.

But it's Jason she's acutely aware of, especially once Elsa's returned to her own booth. "*Jason*," Maris whispers close.

He answers her without turning, keeping his eyes on Celia and Shane. "And you can stop dancing around the subject. Haven't seen you this flustered in a long time,

Maris. Ever since Shane arrived, you've been off." Now? Now he looks at her to deliver a question she can't avoid. "What gives?"

"*Stop it.*" Alarmed at her own angry voice, again Maris leans close in the noisy bar and whispers harshly. "You've been at me *constantly* about this." She hesitates when he looks her straight on. "Too much so."

"And *you're* deflecting."

"We can't talk here."

Jason glances over at the others in the booth behind them before answering. "You can't talk *anywhere*, lately. Not at home, not outside on our deck. Not here."

There's a sudden blur of motion coming up beside them. It's Eva this time. No doubt riled up by Jason's restrained anger, she scoots into the booth seat across from them. Maris drops her eyes closed for a long second, because if anyone always has her back, it's her sister. And she makes no bones about it, ever. It's obvious Eva's about to let loose.

"*Jason!*" Eva begins. "You're making a scene. Everybody's getting uncomfortable. And look." She nods to Maris sitting beside him. "Now you're making my sister cry."

Jason glances at Maris as she quickly swipes away a tear.

"What's the matter with you?" Eva says, leaning halfway across the table and pointing a stiff finger at him. "Arguing here like this."

"Eva." Jason leans equally close over the table. "Fight your own battles," he says, then hitches his head for her to leave. When she finally does—in a breathy indignation—

Jason turns to Maris. He touches her hair and speaks softly this time, near her ear. "Maybe you should talk to Shane."

"What? Why?"

"Seeing you like this? Wanting to book it out of here? There's obviously more of a history between you two than you're letting on. And you *know* how I feel—you cannot hide from the past. So just go say hello to the guy," he says. "Talk."

Her regretful smile comes first because, heck, there's no way out of this now. "I already did," she quietly answers. "We've talked."

In his pause, Jason looks closely at her. "I know."

"What?"

"My thought exactly. I saw you and Shane talking on the beach the other day. Saw you storm off, too, and have been waiting for you to spill it to me. But you won't." He leans closer and presses his mouth near her ear, while watching only Shane as that darn harmonica grows louder. "You're just not talking these days." Jason's low voice fills her ear. "Not to me. Not to Shane tonight. Not to *anybody*."

"That's not true!" she insists under her breath. Her throat is so tight trying to keep her words civil, it hurts. "I just can't talk now. *Here*."

"Okay. But we are *not* abandoning Celia, *or* Kyle, leaving them alone with Shane. No one here is."

Maris starts to talk, but snaps her mouth shut. Sitting beside Jason, she sips her wine instead. It's all she can do to get any of the liquor down her closed-up, tense throat.

Again Jason leans over. Again he presses his mouth

close to her ear. She feels his breath against wisps of her hair as his controlled voice rings clear. "And you're a *helluva* lot stronger than what I'm seeing tonight. So buck up, darling."

# twenty-one

## That Same Night

CELIA NOTICES ONE THING. SHE'S aware of it as she leans her guitar against the stool and walks off the stage area while the crowd whistles and claps. She's aware of it when the waitress hurries over to give her a glass of water.

"Great set, hon," the waitress tells her. "How about an encore?"

Celia, still aware of that one thing, takes a long sip of water to satisfy her parched mouth. "We'll see. Maybe one more song."

"I'll let Patrick know." The waitress pats her arm before hurrying off toward the dimly lit bar.

And still, Celia's aware of that one thing as Shane moves beside her. She'd never expected this to happen, this one thing. Never saw it coming; never would've guessed it earlier in the bar, when all she wanted to do was pack up her guitar and head home. She gives Shane a good look now that she's not preoccupied with playing her songs. He's wearing jeans with a sleeveless tee. A leather cuff is wrapped around his wrist; a shadow of whiskers covers his face. And he's clearly in his element tonight, with that harmonica, in this casual environment. The way the salt air drifts into the dark tavern, Shane must feel like he just stepped off the lobster boat and stopped in for a cold one after a long day at sea. His stance is easy, his expression relaxed.

Seeing him here, having him here, Celia *still* notices that one thing: She can't stop smiling.

And it feels good.

"What are you *doing* here?" she asks Shane while laughing and brushing a strand of hair off her damp face.

"Hoping to talk to my brother," he tells her, fidgeting with his harmonica. "Lauren mentioned they'd be here tonight. Added bonus was catching some of your act."

"That was so much fun! No one's ever jammed with me like that before." She turns and looks at the empty stage. "And you stole the show!"

"No." Shane points his harmonica at her. "*We* did."

Celia sips her water, needing to cool down after the set she just performed. Her songs felt different tonight. More alive. More just plain, well, *fun*. She eyes Shane closely. "You're not really as *bad news* as everyone would have me believe, are you?"

"Do *you* think I am?"

"No." She steps back, her long skirt skimming the floor. "Not yet, anyway."

183

Shane, well, Shane takes two steps closer for the two steps she'd just taken back. "I see you got some sun this morning?" He lightly touches her face. "Got some freckles going on. That tent hold up okay for little Aria?"

"It did! We ended up staying on the beach too long, though. I barely had time to get ready and square away the babysitter."

Shane gives a slight nod. "You look good, Celia."

As he says it, the stage lights come back on. Celia glances to the stool and her waiting guitar, then back at Shane—still watching her.

"One more song to close out the night," Patrick says into the microphone. "Give it up for acoustic singer-songwriter, Celia Gray!"

Celia sets her water glass on a nearby table. "That's my cue," she says, brushing back another wisp of hair and walking toward the stool beneath the solo spotlight.

"Take it away," Shane tells her from the shadows as the bar crowd lets loose with their applause.

Celia stops and turns back. "You coming in on this one?"

"No. The floor's all yours now."

～

Halfway to the stool beneath the spotlight, Celia looks at him for a long second. Finally giving a slight wave, she then grabs her guitar and takes her seat. The whole time, Shane watches from the shadows. He's glad to be in the semidarkness now. Maybe he'll spot Kyle somewhere in the bar. Maybe he'll walk over, shake Kyle's hand. Say hello.

Maybe.

In a moment, though, standing side-stage alone, Shane feels eyes on *him*. So he glances over and sees not Kyle, but the whole beach gang sitting in a couple of booths. Jamming with Celia, he hadn't noticed them beyond the crowded tables on the floor. One thing's for sure. He's taken aback by the surprise of it all—of seeing his old friends right there. Only his brother and Lauren were supposed to be at the bar tonight.

But if there's anything he's learned from fifteen years on the sea, it's pretty much not to expect *anything.* Any wave can crest, any wind can kick up, any boat can pitch, any storm can turn. When it does, you damn well better be ready for it, or you're going down.

So … he's ready.

Standing in the darkness, Shane leans against the wall and simply watches Celia perform then. Watches her hand strum the guitar, sees her tuck her auburn hair back. Returns the discreet smile she sends his way.

✺

*Break the ice. Break the ice*, Kyle reminds himself with a few long breaths as he steps back into the dark room and walks to the bar. He feels Lauren squeeze his hand before she veers off to their booth, leaving him alone now.

Break the ice? Hell, Kyle could break a barstool or two.

Break a glass. Break a few heads.

At the bar, he orders two draft beers. Beneath the beach umbrellas propped at either end of the bar, tea-light candles flicker in crackled-glass globes. Standing there, Kyle wonders how many times in the past year he's actually lit a candle for Shane. For his brother. How many times, for some reason, he's swung into St. Bernard's Church and touched a lit taper to a candlewick with thoughts of the guy he hasn't seen in nearly two decades.

"Shit. Be careful what you pray for," Kyle mutters with a glance over toward Celia taking her seat beneath the spotlight again.

"Say something?" Patrick asks, setting down the two frothy glasses.

"No. It's nothing." Kyle leaves a few dollars on the bar, grabs the beers and walks into the shadows. But he circles around to the back of the barroom, so he can approach the offstage area inconspicuously. Don't need a full audience tracking his every move; witnessing him sweat and stammer his way through some painful reconciliation.

He sees Shane, up ahead. He's leaning against a wall while watching Celia sing. And there it is, that cavalier attitude, obvious in a knee bent as a foot is kicked back on the wall behind him; in his hands casually hooked in his jeans pockets. He and his brother will surely be a study in contrasts to anyone watching—if Kyle can just get himself to keep walking.

Which he does.

Holding the two beers, he walks right into the shadows.

Right into the darkness, and hell, into some nerve-racking unknown.

Yes, for the first time in fifteen years, Kyle finally does it. He stands beside his brother. "Shane," he says, giving him one of the beer glasses. "Been a long time."

"Kyle." Shane looks at him, takes the beer and awkwardly gives Kyle a one-arm hug. "Good to see you, man."

And that's it. They both settle in, leaning against the wall and swigging their beer. But Kyle felt it. He felt his brother's hand slap his shoulder. That's *all* he feels right now.

"Want to grab a seat?" Shane asks a moment later.

Kyle rolls his shoulder as though there's a crick in it. Shoulder slap or not, brother or not, he's no fool. Grabbing a booth means one thing—sitting too long and getting trapped. And a seat at the bar? Well, that's another can of worms. A seat at the bar means too much of an audience all around him … beneath that dim amber pendant lighting, reflected in the bar mirror. Kyle never intended this meeting to end up seated. Standing in the shadows suits him just fine.

"A seat?" Kyle asks his brother. "Nah."

"All right. That's decent."

Neither of them really looks at the other. Celia's their distraction.

After a lengthy pause, Shane raises his glass to Kyle. "How've you been, then?"

*How've you been?* Hell, Kyle's not sure any question could

be more loaded. How's he been? Well, if you mean for the last fifteen years, that answer runs the gamut. How was he when the union steelwork dried up years ago, leaving him with a part-time diner gig while Lauren temped for some local insurance agency? The financial stress weighed heavily on his marriage then. He nearly died in a reckless fall off the boardwalk during that stint, on a night when he thought he'd lost Lauren for good.

Or, how was he when Jerry actually gave him the chance to buy The Dockside? How was he as he and Lauren scrounged every penny of savings, every cent of one last severance check and begged, borrowed and stole the rest just to barely piece together a down payment? Is that what Shane really wants to hear?

Or should he tell his brother how he was two summers ago upon discovering that his son, Evan, was really Neil's? That the child was conceived when Lauren broke off her engagement to Kyle, just a month or so before their wedding. How was Kyle that summer, when learning that secret moved him to mess around with a twenty-something and nearly destroy his marriage? Is *that* what Shane wants to hear?

Or does Shane want to hear how it was moving to Stony Point, and what that took out of Kyle—from a year of house-hunting, when every real estate agent told him and Lauren to keep an open mind at every dump they toured; to throwing out his back on moving day; to unearthing his marriage certificate. While unpacking, he'd lifted that certificate out of a box of paperwork and discovered his misspelled name. Which led to a planned vow renewal ceremony to correct it, and to hope the next decade would fare better.

Instead it all led to this God damn moment. Right here. Right now.

"How've I been?" Kyle asks in the shadows as Celia's voice sings a soft melody.

"Yeah."

"Been all right," Kyle says, rather than all the rest. "You?"

"Not bad." Shane swigs his beer, still leaning on the wall. "Lauren told me you bought the old diner."

"I did." Quiet seconds pass between them. "Jerry sold it to me a few years ago now."

"You always liked that place. I'm glad for you," Shane says, his voice quiet, calm.

Kyle looks at him, right then and there. Gives his brother a good scrutiny. "Are you, Shane?"

"What?"

"Are you *really* glad for me?" Kyle looks over toward the booth where Lauren sits with Jason and Maris. "You didn't give a shit fifteen years ago," he says, pausing before dropping his voice to an impatient whisper. "And honestly? I'm thinking you *still* don't."

"Not true, man."

"Hard to get into things here." Kyle hitches his head toward the booths in shadow. A candle glimmers in a low globe near Lauren; he can make that out. "Got a lot of eyes on us right now. You feel it?"

"I feel it. And it doesn't matter. I don't care."

189

"Fine. I'll go along with this bullshit." Again, Kyle looks at only Celia as she leans toward the mic. "You still lobstering?"

"Absolutely." Silence, then, "It's all I know, Kyle."

"So what are you doing here?"

"Was invited by your wife. For your vow renewal ceremony."

"Well, that day's sure as hell come and gone. So I'm wondering why you're still hanging around. Thought maybe you quit lobstering."

"Can be a lot of crazy chaos out on the ocean, definitely, putting my body through the fuckin' mill. But until things give out on me, and my bones can't take the beating from hauling pots on the seas ... I'll be on the boats."

"You ain't on a boat now."

"The boys got me covered for the time being."

"And how long's that?"

"Two weeks, man. Give or take," Shane says, pausing and glancing over at Kyle. "Shit. I'm here just to see you, brother."

"All right." Kyle pushes himself off the wall, takes a couple of steps and turns back to Shane. "You can check that off your list now." He tips his beer glass to Shane's before walking away.

And that's it. As agonizingly slow-in-coming those few minutes were, just as quickly, they're done. Kyle crosses the dark barroom and returns to his booth. He sees it all, too. Sees Jason slightly raise his drink to him. Sees Maris give him a small smile. Sees Lauren slide over in the booth seat to make room.

But no one says a word. Which means they saw it all go down. And what can they even say? Anyone can well imagine how painfully awkward it was, that reluctant reunion. So they look over to the open-mic stage as Celia finishes her number and thanks the crowd.

They all do, except for Kyle. Instead he looks back to where he stood with his brother moments ago.

Stood with his brother.

It's still hard to believe, even though it really did happen. Kyle squints into the darkness and just catches a glimpse of Shane leaving, walking out the side door, alone.

# twenty-two

### Friday Morning

SHANE'S PLAN TODAY IS SIMPLE. It's to have a grilled cheese sandwich for lunch at his brother's diner. Because there's no way in hell he's letting Kyle off the hook that easily. If you'd call their few, sparse words last night a reconciliation or not is debatable. At least in Shane's book.

So while sitting on the half-wall of his open back porch Friday morning, Shane makes his decision, then sips from his coffee cup to seal the deal. Kyle's not going to call the shots on their reunion anymore. Shane is. He'll stop in at The Dockside and hopefully get Kyle to sit with him—even for ten minutes—and talk more. *Without* an audience.

To sway the odds, he reaches into his button-down shirt pocket for Cliff's domino and gives it a spinning flip. The way Cliff insisted the faded domino brought him good luck, well, Shane wouldn't mind if some of that luck rubbed off on him at lunch today.

But he's got hours to fill until then.

He lingers with his coffee and looks out at the gray clouds churning over Long Island Sound. It's a familiar sight, indeed. Shane knows what's next, and can actually see it start. Further out, a sheet of rain is moving over the water. It's like a silver wall, blurring the sky behind it. And on that distant water? Thousands of tiny drops hit the water surface, making the merest pinprick splashes. That open view is why the porch is his favorite part of the old cottage. Sitting here like he's on a boat's deck, he can have his morning coffee and gauge the sea, the weather—even his life.

When he starts to feel those raindrops hitting his face, he heads inside. Taking his coffee, he crosses the porch, going through the squeaking screen door to the kitchen. Problem is, the way the wind's picked up and blowing that shower almost horizontal, the rain's coming in the cottage windows now. So he hurries first to the living room and starts shutting the windows there. Some stick in the humidity, but with a good shove, down they go.

At the third window, a motion catches Shane's eye. Out on the street, Celia is walking by. While pushing her stroller with one hand, her other hand's shielding her face from the sudden rain. Quickly then, she twists out of her windbreaker jacket and drapes it over the top of the stroller, trying to keep her baby dry.

Shane shoves the window back open. "Celia!" he calls out. He bends low so she can see him. "Hey, Celia! Come in out of the rain." When she stops and looks toward his cottage, he yells through the thrumming downpour, "It's Shane!"

Well, God knows what bullshit the gang filled her head with after he left the bar last night. But something's got her really tentative as she squints through the pouring rain, gauging the skies—and no doubt the distance back to her own cottage. He rushes to the front door and trots outside.

"Come on!" he calls as he runs down the driveway and helps her with the stroller. By now, Celia's hair is soaked, and her clothes are spattered, too. "Hey, come inside and dry off."

It's been a long time since Celia's walked into a cottage like this one. Since last summer, to be exact, when she staged so many old beach houses for Eva's realty. Nothing much changes from one tired cottage to the other: from the wide-planked paneling, to the paned windows framed with sparse cotton curtains that'll puff out in a sea breeze, to the lumpy couches and chairs slipcovered in sun-faded stripes and soft plaids, to the painted end tables, to the clear glass lamps filled with salt-coated seashells.

But what strikes Celia *most* is the dank scent of sea damp. In this little beach bungalow, it's as though it clings to every fabric; is a topcoat on the dull paneled walls; fans from every page of old novels on a shelf. There's something about the pungent coastal scent within these shabby cottage walls—she could be blindfolded and know exactly where she was by that scent alone.

Stopping just inside Shane's cottage door now, she simply takes a long breath.

There's something else she's doing, too. Dripping rainwater. Puddles of it pool around her feet.

"Let me get you a towel," Shane says before rushing down a dark hallway. Moments later, he returns with a few. "Here you go."

"Thanks." Celia reaches for them as she fusses with Aria in her stroller. With the corner of a smaller towel, she bends close and pats her daughter's damp cheeks and forehead, then lightly fluffs her fine dark hair. That done, she glides the towel over Aria's arms and legs. "Okay, sweetie?" she murmurs, leaving a whisper of a kiss on the baby's face.

"Does she need anything else?" Shane asks.

"No. I'll dry off, then wrap her up to keep warm." Celia lifts a second towel, a bath towel, and scrunches her own damp hair in it, then presses it to her face and arms. "Ugh," she says, blotting her sleeveless blouse and denim shorts, too. "What a dirty day." Quickly she looks up at him, standing nearby. "You know. Like you told me about? I feel like I just went overboard."

"You got swamped, for sure."

"I'll try not to make too much of a mess here."

"Don't worry about it. Hey, I've got coffee on," he says, half turning and walking backward toward the kitchen. "Would you like one? While you wait out the rain?"

"Sounds great."

"How do you take it?"

"With cream," she says, looking over from drying off Aria's stroller, which is also dripping wet.

Once Shane's in the kitchen, Celia loosely swaddles Aria in another towel and lifts the baby to her shoulder. Her daughter is very interested in these new surroundings and looks around the room. Celia turns and looks, too, at the thin checked curtains framing the paned windows; at the walls painted white, except for the wood-paneled fireplace wall. The beamed ceiling is unpainted, too, exposing raw planks of wood beneath the crossbeams. Blue and green glass fishing floats hang from ropes in the corner, and a gray rattan sofa is casually covered in white cushions and pillows.

When she turns a bit more, Shane's back and setting their coffee cups on a distressed, painted trunk. He walks closer and touches Aria's towel-fluffed dark hair. "Hi, there," he says.

Celia bounces the baby a little. "I thought I could get a walk in, and give her some fresh air before the rain came." She glances toward the window, where outside, rainwater cascades off the roof now. "Mother Nature had other plans."

"As she usually does. Maybe you'll walk tomorrow."

"No can do. I'm actually bringing Aria to my dad's, in Addison. He's watching her for a few days while Elsa and I are busy with a final cleaning and last-minute things. Before the inn opens?"

Shane nods while stroking the baby's cheek. When the living room grows dark with the sudden rainstorm, he turns on a table lamp.

They're quiet, then. Celia just stands with Aria near the front doorway. The rainfall outside makes a constant whisper; the room is only dimly lit.

"Celia. Come on. Have a seat." Shane motions to the rattan sofa. "You won't be going anywhere for a while with the way it's coming down out there."

"I guess you're right. So … nice of you to call us in," Celia says, cautiously sitting on the edge of a couch cushion. She holds Aria on her lap.

It's quiet again, when Shane takes his coffee and walks over to the fireplace. On the mantel, carved sandpipers stand alongside a tall wooden lantern—its glass paned, a fat candle inside it.

"I had fun last night, Shane," Celia says after a moment.

"Me, too. It was a good time on stage."

"How do you do it, just jump right into my songs like that?"

He watches her for a second and gives a slight shrug. "Fifteen years being out at sea. Gave me some time to work the blues on that harmonica of mine. So I liked your song. *Beach Blues.* When I walked in the bar and heard you talking about it, I pictured the open, blue Atlantic. That song," he says, pausing to sip his coffee near the fireplace, "the way you played it on your guitar … well, it was custom-made for a harmonica riff. I hope you didn't mind."

"No, just the opposite. More like I *appreciated* it," Celia says while stroking Aria's now-dry hair. "Because I'd felt a little off last night."

"How come?"

197

She moves the baby to her shoulder, then reaches for her coffee and takes a sip. "It's been a year since I'd done open mic. Sal convinced me to do it, first time around. He actually inspired that song." She gives a regretful smile while setting her coffee cup on the painted trunk. "*Beach Blues.*"

"Really …"

Celia looks at Shane standing there at the mantel. Dressed in a loose button-down over his tee and jeans, leather boat shoes on his feet, he's completely at home here, pure beach bum. His sleeves are cuffed back as he holds his own coffee. As he listens.

So Celia stands, too, and rubs her drowsy baby's back while circling the living room. "I was ready to leave Stony Point, last summer. It was supposed to be a temporary thing, staying here. And it was time to go." She walks around the sofa, passes a small wood table. On it, a silver tin pitcher is filled with dried beach grasses. Two painted seascapes framed in gray driftwood lean on a wall shelf.

"What happened?"

"Sal happened. We'd started dating, and he saw me one day when I'd begun packing my things. My summer stay was about over. I was sad to leave and told him I had the blues. Beach blues."

"The blues," Shane repeats. "Because you had to leave Stony Point?"

Celia nods, still lulling her sleepy baby around the shadowy room. The rain outside falls steady. Sheets of it, gray and liquid. In the hiss of the rain, she remembers Sal's whisper when he took her hand in his. *Come on*, he said, leading her outside. *I'll show you a different kind of beach blues. The kind that'll only make you smile.*

"Sal took me outside that day," she tells Shane, "and we walked to the beach so he could show me another kind of beach blues. The sea. Wild hydrangeas in the dune grasses." Her sandaled feet cross the cottage's planked wood floor as she goes back in time. "The sky over the water."

Shane is quiet, and moves to a chair near the hanging fish floats. He cups his coffee mug in his hands, waiting as Celia settles sleeping Aria into her stroller. She pulls a light blanket over the baby and wheels the stroller off to the side, into the hallway where it's quieter.

"Beach blues were everywhere we looked," Celia says on her way back to the living room. "Even Sal's cuffed jeans were blue. Sea glass, too. We walked the driftline, and he actually found a piece of blue sea glass. And when I smiled?" She looks over at Shane, silently watching her from the chair. The hiss of rain fills the room in her pause. "He kissed me," she whispers, then sits on the white-cushioned sofa and reaches for her coffee cup again. "I remember that, the way the sea breeze blew my hair, and he pressed it back. And touched my face. And kissed me, right beside the *beach-blue* sea." She glances from Shane to the rain-spattered window. Her voice drops with the memory, and drops further with the words she hasn't once said in the past long year. Words she's felt plenty; words she's swallowed.

Words that have been a long time coming. "God *damn* him."

"What?" Shane leans forward, his crossed arms on his knees. "Celia. That was a beautiful story."

"Oh, Sal made *everything* beautiful. He had that way about him." She stands and presses aside a checked curtain to look out at the rain. "And then that selfish son of a bitch went and died."

"What? Selfish?" Shane asks.

She looks back at him with a raised eyebrow. "After stringing me along *all* summer? Making me *think* we'd have a perfect life together? Yeah." She turns and crosses her arms before leaning against the wall. "Had me believing we'd get married, live a beach life. He got me—stubborn as I was—to fall in love with him."

"But Celia. Maybe—"

"Oh, no. Don't you defend him. I did *not* want to get involved with anyone, and he knew it. I came to Stony Point fresh out of a divorce and only wanted some quiet time, you know?" She presses back a strand of auburn hair. "A couple months at the beach to clear my head. *Not* to fall in love again."

"I'm not getting how he strung you along, though," Shane admits.

Celia looks long at him, directly—without wavering. "Sal never told me he wasn't well. Even when I suspected something, he actually *denied* it." She stamps her foot then. "*Denied* it!" she says again, this time as her eyes fill with angry tears. Tears that have her swipe at them.

"What was wrong with the guy?"

Surprisingly, Celia's answer comes at him like one of

those rogue waves Shane encounters on the lobster boats, hundreds of miles offshore. Yes, just like on the vast waters in the Gulf of Maine, Celia's words overtake him, catching him off guard, off balance.

*As a child growing up in Italy, Sal had rheumatic fever … Damaged his heart, his valves … Symptoms came and went throughout life … Chest pains, palpitations … Breathlessness, fatigue … Kept it secret until right before his valve-replacement surgery … But it was too late, too late, too late.*

"You had no idea?" Shane says in disbelief.

She shakes her head. "He hid it from me well. One day when I went and asked him if he was okay—because I had some doubts—instead of telling me the truth, he took me to this godforsaken shack he'd found." She paces behind the sofa now. "Threw me off the topic. Distracted me from his health issues. Said he was fixing up that shack for us, for a getaway. He *acted* like everything was fine."

"What do you mean, a shack?"

"Oh, yeah. You'd know the kind. It looked like something straight out of Maine." Celia picks up one of the damp towels and begins sharply folding it. "Silver shingles, strung with buoys," she's saying as she tosses the folded towel on the painted trunk. "Supposedly it belonged to Neil, back in the day."

"A shack? Where is it?"

"It *was* out past Little Beach. You could only get there by boat." Again, she brushes away a tear. "But of course Maris has the shack now. Jason had it towed on a barge and it's in their yard. Maris does her writing in it."

Celia's pacing gets more agitated, Shane notices. She walks a few steps, abruptly turns, stops with a quick breath. "Maybe you want to sit down, Celia." He stands and takes a step closer. "You're upset."

"That's right, I *am* upset. Sal used me, didn't he? That bastard used me. *Didn't* he, Shane?"

"Celia." Shane turns up his hands.

"No. *No.* Sometimes I hate that man so much. He kept his dirty little secret to get what he wanted from me. To get my love, my *life!* Now I just want to wipe it all off me," she says, her hands slowly swiping at her arms. "Wipe last summer off. Wipe *him* off," she insists through more tears as her hair falls across her face. "And the thing is? I can never get upset with the people here. I have to be *smiles.*" She looks at Shane through those tears. "I have to say what a *blessing* Aria is. And she *is,*" Celia says, briefly cupping her crying face. "Oh my God, she is, she is. But … maybe I didn't want to bring her back to Stony Point. And I can't really tell anyone here how I feel now, can I?" she asks, her hands drawing her damp hair back.

Shane steps closer. "Tell me."

⁓

Celia only looks at him with a teary smile. Something, she starts to say something, but stops and shakes her head.

Shane steps closer still. When he moves a strand of auburn hair off her damp face, her eyes drop closed at his touch. "Why did you come back, then?" he whispers. "To Stony Point."

"Jason Barlow asked me to," she answers, softer than the whisper of rain outside. "For Elsa. She was selling her inn." Celia spins around, her hands sweeping open. "Everyone wanted to save her dream. But what about *my* dreams? *My* life?" Celia looks back toward the kitchen, then toward the hallway, almost panicked. Finally she rushes to a window and tries to open it, but it sticks in the humidity. "Come on, come on," she pleads.

When she gasps, and pushes at the window so roughly, Shane fears her hand will go through the glass. So he silently walks to her. Without a word, he stands behind her and takes her in his arms. Folds his arms right around her— locking her arms to her side, setting his chin on her shoulder, giving her not an inch of space to move.

And he takes it, all of it. All of Celia's struggle. All of her pain as she tries with all her might to twist out of his hold, to push him away. To whip her arms free—but her strength is no match for his.

"Sal used me. He used me, used me, *used me*!" she sobs then. Her shoulders begin shaking, but she doesn't give up the fight.

When Shane turns her to him in his arms, Celia tries to punch his chest. But he doesn't loosen his hold and instead takes every bit of her anger. Every bit of the sadness and grief that she'd long held inside. Takes her every blow until her body goes lax. She feels fragile in his arms then, and when he realizes she's simply weeping now, he presses her face against his chest. "Shh. Shh," he whispers at the side of her head. "It's all right, Celia," he says, stroking her rain-mussed hair, holding her close until she quiets. When he finally relaxes his arms around her and steps back, he bends low to see her downturned face. "You'll be okay," he whispers again, then leads her to the sofa and sits with her for a few moments. She leans against him such that he fixes her hair, touches her tear-streaked face, her arm.

A gust of wind blows outside, bringing a spattering of rain to the windowpanes. For whatever reason, Celia wanted a window open. Rain or not, she wanted to breathe that damn salt air, maybe to cure what ails her. Maybe to just catch her breath after letting out a pent-up anger that's festered for a year now.

An anger she could direct at no one.

An anger at Sal for leaving her the way he did—pregnant and heartbroken. And alone.

So Shane gets up and goes to one of the windows, opens it halfway and looks out on the summer rain. A cool mist of it comes through the screen. He turns, then, to Celia. Her breath is still shaking; her hand wipes her cheek. She is spent.

"A dirty day?" Shane asks, then crosses the room and sits beside her again. She's been completely undone by the direction her life took. Yet no one knew it. No one even *suspected*. But Celia unraveled, right here in his cottage.

Right in front of him.

He hooks a gentle finger beneath her chin and lifts her wet face to his. "You've had a helluva dirty *year*."

# twenty-three

THE RAIN STOPS AS QUICKLY as it began. One second, it drummed on the little beach bungalow's roof. Shortly afterward, the rooms inside go oddly quiet. It takes Shane and Celia a moment to realize why. But as soon as she sees the sky outside lighten, Celia gathers her jacket and little Aria in her stroller, and goes on her way.

Unlike the rain, though, Shane doesn't let up. Not after seeing Celia break down the way she did—silently, her shoulders shaking, her tears caught in her hands. So he walks with her and her daughter down the beach roads to the boardwalk. The air is damp, the stroller wheels gritty on the wet pavement. On the beach, they stop beneath the roofed pavilion, which kept the boardwalk dry from the summer shower.

"Aria and I will sit here for a few minutes. Get some fresh air," Celia says. "Then I'll take her home for lunch."

When Shane nods and starts to leave, Celia calls out his name. He turns, tipping up his newsboy cap and waiting. It's been a long time since he's worried like this for someone.

"I'm sorry," she quietly says. "You know, about before. It's just … one of those days."

One of those days.

He's been having *one of those days* every day here at Stony Point. He salutes Celia and hurries back to his cottage so that he can get to The Dockside in time for lunch.

Lunch with Kyle.

～

Fridays are always busy at the Dockside Diner, but add rain? It's standing room only out there. Kyle can tell from where he's cooking at the big stove. The hum of talk, and clatter of plates and silverware, carries right into the kitchen. Today, he's thankful for the rain making it this busy. Being busy keeps him distracted from thinking. If he wasn't filling stacks of white dishes as fast as he is, all he'd think about is his talk with Shane last night. Wondering if he should've said more. If he should've asked Shane to sit with the gang. But Kyle *couldn't* keep talking. The moment was too big, with too many thoughts and words bottled up for fifteen years. It was all he could do to just stand beside his brother in the shadows and say a few of those words.

"Let it rain, let it rain," Kyle mutters as the waitress hooks two more orders on his carousel. Cooking beats coming undone by his own thoughts. And at least it's Friday. He steps away from the stoves to catch a glimpse outside. The rain's actually let up now. He bends for a better look out the booth-side windows. Yep, the sun's breaking through the clouds so things will dry out in time for Friday night fishing.

Which is just what he needs at the end of this long week: a few hours sitting on the rocks with the guys, casting their lines, bullshitting with some cold brews, breathing that sweet salt air.

Back at the stove, though, he gets to it. Lunch is quick cooking. People stop in for a bite and breeze right out. So Kyle's grilling sandwiches and making wraps, while Rob's manning the burgers. Patties sizzle on Rob's stove; rolls are toasting on the grill top. Burgers are lined up on several plates, too, as Rob goes down the burger assembly line, adding lettuce, tomatoes, fries, before setting out the plates for the waitresses.

All the while, Kyle's working on turkey wraps, loading up tortillas with Dijon mustard sauce, baby spinach, and sliced turkey sprinkled with shredded Swiss cheese. Quick, quick, as the waitresses come and go, leaving orders, taking plates. Add chopped tomato and roll up the wraps, slice in half, go. Back to grilling chicken for sandwiches. Slide spatula beneath, flip, flatten.

"Kyle!" his head waitress says as she zips into the kitchen. "I didn't know you had a brother."

When Kyle glances over at Stacy, he burns himself on the stove edge and quickly shakes his hand.

"I saw this guy in one of the booths and thought it was you," Stacy's saying, leaning in the doorway. "Spittin' image, I'll tell you. So I said, *What are you doing out here, Kyle? You know what he said?"*

"No." Clearing his throat, Kyle slathers mayonnaise onto toasted bread off the grill, then drops cheese onto the sizzling chicken cutlets.

"*Not Kyle*, he said. *Kyle's brother.*"

"Shane."

"Unbelievable. You never mentioned you had a *brother.*" As she says it, she sets her pencil behind an ear.

Kyle adds lettuce, salt and ground black pepper to the bread, halves the cheesy grilled chicken cutlets and drops them on the sandwich bread. More mayo, tomato slices, done.

"Well, your brother—Shane, is it? He requested that you *personally* deliver his lunch."

"It's really busy, Stacy." Kyle dabs his forehead with a towel, then tosses it over his shoulder. "So I don't know about personal service today," he says, leaning to the side to glance out at the packed diner.

Stacy shrugs, rips Shane's lunch order off her pad and walks to Kyle's stove, clipping the order on the carousel right in front of him. "Up to you," she offhandedly tells him, then lifts the two plates of turkey wraps he'd already finished up.

So much for being busy.

So much for rain, and mobs of customers keeping his thoughts at bay.

208

So much for loading up his second stack of white plates with quick, fresh-cooked lunches.

So much for working his stovetop like there's no tomorrow.

Shane just cut through it all—right to the chase.

Or not. Kyle finishes the toasted chicken sandwiches, adds pickle spears on the side—creamy coleslaw on one, fries on the other—sets out the plates and reads Shane's order hanging on the carousel. As he considers it, he's wiping his hands on his white chef apron.

A grilled cheese sandwich. *Seriously?* Kyle squints and leans closer. That's what his badass brother wants?

"Hey, Rob," Kyle calls to the other cook as he preps the sandwich bread. "Where are those peppers from the farmers' market?"

"The what?" Rob's flipping burgers on his grill top, then using his spatula to clear off some grease.

"Those hot peppers delivered with the vegetable order."

"No, man," Rob warns him. "They're the wrong ones, remember? *Waaay* too hot. Shit, they're dangerous. Can practically set your mouth on fire."

"Yeah. Those are the ones. Where they at?" As he asks, Kyle's putting on protective gloves so as not to get any pepper-seed oil on his skin. He wants that formidable burning to hit one person and one person only.

Rob walks over and drops the container of peppers at Kyle's cooking station. "Here you go. Thought we were tossing them," he adds on his way back to his stove.

"Just need a few," Kyle tells him. "For a special order."

Because Shane wants lunch? Personally delivered? Kyle slices one of the peppers and lifts it to his nose, inhaling deeply. A burning sensation from the scent alone brings tears to his eyes. Whistling, he spoons out more peppers, preps and slices them before drizzling oil on a hot skillet and adding the peppers.

"*I'll give my brother a lunch to remember*," Kyle whispers as the pan begins to sizzle.

There's no mistaking that Kyle runs a tight ship. From where Shane sits in a window booth, he can see that. Each red-padded booth seat is wiped clean; old, vintage buoys—red, yellow and blue—hang from the ceiling like pendant lights; each silver napkin dispenser shines like glass; lanterns sit perfectly centered in each booth's window. And in the far corner, a display of seaside scenes painted onto driftwood is for sale, along with stacks of neatly folded diner T-shirts.

Shane can also see Kyle walking out of the kitchen. A white apron covers his black tee and black pants. A small towel is tossed over his shoulder. His light brown hair is cut short, and sort of spiked—as though he'd been to the barber's recently for his vow renewal. And his face is dead serious as he personally delivers Shane's lunch on a tray. Which he sets on the end of the table, then sits in the booth seat across from Shane.

"There you go," Kyle says, nodding to the plate on the

tray. "Dockside Diner makes one mean grilled cheese."

On the plate is a sandwich perfectly toasted and oozing with thick, melted cheese. His brother must've doubled up on that cheese, just the way Shane likes it. A hefty pickle spear sits against the sandwich, with a helping of French fries off to the side.

"Thanks, man," Shane says while grabbing a paper napkin from the dispenser. "By the way, awesome décor here, Kyle," he says, nodding to the fishing net draped along a far wall. Starfish and seashells cling to the ropy net. "Looks like I'm out on the lobster boats."

"Nautical is nouveau these days," Kyle says with a glance at the net. "Guess we both feel at home by the sea."

"Well shit, after you spent years building ships, being a union steelworker and all. Totally get that."

Kyle sits back, arms folded over his chest.

"Really nice digs here, bro. You did all right," Shane tells him, motioning to the diner that's chock-full of patrons right now.

"Don't need no pat on the back."

"It's not like that. I'm just saying—"

"What're you doing here today, anyway?"

Shane reaches for his sandwich dish and sets it on the table. "You *know* why I'm here. I told you last night. Lauren invited me."

"No. Not why you're *here,* in Connecticut." Kyle points out the window where the parking lot's still wet from the rain that's stopped. Down the street a ways, sunlight now glistens on the blue harbor waters, where white sailboat masts dot the view. "Why are you in *my* personal space? Still."

"Thought we could talk more. You know, work some things out over lunch together."

"Lunch?" Kyle looks at the mobbed diner, then at the watch on his still-folded arms. "You've got five minutes."

"Five minutes. Okay, better dig in." Shane notices that Kyle didn't bring out a lunch of his own. His brother just sits there, rubbing a hand on his jaw, watching him. So Shane lifts the sandwich. "You make this?"

Kyle nods. "Want some ketchup with it?" As he says it, he shakes the ketchup bottle before squirting a puddle onto Shane's plate. "Enough?"

"Perfect." Shane dunks his cheese-oozing sandwich into the ketchup before taking a big, double bite. The funny thing is, his eyes instantly tear up, and a bead of perspiration emerges at his hairline. He feels it all—the tears, the sweat— right before some godawful fire ignites in his mouth.

And he knows, hell does he know. His brother set him up. Set him up to fall, right here in the Dockside Diner. Problem is, Kyle doesn't know just who he's dealing with. So Shane fights a gag—which he can tell Kyle notices— and keeps chewing. "Really good, Kyle," he manages to say while thinking, *You rotten scoundrel.*

"Thanks." Kyle shifts in his seat and leans an elbow on the table.

So, his brother got him good. Caught him off guard and off his game—giving their reunion lunch a new spin. Shane winces over at Kyle. That'll be the end of this shit. No way is he going down at his brother's hand. Instead, Shane takes an even bigger bite of that cheesy sandwich cloaking some friggin' ammunition inside it, while not once taking his eyes off Kyle's. Even though Shane's burning mouth feels like it might need medical attention. If he can only swallow this—before his throat closes up—he might be okay.

"Still good?" Kyle asks, dropping his voice while leaning closer across the table.

Shane, hell, he can't even talk. But he can still think, though. Think, *You fucking prick*. Because now even his face feels engulfed by flames. He must be red as a beet.

A worry confirmed when the waitress walks by. She gives a panicked double take and backs right up to their table. "Everything okay here?" she asks, looking only at Shane.

"Water, please," Shane barely manages while fanning his face.

"Make it milk, Stacy." Kyle looks at Shane with a slight grin. "Dairy's better for neutralizing the burn, you *wuss*."

"Oh my God, I'm on it!" When the waitress is back only seconds later, she practically spills the milk as she sets down a tall glass. "Anything else?"

"We're all set," Kyle tells her.

Shane stops guzzling the milk long enough to call out, "Wait!" After suppressing a gag, he gets out some hoarse words. "Bring seconds!"

"Of course." After returning with another glass, she walks away, slowly, stealing a glance back at them.

Shane glares at Kyle while gulping down more milk.

"You fuckin' asshole," he whispers then.

"Too hot for you, tough guy?"

A quick laugh first, before Shane picks up that sandwich and takes another bite. "What'd you do?" he asks around the furnace in his mouth. "Sneak hot peppers in there?"

"You got it. Getting back at you for what you pulled— not RSVP'ing to Lauren and setting us up like you did."

"I didn't have *time*. I told Lauren that," Shane manages between coughs. "I just got off the boat and booked it here."

"There's always time. Our night wouldn't have been blown to oblivion if you'd made one *single* call. Sent one damn email."

"So … your payback is a hot pepper?"

"For starters."

They have a showdown, then.

A staring showdown when neither one looks away. Not until Shane stuffs the rest of the sandwich in his mouth, still holding teary eye contact until finally Kyle stands, shakes his head and returns to the stoves in his incredibly busy diner.

# twenty-four

## Friday Night

AT LAST, AFTER A FRIGGIN' long day, it's here. And it's enough to get Jason to gulp one just-as-long salt-air breath.

Yes, it's Friday night, and with a fishing pole slung over his shoulder, he's walking across the beach. The week's done. Work's done. Let the downtime begin. While walking, he rolls a few kinks out of his neck. Madison runs ahead of him on what should be a well-worn path in the sand, given the infinite number of times Jason's walked this beach. Walking it usually does the trick. Usually sets his mind at ease while easing his gait, too. Often, by the time he's walked across this stretch of sand, life is good again.

But tonight, though the rain has let up, Jason's agitation hasn't. One week ago, Shane Bradford arrived at Stony Point—and the place hasn't been the same since. Everyone's bristling. Everyone's on edge. That couldn't have been more obvious last night. While sitting at The Sand Bar with Maris, the tension amped up only once Shane showed up at the bar.

So Jason slows his step. Fishing can wait a few minutes, because his brother's voice sometimes comes when he's alone like this. A whisper might drift in with a sea breeze, or in the rustling dune grasses. Whether it's real or not, all Jason knows for sure is this: He feels his brother's spirit in the places he'd walked; he'd loved. What he wouldn't give to talk to him now.

"You there, Neil?" Jason quietly asks. His hand goes to his father's Vietnam War dog tags hanging on his neck, and he slides those tags back and forth along the silver chain. "See all the shit going down this week? With Shane, and Kyle?"

*Christ, Jay. Crazy. With Maris, too*, Jason hears as a frothy wave gently breaks beside him. *Things'll settle down eventually*.

"Yeah." Jason bends and picks up a driftwood stick, which he tosses for the dog.

*Just stay out of the crossfire in the meantime*, comes Neil's voice, right as another hissing wave retreats back across the sand, into the dark Sound.

"What?" Jason barely says, stopping at the water's edge for a moment. The rising August moon, just past full, hangs heavy over the water. "Crossfire?" he whispers. "Between who?"

Right then, a sharp whistle cuts through the damp sea air. "Yo, Barlow," Kyle's voice calls.

Jason looks over his shoulder to the rocky ledge at the

end of the beach. The guys are fishing there, and beyond them, the patch of woods rises like a dark phantom. Tall pines and oaks cast the nearly hidden path to Little Beach in night shadow.

Turning to join the fishing crew, Jason trips—on a forgotten sandcastle? A dip in the sand? Honestly, it felt more like he'd been lightly shoved. Looking back, he gives a discreet salute toward where his brother's spirit might linger. Ghosts, memories, spirits, they sometimes feel one and the same—visiting him, hovering, guiding. But when Maddy's dog collar jangles as she runs ahead to the guys on the rocks, any whispers behind him fade away.

～

Kyle thought Friday night fishing would never get here. But still, knowing it was on the horizon helped him through the week. Finally, here he is, leaning against a good-sized boulder while tying a lure on his line. The water's calm, the tide's going out—sloshing around the small rocks down below—and that low-slung moon throws just the right amount of misty illumination. Don't even need a flashlight tonight, with that silver moonshine.

"What's biting?" Jason asks, walking up with his fishing pole.

"Snappers," Nick tells him. He reels in his limp fishing line. "The reports say lots of stripers, too. Especially at dusk."

"You're late," Kyle calls out, giving Maddy a good pat

when the dog scrambles over the rocks to him. "Where've you been, guy?"

Jason heads over to where Kyle's stationed. "Where *haven't* I been? Beach Box, Fenwicks' place, and that shotgun cottage I told you about. Plus on the phone with Trent between each."

"Trent." Nick moves closer to the water. "That's your show's producer, right? Cool dude, I met him when you were filming Elsa's reno."

"He's the boss," Jason says. "Then Carol stopped by my studio this afternoon to review blueprints, which are just about finalized." Jason sets down his gear on a large, flat boulder, right beside Kyle's tackle box.

Cliff, standing lower down on the rocks, reels in some line, then lets it go slack. "And when's the *Castaway Cottage* filming begin?" he asks Jason. "For the Fenwick job."

"After your God damn Hammer Law lifts." Jason plucks a lure from Kyle's tackle box and strings it on his fishing line. "The one to which you give no exemptions."

"The rules are the rules. You know that, Jason," Cliff tosses back. "And your *Castaway Cottage* filming would be right on the beach! Construction noise in that prime location during peak vacation season is unacceptable."

"All right, all right." Jason waves Cliff off and fusses with his fishing rod before scoping out the water. "Where's Matt? Couldn't make it tonight?"

"Our resident state trooper's putting in the overtime, as usual. Saving up for that RV he's been hankering after," Kyle tells him. "And what about you?"

"What about me?" Jason asks back as he maneuvers toward a spot among the lower rocks.

Kyle tips up his *Gone Fishing* hat and looks down at him. "How's your leg, man?"

"Seriously?" Jason slows his slippery trek, his hand touching a nearby boulder for balance. "You still asking me that, Doc?"

"Always will." Kyle's voice turns serious. "After what you went through."

"Well, it's okay. Humidity's a bitch today, so had some perspiration at the socket. Wiped it off earlier, at home."

"Hell, it's damp *here* tonight, too. On the rocks. Maybe you should settle up there, where it's drier." Kyle motions further up the rocky ledge near where he's parked himself.

"Nah." Jason moves even lower, carefully climbing over the rocky terrain, and casts his baited line. "Feels good to be moving around, fishing. Especially after the ordeal at the bar last night." He glances back at Kyle. "With your brother and all. Can't believe you finally talked to him."

"Last night was nothing, compared to what happened today," Nick says before swigging from his beer can.

"Today? What'd I miss?" Jason asks.

"Kyle's lunch story," Nick tells him. "What a hoot."

"Really." Jason looks over his shoulder to Kyle. "What happened?"

"My brother stopped by the diner for lunch."

"You shitting me?" Jason asks.

"Nope." Kyle casts his line and squints to watch his lure soar over the dark Sound, landing right where he wants it to, in that swath of moonlight. Further out, he sees the silhouette of a large barge being towed across the water. "Shane wanted to have a sandwich with me, and to *chat*." Kyle air-quotes the word with his free hand.

"Oh, man. It was classic, Barlow." Nick sets down his fishing rod and opens the nearby food tote. "Kyle detonated a bomb in his brother's sandwich."

Jason gives his line a sharp tug, then looks back at Kyle. "What are you talking about? A bomb?"

"Hot peppers. Had a batch *way* too hot for diner food. I mean, they're dangerous. So," Kyle says, smiling at the thought, "I made my brother a sandwich to remember. Sliced up a few peppers, grilled them and hid them in the thick, melted cheese on his sandwich."

"Shit. You didn't." Jason's shaking his head. "Must've set his mouth on fire."

"Eh. Serves him right," Kyle sets down his fishing rod and grabs a beer, too. "Maybe he'll hit the road now. Get the damn message and head back to Maine."

"I don't know about that," Cliff tells them while casting his baited line further out. "Shane seems pretty well settled into that little beach bungalow."

"Yeah," Jason says. "But he's only got the place rented for another week. And Bradford, I thought you were open to hearing him out. When I found you at the cabin last weekend, you said Shane had been on your mind lately."

"Listen, Barlow. Just because I might eventually have a legit conversation with my brother—make peace or some shit like that—it doesn't mean I'm going easy on him. Hell, no," Kyle insists. "If he really wants to mend fences, Shane's got to sweat for it."

∽

A few minutes later, Kyle calls across the rocks, "Yo, Nick. Bring me up a piece of that leftover cake."

"Oh man, good stuff." Nick lifts a wrapped hunk of cake from the tote. "Elsa even sent *me* home with leftovers from your event. Which," he says as he tosses Kyle the cake piece, "I'm very sorry was cancelled, except for the leftover part."

"Whoa!" Cliff yells while pulling on his now-arched fishing pole. "Got one. Oh boy!"

While biting into the cake, Kyle makes his way to the lower rocks. Nick's reaching for the nearby net at the same time, then hurrying to Cliff's side, too.

"Get your phone, Nicholas!" Cliff orders while some monstrosity beneath the water unreels his fishing line in a loud whistle. The noise gets Maddy running closer—her radar ears up, her paws slip-sliding across the wet rocks. "I want a picture of this one. It's a *doozy*!" Cliff is saying as his rod strains even further with some bad boy clamped onto it. "Feels like a big blue. I'll put the photo in the next newsletter."

They gather around Cliff as he reels in the taut line, releases to give the monster fish some play, then barely reels in more line.

"You got it," Jason's telling him, all while grabbing his

221

anxious German shepherd's collar and approaching Cliff at the same time. "Easy does it, Commish. *Easy*. Bring him in now."

Kyle stuffs the last of the cake in his mouth. "Let me help," he says around the food. He moves beside Cliff and takes hold of his fishing pole, too, giving it a sharp pull back, then stepping away as Cliff reels in the slack line. "Shit, that's a beast, Judge."

"Go, go!" Nick inches closer, holding out the large net to scoop the fighting fish once Cliff raises it up. The water surface splashes with the fish's struggle. "Get that sucker out, boss. That's the biggest fish *any* of us ever nabbed!"

"Ride it out, man," Jason tells him. Maddy whines and struggles against his hold when he moves beside Cliff. "Don't lose it. You're almost there."

"Moment of truth, fellas." Cliff reels in the line, pulls back on his bent rod to get more slack line, then quickly reels that in, too.

And suddenly? Nothing. No whizzing fishing line. No cheers and whoops. Just silence when Cliff's fishing rod goes perfectly straight. At the same time, the fishing line hangs slack in the water just yards off the rocks where they're all clustered together. The seawater goes calm, with only wavelets swirling among the smaller rocks.

"Ah, fiddlesticks," Cliff mutters. He pulls the limp line this way, then that.

"Seriously, boss?" Nick steps into a tidal pool and snaps a picture of Cliff's pathetically slack line.

"Oh, man," Jason says, tossing up his hands. "Gone."

The dog is, too. Gone—just like that. As soon as Jason releases her collar, she bounds over the lower rocks and splashes straight into Long Island Sound.

"Aargh, Maddy!" Jason calls out. The dog paddles around and snaps at the dark water as though looking for that monster fish. "Maris hates when she goes for a saltwater swim and reeks afterward." Jason gives a sharp whistle. "Maddy! Let's go. *Out!*"

And out she comes, bounding out the same way she bounded in. Except this time, the dripping wet dog scrambles over the rocks and stops at their feet—where she gives a good and thorough dog-shake. Drops of the sea spray everywhere, on everyone.

"Oh, no you don't," Kyle groans, jumping back and brushing off his shorts. But when the dog thinks he's playing and bows low at his feet, Kyle gives her a head rub. "Atta girl," he says as her tail does a slow swing. "You got us good."

"It's *your* fault, boss," Nick insists while wiping water droplets off his fishing vest.

"Mine?" Cliff asks.

"Yeah. You got us all worked up with that catch of yours, the dog included, for … *nothing!*" Nick says.

"And I'll tell you why." Cliff reels in his now-baitless hook. In the darkness, there's only the click and hum of his reel. "Ever since I lost that darn domino, I've had nothing but bad luck." He tosses his fishing pole onto the rocks as Kyle snaps open a can of beer and hands it to him.

"Drown your sorrows, Judge," Kyle tells him.

223

"Will do." Cliff takes a long swallow of the brew. "Just saying, I'm finding it very distracting, too, wondering where that domino even went. Where the heck is it?"

"Seriously, Cliff?" Jason asks as he tosses his dog a biscuit from his cargo shorts pocket.

"Yes, seriously. It's the not-knowing that's eating away at me."

"Let it go, already." Jason picks up his fishing rod and sits himself on a rock. "Christ, it's a blessed *domino*."

"Yeah, boss. Do you hear yourself?" Nick asks while unwrapping a chicken salad sandwich from the cooler.

"Hey," Jason interrupts. "Those from the diner?"

"Sure are," Kyle calls over. "Brought a few for snacks."

"Give me half of that." Jason holds out his arm and snaps his fingers at Nick, who obliges.

"Anyway, that domino's probably in your desk drawer," Kyle says. He grabs his fishing rod and parks himself beside Jason now.

"No, I looked everywhere," Cliff tells them. He leans against a large boulder and takes another swallow of his beer. "Even checked at Elsa's. Who, by the way, hasn't given me the time of day since I lost that good-luck charm. I can't book a date with her, either. She's so busy fluffing pillows and filling happiness jars for the inn's grand opening. Whenever I stop by, she puts me to work wrapping twine around Mason jars. Stringing twinkly lights."

"Listen, Commish. Maybe you two need a getaway after the inn opens. You know," Jason explains while pressing the last of that chicken salad sandwich in his mouth, "after things quiet down. Like Maris and I are taking this weekend."

Cliff walks closer to Jason, reaching down and touching the boulders to keep his balance on the rocks. "Really? Now that's not a bad idea."

"Is that trip this weekend *already*?" Kyle asks from beside Jason. He stands straight and casts out his line. "You're going to Vermont, right? To the chalet where you honeymooned?"

"Absolutely," Jason says, nodding.

"Congrats, guy." Kyle gives Jason's shoulder a shove. "Two years wedded."

"Or shackled," Nick puts in. "Depending."

"Shackled? What would you know about being shackled?" Jason asks.

"Shit, I know everything I need to just by watching you dudes. Sometimes being a husband seems like it's nothing but a headache. Case in point, last night?" Nick eyes Jason. "You and the wife at The Sand Bar? A little stressed, no?"

"What?" Kyle asks. "You and Maris? Did I miss something?"

"Nothing." Jason glares at Nick before checking his watch. "Nothing worth mentioning anyway."

They all quiet, then, so Kyle figures something went down when he was preoccupied with his brother's intrusion into his life. Out on the Sound, a lone rowboat paddles through that swath of moonlight. Onshore, lamplight spills from the windows of the last-standing cottage on the beach. Kyle looks at it all, then at Jason.

"What's going on, bro?" he asks, his voice low.

"Nothing, I said."

But it's Jason's next words that say it all to Kyle. That say there might be a little trouble in paradise for his friend.

"It's just been a long week, okay?" Jason casts his line far out, where a beam of the Gull Island Lighthouse sweeps across the water. "So another hour fishing and I'm outta here to go home and pack a bag. Because seriously? Maris and I *really* need that getaway."

# twenty-five

## That Same Night

SHANE HAD TO SEE IT for himself.

Once Celia told him about some old fishing shack being towed to the Barlow property, he couldn't get it out of his head. So Friday night, he takes a walk down Sea View Road. The painted bungalows and shingled cottages are bustling with folks arriving for the weekend. Front porches are illuminated; car doors slam; overnight bags are hauled from trunks. Couples stroll along the sandy beach roads. The heavy moon rises low over the Sound. Shane takes it all in before slowing in front of Jason's rambling cottage sitting high on a sloping yard. From the street, only a glimpse of that rescued shack is visible. It's in the Barlows' backyard, beside the big barn. In the moonlight, some of the shack's silver shingles catch his eye.

So he decides to get a better look. First, he studies the Barlow place for any sign of activity. The old beach house rises in dark silhouette—its peaks and gables black against that moonlit sky. Most of the home's paned windows are dark; only a few glow with pale lamplight. Beach grasses and unkempt tiger lilies grow wild behind a low rock wall alongside the front entranceway. With all looking quiet, Shane ventures up the driveway winding beside the imposing home. Halfway up, he stops in dark shadows beside a tall maple tree. Crickets chirp; a whisper of breaking waves comes from out on the bluff. Squinting into the yard, he sees more of the fishing shack.

Sees something else, too. Looking at that weather-beaten shack—its silver shingles tinged with black, vintage buoys of red, blue and yellow strung from them—what he sees is surprisingly painful. Shane steps a bit closer. So much of the sea is evident on that shack: from the deep wood grain of the faded shingles, to the seaworn-smooth surface of those buoys, to the paint peels curling from the window frame. The shack must've sat right on some untamed beach, with years of sea spray leaving it tired and worn down. Oh, doesn't he know that feeling? That tired weariness from facing the constant energy of the sea.

But that's not what's painful. No, looking at the tiny silver shack that Jason towed here special for Maris, something else bothers him. Something really personal. Something stirring up feelings Shane had thought were long gone. It's why he had to walk here tonight—to see if his suspicion was true.

It is.

From where he stands, what he sees in that old fishing

shack up on the hill is this: It's the *exact* life he offered Maris all those years ago. When he proposed to her in front of the shingled dockside home he bought in Maine, it was with the intent of giving her what he sees here, tonight. A good life working beside the sea, living in a weathered beach house.

It wasn't the life she wanted then. But from the looks of things, it certainly appears to be the life she wants now.

The problem is that when he walked down Sea View Road minutes ago, he'd thought stealing a glance at this shack would be enough. Now that he's here, it's not. Not when he sees the coastal reality of Maris' everyday life—a life mirroring the one she'd turned down with him.

And especially not when he sees that the shack is all lit up. Lanterns flicker in the windows, in the doorway, with its wooden door propped open to the night.

Shane knows, too. If that shack's lit up, it means one thing: Maris is working inside it. He also knows that all the guys are out on the rocks. It's their Friday fishing night, after all. According to Lauren, that weekly fishing happens like *religion*. And he could figure that with the hanging out, and beer and food and bullshit going down, those guys would miss their fishing night as well as any devout Catholic misses Sunday mass. Never.

Which would mean Jason's not home.

So in the evening darkness, Shane takes one step, then another, and walks up the twig-and-leaf covered driveway, passing the Gothic-looking beach house sitting near the bluff. When he rounds the corner to the backyard, he pauses off to the side. Uncertain still, he first takes in the sight of the Barlow deck. It sits high on top of a stone foundation, the deck railings weathered and splintered. In shadow beyond it, a large barn with brown, rough-hewn walls is also covered with buoys. Though Shane knows it used to be Jason's father's masonry workshop, it's obviously been renovated. Low, wide steps lead to a double slider. A couple of old-fashioned wooden lobster traps sit on the side of the steps. Shane can barely see inside those wide glass doors. But he sees enough. Picture lights cast soft illumination on immense photographs hung on a large wall. Each framed image is of a stunning seaside cottage, surely ones Jason must've designed and restored. Absolutely impressive.

But Shane keeps walking. Doesn't stop, actually, until he's standing in the open doorway of that shingled fishing shack. And he was right. There's Maris inside, sitting at her computer. It catches his breath, the way he recognizes her posture—it's the same posture she'd assume while bent over fashion sketches years ago. Now, like then, she barely moves except for her creating hands. Her head is tipped, just a bit, as she focuses intently. Her fingers glide over the keyboard; text fills the screen. Wherever denim design took her years ago, the written page takes her now. She wears a pale yellow tee and frayed denim shorts; her hair is gathered in a loose ponytail; a lacy sweater hangs over her chairback. And tiny grains of sand fall in a pewter hourglass flipped beside her open laptop.

Shane watches for a second, then gives a light rap on the doorframe.

"Jason?" Maris asks without turning around. "I'll just be a sec."

"Not Jason." When her hands freeze over the keyboard, Shane quietly continues. "I offered you this life. Working in a shingled seaside home. Breathing that salt air every day. Hearing the gulls cry." He crosses his arms and leans against the doorjamb. "But it wasn't good enough for you then."

Maris spins around in her seat. "Shane."

"And now it is?"

"Shane." She wheels her chair back. "What are you doing here?"

Still standing in the doorway, he takes in the shack's white-painted wood walls, the rustic beamed ceiling, dusty hurricane lanterns, and old fishing poles hung above a shelf of duck decoys. "Heard through the grapevine that you work in a fishing shack. One covered in lobster buoys." Now? Now he looks at Maris. "After you turned down that very life with me, I had to see this with my own eyes."

"Shane. You're at my house? Come on," she says, shaking her head.

"You know, when I arrived at Stony Point last week, you were the last person I thought I'd *ever* see. Surely you would be living in New York City with some hotshot fashion job. Your own state-of-the-art design studio, maybe." He steps inside, feeling the wooden floor creak beneath his foot. "But ... you work *here*? In your shack?"

"It's not really mine. Or Jason's, for that matter. It's actually Neil's, Shane. And *okay*," she says, standing and fiddling with that star pendant she wears. "Fair enough. It must be shocking to see me, well …" Maris stops and gives him a quick smile, then turns to the shelves on the walls. "Okay, look." She picks up a leather journal, then another, before setting them back on the shelf. "These are Neil's things." After tucking a fallen strand of hair behind her ear, she motions to the mugs beside a two-burner camping stove. And to a dingy round table, its wood finish streaked and worn. Her fingers brush the top of a glimmering Mason jar, out of which rises a wisp of candle smoke. "All Neil's."

Still Shane hasn't moved from inside the doorway. He's not sure he's ever seen Maris this unsettled as she flits about the tiny shack—picking things up, glancing at him, touching various trinkets.

"And this," she's saying now, lifting a stack of white papers, "is Neil's, too. His unfinished manuscript."

"The book you told me you're writing?"

Maris nods. "We found it in a drawer here. I guess he started it years ago," she says, her voice quieting. "Before he died," she almost whispers. The rest, the *And before his shack ended up abandoned past Little Beach*, Shane barely hears, her voice fading to nothing as she stands at her writing area and sets down the papers.

"Until Sal found the place, I've heard." When Maris glances over her shoulder at him, Shane walks further into the one-room shack. Celia was right; he'd recognize it. It's straight out of some seafaring storybook tale and pure New England coastal—briny and alluring. Even with the door and window open, the shack's mustiness is salty and wild. That scent will never fade, a part of its very walls. "*Fascinating,*" Shane says, mostly to himself. There are white shells nestled in a wicker basket; and dusty glass-domed hurricane lanterns—the kind that foreboding, late-night stories are spun around. The window's curtain—a white-linen topper—looks like a sun-bleached sail. Candles are lined with dribbles of hardened wax, evidence of being burnt long into seaside nights.

There's more, though. As Shane pokes around the close quarters of this fishing shack, running his hands along the salt-coated shelves, touching threadbare chairs covered with thick throws, he's actually doing something else.

He's hearing Maris move. Listening to her breathe. His every sense is tuned to her in this musty room. When he takes a journal from her, and their hands touch, he better senses the life *they* might have had.

"You still have that shingled house on the docks?" she quietly asks. "The one you showed me that night—"

"It's always been home," Shane answers.

"With a wife?" she asks, hopeful. "Family?" A small smile, then.

"No."

"No wife?" She tips her head. "Divorced?"

"Never married, Maris."

When she says nothing, he looks at the journal he's still holding. A seagull feather serves as a bookmark, and he flips to that page. Neil's handwriting covers it. Shane skims the lines but is unable to focus on his old friend's thoughts on the beach, or Neil's commentary on some weathered cottage he came upon. No. All he's aware of is Maris.

Maris, hovering in the shadows. Her silky brown hair pulled back. Her denim shorts faded. A turquoise cuff bracelet on her wrist. Barefoot. Casual as ever. And wary.

"I offered you all this," Shane finally says again, stepping closer to her. The planked floor creaks. "But it wasn't good enough back then." He sees that her eyes are moist. "Now it is?" Another step closer, another quiet moment. "I'd really like an answer, Mare."

"Shane." She takes a deep breath. "It's not that. Not you, I mean. Or Jason. No, no." Looking out the window, she continues. "It's actually none of that keeping me here now, living my life this way. It's … It's *Eva*, who—come to find out—is my sister."

"I've heard. Elsa filled me in on some things."

Maris looks from the window to him now. The room grows even quieter, the air closer. She squints through the shadows. "And it's *Elsa*, too, keeping me here. My dear aunt Elsa. Shane. No one else could come as close to being the mother I lost when I was a girl."

He says nothing, just slightly shakes his head while stepping closer. He sets Neil's journal aside before talking again. "Family."

A quick nod of her head as she steps closer to him. "*Yes!*" she whispers. "That's all we have sometimes, don't you think?"

"Family?"

More silence. Maris stands in front of him and turns up

her hands. The moment is alive. Somehow, being here in Neil's shack frees them. It puts them in neutral territory.

They're not in Rockport, Maine. Not outside the shingled harbor home where he proposed to her years ago.

Not on the Stony Point beach where anyone can witness their talk.

No.

They're alone in Neil's old shack where the closeness of the sea shows on everything. There's a salty coating beneath Shane's every touch, a mustiness—all of it wearing the place down to its raw form.

Wearing them down, too. Stripping away the layers of years between them.

"Yes. Without family ... Well, listen," Maris tries to explain. "You received an invitation from family."

"Lauren."

"Right. Your brother's wife." Maris reaches out and clasps his hand. "And you stopped your *life* to be here."

Shane looks long at her, then takes her hand, runs his thumb over her wedding band. "So now this works for you? Because of family? *This* life."

She barely nods.

"But you didn't really realize this until recently, this family connection. So what was it back then?" He has to look away, at a tattered celestial guidebook on a shelf; at an old manual typewriter and its round, clicking keys—at anything other than the woman who *still* has his heart. Finally, in flickering lantern light, he looks at her again. "When I offered you this same thing, this life, you agreed at first. What made you change your mind and say no, if it wasn't me?"

"Fear," she whispers.

"Fear." Still holding her hand, he moves closer. Around them the shadows grow long; not a breeze stirs. "You were afraid of me?" he asks, his voice low.

"I wasn't afraid of you then, and I'm not now." She pulls her hand from his, turns and walks to the wall where a black sweatshirt hangs on a hook, and a small nautical steering wheel leans on a shelf. When Maris turns back, her eyes are sad. "I was afraid of oh, so much else. But not you."

Shane walks to her, backing her against the wall. "You sure?" he quietly asks.

"Shane. Please." She looks away, then at him again. "Maybe you should go."

"I'll go if you tell me to."

She doesn't answer.

The room's darker now—the moment's darker—as the night minutes tick past. In the shadows, he hears Maris breathe. Sees her chest rise with each uncertain breath. Leaning against the wall, she shifts her body as he stands so close. He puts a hand on the wall behind her, blocking her in. How many times, years ago, were they purely quiet with each other like this? They didn't need any words. Everything was said in a look. A touch.

Still is.

Some guard's come down, and Maris' eyes have softened. So he touches a strand of her brown hair, loose from her ponytail. Gently he rubs the silky strands between his fingers. And it feels nice, nostalgic. He used to touch her hair like that when he got off the lobster boat in New London and found her waiting on the docks. Touch her that way in his pickup truck. In bed. His hand drops to her neck, her shoulder. His finger hooks beneath the gold chain of her etched-star necklace.

Her hand, then, moves next. It clasps his, pressing it close between them.

"Shane," she whispers as he bends low, and tips up her chin.

There is only the two of them in this seaworn fishing shack. The salt air is heavy. But sweet. Candlelight flickers. Shadows trick the eye. It's a powerful, private feeling bringing them back to a time they *nearly* had—married, living in a shingled house on the docks.

Back to a life once within reach, until some tide turned.

But here it is again, returned like those beautiful tides, the two of them together. Intimate. Raw. Painful in that the scene lays bare the truth of what they once meant to each other. And what they lost. Maris says something, her voice so low it's more just a sound. A pleasure. A satisfaction as she touches his jaw, her fingers a feather on his skin.

"Mare," he whispers, leaning so close his lips press against her ear.

She's quiet as he feels her soft hair against the side of his face. As his eyes close. As he hears her murmur his name now that every minute of the past fifteen years is swept away in this old shack. The curves of her body press against him; her fingers touch his neck, his hair.

237

"When I called you, that day," she says when he pulls back and looks at her in the shadows, "I wanted to … We were cut off …" She pauses—surprising him when her hands hold his face, as though she's about to kiss him. "On the payphone, I ran out of coins," she says instead, so close, her whisper as soft. "But there was more I had—"

"Maris?" a voice carries then from out in the yard. "It's late. Let's call it a day."

Like that, it's done. The movie's over. The curtain's dropped. Reality washes back in like that God damn tide that can't *ever* be stopped.

In a blur, Maris slips away from Shane and hurries to where her laptop is. Though she pulls out her chair, there's not even time enough to sit. Not before Jason's next words.

"We have to pack," he calls out.

No, Shane can see it, the way Maris can only spin around, her hands—hands that had just touched his face, hands that had stopped resisting—now grip the top of the chair behind her as she stands there.

Stands there barefoot, in her frayed denim shorts and pale yellow tee, with one telltale strand of brown hair fallen alongside her face as she looks at Jason standing in the shack's open doorway.

# twenty-six

*Moments Later*

J ASON STANDS IN THE DOORWAY. He'd given the dog some kibble in the house, before catching up with Maris in the shack. He sees her standing near her writing space. He actually sees a lot: loose manuscript pages stacked beside her computer; a basket of seashells nearby; her lacy cardigan draped over her chairback; grains of sand dropping into the bottom bulb of the pewter hourglass. It's the same hourglass his father used. After coming home from Vietnam, he'd often take an hour to calm his thoughts of the jungle. Now Maris uses the hourglass to time out her writing sessions.

And all is good. All is normal. Mundane, even.

Until his eyes catch sight of Shane Bradford standing in the shadows. Instantly then, Jason's blood boils. His heart pounds. It's like someone flipped a switch on the night.

239

Because every which way he turns lately, there's Shane. Just like in that hurricane photograph hanging in the Fenwicks' cottage on the beach, the one where the monster wave overtakes all. Again, Jason remembers his father's dire words: *Never turn your back on the sea.*

For one night, Jason did. For one God damn night he took his eyes off the wave that rolled into Stony Point this week. Took his eyes off of Shane Bradford. For one night, to go fishing.

And now Shane's crashing into his home.

"What the hell are you doing here?" Jason asks, still not moving from the doorway.

"Jason." Shane stands at the side wall, where Neil's old black sweatshirt hangs.

"It's okay," Maris says, walking to the doorway.

But she's too late. Jason's already crossing the room—a room too small for the three of them. All Maris can do, Jason feels it, is grab onto his arm. So he turns to her.

"Shane's just visiting," she whispers, her face flushed.

Jason looks at her, at her disheveled hair. At her pale yellow tee, frayed shorts. Then he turns to Shane and gives him a one-handed shove. "I asked you a question."

"Stopped by to see my old friends," Shane tells him. He puts out a hand for a shake.

A hand Jason ignores as he steps closer. "You're not a friend. And you're so full of shit."

"Jason, man. Not sure what's got you riled. Maris and I were just talking about old times."

With two stiff fingers, Jason jabs Shane's shoulder.

"And you're *done* talking," he says. If he has to, he'll deck the guy. "I told you a week ago at Elsa's inn, and I'm telling you again for the God damn last time." He steps closer, still, with another jab at Shane's shoulder. "Get the *hell* out of here."

Shane tips his head back and looks closely at Jason. Doesn't say a word. Just eyes him. And Jason knows it. He knows Shane can lay him out flat with those jacked arms. One hook shot to the jaw. A straight punch to the gut. Nearly two decades of hauling lobster traps can throw Jason to the floor. But he doesn't give a shit. He figures Shane doesn't either. They're in a standoff right now, one that can be triggered by Shane's next move—some left hook to the chin, some shove to the shoulders.

Shane doesn't make that move, though. Instead, his eyes shift to Maris, then back to Jason as he hitches his head at him to get out of his way. But he doesn't wait for Jason to step aside. Shane just pushes past him, knocking a tin coffee mug off a table as he does, sending the cup clattering to the floor.

"Stop it!" Maris calls out as she rushes over and scoops up the camping mug. "Both of you! Jason, it's nothing." She clutches Neil's metal cup close. "Shane *is* an old friend. *Both* of ours. And he just stopped by."

Jason whips around to Maris. "On a Friday night when I'm not around?"

"Which he wouldn't have even known."

Shane takes the cup from Maris and sets it back on the table. "I'm sorry, Maris."

241

"Get away from my wife," Jason tells him point-blank. "Leave everyone—Maris, your brother—alone. Don't you get it? No one in Stony Point wants anything to do with you. Not after what you put Kyle through all those years ago."

Shane shakes his head with regret. "You don't under—"

"I understand plenty," Jason says, his voice controlled. "Now get out of here. And stay out."

Maris comes up behind Jason and takes his arm. "Jason, please," she whispers.

"Jason." Shane turns back from the doorway. "Maris. Didn't mean any trouble." He steps out into the night. But he stops then, and turns back—eyeing the run-down fishing shack. "Just wanted to see this infamous shack I've been hearing about. I mean, come on." He looks at Jason. "It was Neil's?"

Jason says nothing. He stands there, silent. Waiting.

"Pretty incredible," Shane tells him, then shrugs before walking off into the night.

Maris stands beside Jason. He senses her there, but still, he doesn't move. What she can't see, can't know, is that it's taking every bit of bloody restraint, in every molecule, of every muscle, to not run outside. To not haul off and pummel this Shane Bradford who seems to still have a thing for his wife. Though he tries to take a long breath, it's not working too well. Suddenly it feels like everything's closing in on him. Like he's going under beneath that wave he was *not* supposed to turn his back on.

Finally, after managing a deep breath, he turns to Maris.

"I'm going inside to pack for Vermont," he says. "We need to get away from all this. You and I."

He walks out then without waiting for a reply. Without talking more. Just walks out of the shack and crosses the lawn toward the house, to the stone steps leading up to the deck. The whole way, he tries shaking off the tension in his arms, his neck. If only he could shake off the phantom pain that's suddenly shooting below his knee, through his missing limb. Already he knows just what he'll be doing once he removes his prosthesis later. He'll be sitting on the edge of the tub going through the routine: taking off the limb and sock, then unrolling the silicone liner before setting it all aside. Next comes the scalding hot towel he'll wrap around his thigh and stump, displacing one pain with the other. He glances down the driveway, where Shane's in the shadows, leaving. There's a lot in Jason's life lately that he'd like to displace.

But Jason never stops walking, over the lawn, up those stone stairs, across the deck.

By the time he opens the slider to the kitchen, he feels the complete, insidious ache of all that restraint he just employed. Every muscle in his body hurts with it.

As he closes the slider, Madison dances around his feet on the kitchen floor.

⁓

Oh, Maris knows it.

Knows it as she straightens her papers in the shack, and

243

JOANNE DEMAIO

extinguishes a lantern. As she lifts that tin coffee cup off the table, and sets it back down. Looking out the doorway at the dark night, then pushing in a chair at the round table, she knows it, and knows it but good.

Yes, she knows now what she'd feared all these years: that there would be a day of reckoning. Here it is.

Fifteen years ago, from a payphone near the creek, she'd left Shane in the lurch. They were in love and she walked away without much reason. Tossed him overboard without even a life ring. And all these years, he struggled for understanding.

So Maris knows, too, at the very least, this: She owes Shane the explanation she never gave him fifteen years ago when she ended their engagement.

But how? And when? How can she say the right words, ones that'll erase some long-buried hurt she just saw? When he stood inches away from her tonight, she saw in his eyes what she *couldn't* see that sad winter day. Couldn't see that moment she broke off their engagement from a payphone, just minutes before running out of coins—prompting the operator to end the conversation.

Maris had never spoken to Shane again. Not once. Not until this past week, on the beach.

And again tonight, in the privacy of the shack, when a certain intimacy reeled them back fifteen years to that heartbreaking conversation.

Pacing around the faded table, past the doorway, by the dusty wall shelves, Maris finally sits at her laptop. Just sits. Sits and breathes. After rereading the page she'd last written

244

simply for a distraction, she lifts her hands to the keyboard and begins typing …

*The hurricane is hitting the beach directly now. Their cottage had been taking the brunt of gale-force wind for hours, though, so she's grown used to the noise. Gusts of wind rattle loose shingles and pelt the cottage with rain and sand. Windows were shuttered, doors barricaded. Still, the sound of the wind makes it inside. That whistle of the storm is almost unreal, the way it howls. Like the wind is in some sort of terrible pain.*

*But it's the waves that get her to jump just now. That get her to quickly stand and look at the floor in horror. Okay, so the cottage is raised on stilts, but this? This is something new. The monster hurricane waves meant to roll in beneath the raised structure are roiling and churning so fiercely, they hit the underside of the floors. Slap across them with more angry force. Could the hurricane waves do damage beneath where she now stands? Could a floor be washed out? She remembers him telling her that waves keep at something until they find a weak spot, almost like an attack. Over and over again, they'll wear down whatever is in their path. Are they safe anywhere?*

Okay, so everything Maris is writing *isn't* purely fiction. Because the parallels with her personal life are uncanny. Like now. Shane? Shane is that hurricane wave, somehow. And without even knowing it, he's finding the weakest spot in her and Jason's marriage. The weakest spot in her thoughts, her heart. The spot that aches knowing she left him behind fifteen years ago without even a goodbye.

Now there's nothing left to do but turn off her computer, and extinguish the candles and other lanterns. To wrap a string of fishing line around one of Neil's leather journals left open on her worktable. The same journal Shane had just held. She puts it back on the shelf with the others.

But before walking out into the night and crossing the backyard to her home, Maris stops right there in the shack's open doorway and looks out. Not toward her house. No. She looks toward the rocky bluff, where those damn breaking waves remind her of too much.

Because all the what-ifs of her life crested through that shack door tonight. Wave after wave.

What if ... What if ...

What if she'd *stayed* in Maine fifteen years ago?

Stayed and accepted the job at MaineStay?

Been a fashion designer for the now-untouchable outdoor lifestyle brand?

Stayed, and had children with Shane there in Rockport, a quaint harbor town?

Bought a bigger house together?

What if she *liked* it there, by the wild Atlantic Ocean instead of on tranquil Long Island Sound?

Where she'd have hugged Shane, her lobsterman husband, after every voyage.

Where she'd have talked on the dock about his sea stories. His adventures. His near misses.

Would it have been a life that scared her?

Or satisfied her?

# twenty-seven

*Early Saturday Morning*

ONE THING SHE AND JASON always do when they go away is get an early start. Today, on the weekend of their wedding anniversary, is no exception. Jason loaded their overnight luggage into the SUV first thing, so they'd be on the highway by the crack of dawn. Finally, every mile passing beneath the SUV's tires is bringing them that much closer to their rented chalet in Vermont. To dinners out, and trail hikes, and a bottle of wine at night, and, well, breathing space.

They'd been so tense lately, Maris thought for sure the car ride would take them away from their troubles. Would offer them a respite. Would help.

Instead, it's amplifying everything. Or, more to the point, the car ride's amplifying the strained silence between the two of them.

So to fill that silence, she's telling Jason—for five

247

minutes already—how Maddy dove right into the marsh when she dropped the dog off at Eva's for the weekend.

"Completely in. I mean, she went and just plunked herself in the water and began paddling! Jumped right off Eva's dock. I couldn't even stop her. And then she swam after an egret, until the bird flew off all irritated. Still, Maddy was *soaked* when she got out. I mean, what a water rat, right? So Taylor? Well she's at least going to give her a bath, with their outdoor shower nozzle. Which is good, because the dog already stunk from her saltwater swim with you and the guys fishing yesterday."

Nodding, Jason only glances over at her, then focuses on the road again. But she keeps her gaze set on him. On his shadow of dark whiskers, nearly concealing the faded scar along his jawline; on his hair, wavy in the midsummer humidity. When he says nothing, she looks out at the passing view instead. In the silence, as every bit of the broken centerline blurs ahead; as the scenery turns more green with lush northern forests; as the summer air rushing in through Jason's partially open window slightly cools, Maris hears every silent, unspoken and unanswered question between them.

His. *What was Shane doing in Neil's shack last night? You didn't invite him?*

Hers. *Why don't you trust me?*

His. *Why didn't you tell me you were engaged to the man?*

Hers. *Why does it matter now?*

His. *Why doesn't it matter now?*

Hers. *Do you really think I'm still in love with him?*

His. *Are you?*

But instead of asking any of those questions, after a few more miles pass by—the terrain more hilly, the skies hazy blue—Maris pulls a Vermont guidebook from her handbag. They've got another hour of driving to go, at least. This guidebook can supply plenty of *safe* questions to fill their ride, to pass the time, to distract from the other dangerous questions.

"Want to stop at a covered bridge?" she asks. A red-painted one with open lattice windows caught her eye in the book. When Jason says nothing, she glances up from the pages of glossy color photographs. "Well?"

"Not much in the mood for bridges."

"I just thought …" She looks longer at him, at the dark sunglasses concealing his tired eyes, then back at the guidebook. "Well, there's usually parking at pull-offs near the bridges. And it says here that most of the covered bridges are historical. Here's one that's a … Town lattice truss? Its construction uses the crisscross elements." Her voice quiets as she turns the page. "I thought you might enjoy the historical architecture, that's all."

A moment goes by, then, "We'll see."

She turns another page, looks out at the passing scenery and tries again. "How about hiking somewhere new? There's a place where we can do a zip-line *aerial* tour of the green mountains. You know, *soar* through the treetops?"

Jason shakes his head this time. "A hard landing can be jarring on my prosthesis, Maris. Don't really feel like messing around with that." Just those words. Not a glance, even. Just that.

249

"But I ... Okay." She pages through more of the guidebook. "Hey, there's a restaurant right in Woodstock, close to our chalet. The restaurant's pretty inside, a little bit rustic with some paneling. And they have that Yankee Pot Roast you love. This one's served on mashed potatoes?"

"Maybe."

The silence keeps volleying between them. A question, an answer. Then nothing. Until another question gets tossed one way or the other, an answer tossed back. Well, it's his turn now, Maris figures. She closes the guidebook and tucks it back in her purse.

A few minutes tick by. Minutes when first her eyes burn with restraint as tears well in them. That feeling passes, thankfully. But only because she distracts herself by watching a distant field of grazing cows. She'll be damned if she asks another question to break the silence.

"What time's check-in at the chalet?" Jason eventually asks.

When Maris only looks at him, her words oddly lodged in her throat now, Jason finally looks over at her in the passenger seat. Seeing her like that—her eyes moist again, her expression drawn—he does it. He asks the *only* question that really counts. The one question they've circled around for the past two hours.

"Something's wrong," he says, his voice level. "Don't you think we should talk?"

"Okay," she whispers.

Jason nods, and for the next excruciating mile of silent driving, for the next mile of hearing only the hum of tires on pavement, what it feels like is this: Someone's in the car with them. Yes, it feels like Shane Bradford's sitting right there in the backseat, tattooed arms crossed, watching her and Jason from beneath the brim of that newsboy cap he wears.

~

Jason finally spots it, the turnoff to the scenic lookout area he remembers stopping at before. He hits the blinker, slows the vehicle and pulls into a parking space. They sit there for a minute, looking out the window. There's a wood-sided building here housing a gift shop, snack area, and restrooms. The SUV engine, which he's shut off, clicks as it cools down.

Maris digs into a tote and finds a trail-mix bar and bottle of juice. "I'll bring this out," she says.

Jason, watching her, can think only that nothing will help. Not food. Not drink. Not even alcohol will do the trick. Nothing will move them forward except the words neither of them wants to begin saying. At least, he certainly doesn't. Especially on what *should* be a happy occasion: their two-year wedding anniversary.

Because, hell. Where will those words lead? Or worse, what will those words disintegrate to? Instead of finding out, he's been riding out the silence.

Now, he opens the door of the SUV. Beneath the August sunshine, he rolls out a shoulder kink and walks to the lookout spot. But they just can't get away from their troubles—troubles that stem from the beach. Because the entire lookout walkway is a wide-planked boardwalk surrounded with post-and-rail fencing. How many times have he and Maris walked the planked boardwalk at Stony Point? Had coffee on it. He even proposed to her on it, one snowy Christmas Eve.

So he walks this Vermont boardwalk now, pausing halfway along. There, he lifts his sunglasses to the top of his head, leans his arms on the railing and takes in the view. Instead of it being Long Island Sound, from *this* boardwalk the view is a sea of rolling mountains. Waves and waves of green unfurl before him. He takes it all in. The view is so similar to the sea, the way the green spreads right to the horizon, where it meets up with the summer-blue sky. A sky so vast, it makes him think of his brother's words— *Don't forget the sky, Jay. It's the true masterpiece, always changing.* Neil was adamant about Jason incorporating the sky into every cottage design.

Standing there, Jason hears Maris' door slam shut behind him. Her footsteps eventually approach until she stops at his side.

"Pretty view," she says.

"It is."

She looks out for a few seconds before turning away. Picnic tables are scattered here and there across the long boardwalk. When she sits at one nearby, Jason follows and sits across from her.

"Want a piece?" she asks him while unwrapping the snack bar she'd brought.

"I'm not really hungry, Maris."

"Jason." She hands him a napkin and half the trail-mix bar, regardless. "I'm *trying*."

"I know you are."

Though he says it, Jason can't help but wonder if Maris is actually *trying* to deny that Shane has a hold on her, still.

"You have to know that Shane Bradford doesn't mean anything to me," she says then, as though reading his mind.

"I *don't* know that."

After pouring juice into a cup, Maris sips her drink. "Jason," she says, reaching across the table and squeezing his hand. "We can still have a weekend together. The weather's perfect. Our chalet is waiting. We'll have dinners out. A sweet getaway, like we do every year."

Jason thought they might. While fishing on the rocks last night, he'd hoped they could somehow salvage these days. But he only thought it until he walked in on Shane and Maris in that shack. Even then, after a fitful night's sleep, he *still* convinced himself time away might do them good. With that hope, he'd packed their bags in the SUV this morning.

Oh, was he ever wrong.

The weekend can't be saved. Too much happened yesterday. When he stood in that shack's doorway—Maris disheveled at her desk chair, Shane in the shadows—it felt like he'd walked in on something. Something personal. Intimate, even. The way they stood so still, it was as though they'd gotten caught. Too much silent tension filled the space. And what it ultimately did was this: It left Jason

253

wondering what would've happened if he *hadn't* interrupted.

Maris gets up from her seat now and walks around the picnic table to sit beside him. In a moment, he feels her hand on his whiskered jaw as she turns his face toward her. When she does, she leans close and gives him a kiss. Just a little one, soft, on his lips.

"Come on, babe," she whispers. "Let's give the weekend a chance. *Please?*"

He looks at her for a long second. Sees how she put her brown hair in a side braid for the drive north. Wore her white shredded jeans with a half-tucked blue-and-white striped blouse—the sleeves turned back, the neckline a deep V. Pure Maris, pure summer style.

"Jason," she says with a small smile that quickly fades.

As though she knows. As though she reads his tired face. His resistant eyes. Hears his reluctant breath before he tells her, "We should just go home."

"Home?"

"Yes."

"Why?"

"That waiting chalet?" he asks while watching her blink back tears. "With the wraparound deck? Mountain views from the bedroom? It was our *honeymoon* chalet. With so many beautiful memories there." Jason stands up and pulls his keys from his cargo shorts pocket. "And I'm not about to ruin that."

# twenty-eight

WHENEVER CELIA TURNS ONTO SHORE Road, life changes. It grows more mystical with each shingled cottage she drives past. More golden with each view of a saltwater marsh—the tall grasses swaying in the breeze. More evocative at the sight of lone rowboats anchored in bays. A little more nostalgic with each old-fashioned ice-cream stand, where sun-bleached umbrellas shade patrons from August's rays.

Shore Road. It's the place where salt air first reaches her lungs.

Usually she loves to point out the scenic views to Aria in her car seat; but today, Celia's alone. She'd left Aria in Addison for a few days, so grateful that her father loves babysitting his granddaughter to help out Celia. Now there's a quiet afternoon ahead of her before the busywork begins at Elsa's inn.

So Celia treats herself. She pulls into The Pizza Palace to order a sandwich for lunch. Yesterday's rain shower did nothing to cool off the temps. If anything, the rain made it more humid. So inside the restaurant, the air-conditioning is refreshing. She sits on a padded stool at the counter and waits. On the other side of the counter, piles of plates stand ready; coffee mugs are lined up; stacked drink cups tower; a coffeemaker steams. Through an open half-wall, Celia sees the shop's owner. His arms move, and slice, and slather, and dab, and finally wrap the lunches he's preparing.

"I'll have a grinder. To go, please," Celia says when her waitress approaches. Celia glances at the wall-mounted menu, where every type of pizza and grinder is listed in black plastic letters, the prices in red. "A ham grinder. Small."

"Cheese?" the woman asks while jotting the details on her order pad.

"Provolone."

"Shredded lettuce and tomato?"

"Yes."

"Mayonnaise?"

"Mm-hmm. Oh," Celia adds, "and a drizzle of oil, too."

"Toasted?"

"No. Cold."

"Be a few minutes," the waitress tells her while ripping the order off her pad and setting it on that half-wall for the cook there.

Which is fine by Celia. She always likes lingering in this little pizza shop, with its sports memorabilia hung on the walls, and TVs mounted on either side of the long counter. There's something comforting about the dark padded booths, the large rack of snack-size potato chips, the countertop case of pizza-by-the-slice. From her stool, she checks her phone first, then watches the noon weather report on one of the mounted TVs.

⌒⌣

If a place could be frozen in time, The Pizza Palace sure is. Shane feels like he's in one of his family's old home movies right now. Or watching a decades-old TV sitcom taking place in a pizza shop. As he sits in a booth waiting for his lunch, he looks around at the other tall-back booths with brown Formica-top tables; at the empty pizza boxes stacked on shelves by the back wall; at the faded beadboard reaching up half the wall—beadboard topped with a swirled wallpaper border. Announcements are tacked on a bulletin board near the doorway: a sofa for sale; babysitter for hire; bingo night at the local church hall.

He takes a long breath and sits back, clasping his hands behind his neck. How many times has he craved a Pizza Palace grinder while out on the lobster boat? A toasted grinder loaded with fresh-sliced meat, dripping in dressings. Seven days left at Stony Point? Hell, he could eat dinner here every night and be happy enough.

"Thanks," he says when his waitress sets down an overloaded grinder with a tall soda, the ice in it swishing against the cup.

"Grab a bag of chips from the rack. Over there." She motions behind him before breezing off.

Shane looks over his shoulder. What he notices first is the multi-shelf rack holding assorted bags of chips.

Second, he sees Celia.

She's sitting alone at the counter, near the cash register. Seems like she's waiting for a take-out order. So he slips out of his booth and approaches her from behind. From the left, he stretches around and taps her right shoulder. Celia turns right and looks at no one there, then laughs when she turns left and sees him behind her.

"I fell for the oldest trick in the book," she says.

"Hey there, Celia." Shane sits on the stool right beside hers. "Where's your sidekick?"

"Aria?"

"Yeah."

"She's actually with my father for a few days."

"That's right. While you and Elsa get the inn ready to open." He glances over at the bantering cooks prepping sandwiches. "What'd you order?" he asks her.

"Ham and cheese grinder. You?"

"Large Genoa. Toasted." He points to the lunch waiting at his booth.

"Oh, don't let me keep you! It'll get cold."

"Join me?" he asks. When she hesitates, he doesn't take his eyes off her. She wears a loose, off-the-shoulder white peasant top over faded denim cutoffs. A thick gold rope necklace hangs around her neck. Large brown-tinted tortoise sunglasses are propped on top of her sideswept auburn hair.

Celia looks to his booth, then back to him. "I was taking mine home," she says with a small smile. "Felt like eating outside today."

"Yeah." He spins on his stool, props his elbows on the counter behind him now and looks out the restaurant windows. The August sun's burned through some early morning haze. "Me, too," he says, then spins back and calls to the waitress. "Would you mind wrapping my lunch, to go?"

"Sure thing," she says, hurrying to retrieve his food.

Shane turns to Celia now. "You know, I've got the perfect outdoor spot. There's a great water view, sea breezes. Lots of shade, too," he adds, touching her lightly freckled nose. "Have lunch with me on my cottage porch?"

# twenty-nine

*Early Saturday Afternoon*

THE DRIVE HOME FELT TWICE as long to Jason.

After leaving the Vermont rest stop, the SUV seemed to move slower; stretches of scenery were never ending. On and on and on went the green forests. Farmland only slowly gave way to more of a cityscape before river views gradually passed outside the window, and finally—*finally*—the shoreline's marshes.

Never has a two-hour drive been more eternal, Jason thinks.

Now, they're both standing in their suddenly-too-small bedroom. The walls are pressing in; the air is close; and it's hot up here on the second floor of their gabled beach home.

When Maris tosses her bags on their bed and yanks open a suitcase zipper, that one angry sound says it all. Loud and clear. She's done trying.

"I can't *believe* we came home. We really needed that getaway," she says through clenched teeth.

"Getaway?" Jason asks from his dresser. "Or were you running away?"

Maris whips around to face him. Her side braid is coming loose; her face is flushed. "Would you stop that? I *tried* with you today. And now I'm really mad."

"Mad at me?"

"Yes! Because you said you didn't want to *ruin* our honeymoon chalet? Well, congratulations, Jason. You *ruined* our wedding anniversary instead."

"Listen, darling," he says as he sets his own suitcase on the other side of the bed and carefully opens it. "This past week was shit. Kyle and Lauren's vow renewal was called off. Shane made his grand entrance. Not to mention I've been so damn busy at work, I can't keep up." Jason stops and goes to the window. When he turns on the air conditioner, it gurgles and spits out some misty water. "Then, Shane again—this time at the bar. And hell, Shane *again*, in my own home last night." Jason lifts a few neatly folded shirts out of his luggage. "Do you know what it's been like getting through each day?" he asks, holding those shirts. "Exhausting. A helluva week."

"For *both* of us. Which is why I *tried* to make a nice weekend." Maris walks around the bed and shuts off the air conditioner. "The a/c is *broken*. Yesterday's rainstorm clogged it all up. And it's really hot out, so it would've been nice to go north, where it's cooler." She swipes her damp forehead. "I finished a chapter in the manuscript and was sure to get my notes squared away to work fresh. Next *week*."

Jason looks long at her wilting there in her striped blouse, distressed white jeans and partially unraveled side braid. Then he turns on the window air conditioner again.

"Jason! It's filled with water. Don't you hear it gurgling? And it's spraying drops on the wall." Again, Maris walks to the window and snaps the air conditioner off. Not only that, she also unplugs it before opening the other windows—making it real clear she's doing so, the way she slams them up in their tracks. "It's so goddamn hot in here. We can still change our minds and go to Vermont, you know," she says over her shoulder.

"No, we can't." He sets the small pile of shirts he's been holding back in his open suitcase. "Not until the air's cleared between us."

"There's nothing to clear. So *stop* that now." Maris opens a dresser drawer, then picks up a pile of shorts from her suitcase and drops it in the drawer. "You act like I'm still pining for Shane Bradford," she says while slamming shut the drawer. "Come *on*, already!"

Jason looks across the bedroom at her. Fine, if it has to be this way, it will be. "What there is to clear," he says, his voice low, "is that you don't confide in me, Maris. I've told you everything about myself. Everything. You know all about my insecurities, about my living without a leg, about dealing with that accident. You *know* I miss my brother. That I privately talk to him sometimes. I've held *nothing* back, only to find this? Find *you* hiding things?"

"Jason—"

"No. Let me finish. You're my wife, and that you don't confide in me is a big deal, Maris. Walking away from your denim-design career last year without even *talking* to me first? Your secret engagement to Shane? There's a trust issue going on here. And that really bothers me."

"Trust? You *know* you can trust me."

"I used to think so, but not lately. Because it just doesn't stop with you." He walks to her jewelry box and lifts out the sailor's knot engagement ring. "What *else* are you hiding?" he asks while holding out the ring.

And he doesn't miss how she won't take it from him. Instead, her eyes drop closed in some sort of defeat.

"This *is* what I think it is, right?" he asks. For a long second, there's only silence—charged between them. "Your engagement ring from Shane?"

"Anything I say," she practically whispers, "you'll twist up."

"What's to twist?" He takes her hand and drops the ring in it before returning to his suitcase. "You kept that ring for fifteen years," he says while lifting two pairs of cargo shorts out of his suitcase and setting them on the bed. "Tell me, Maris. What do you do when you put that ring on? Think of Shane?"

"What? No!"

"Get sentimental? Remember when?"

"No. I don't do anything. The ring … It's just a nautical knot. It goes with some of my outfits, that's all!" She opens the closet and tosses in her hiking shoes. "And at the very least, I can *assure* you that *nothing's* happened between me and Shane. Nothing." She lifts a rolled-up sundress and lacy cardigan from her bag, stops and brushes wisps of hair off her perspiring face, then looks directly at Jason. "Which is far more than I can say about you and Celia."

"What?"

"Oh, come on. Don't you play me for a fool. I know *damn* well something happened between you two last year when I was away for Fashion Week. Right after Sal died. Celia, by your own admission, was drunk. Were *you*, Jason? Did you have too many drinks and cross a line?"

"Maris." Jason picks up the two pairs of shorts on the bed. "I told you more than once already that nothing happened that night at The Sand Bar."

"Fine. But what about *here*? In our house?" she asks, walking to stand inches away from him. "Here?" she whispers, motioning to the bed. "Celia slept it off in *this* house, for God's sake."

"On the couch." Jason drops those shorts back into his suitcase. "You're overreacting," he says without looking at her. "And I'm not getting into that again."

"Well, I am." Maris crosses the room, her one hand clenching that engagement ring, the other still holding the rolled-up dress and cardigan. "Because last year, I was silently expected to understand that things happen in the heat of grief. In the heat of an emotional moment."

Jason walks to his bureau and picks up his sunglasses and a key from his valet there.

"Oh, no. No, you don't." Maris rushes after him. "Don't

you walk away from me, Jason Barlow. Because even worse," she says, tucking back her utterly fallen braid, "I was expected by you to *ask* nothing. *Say* nothing. *And* to forgive Celia. Which I did. All of it."

"With good reason. Because nothing happened that night."

"And I'm telling you nothing happened between me and Shane. And I'm also asking *you* to do the same thing I had to do. Ask nothing. Say nothing, and forgive Shane. Who did nothing more than show up at Stony Point, invited."

"Shane was spoiling for a fight from the minute we spoke, when he tossed that fiancée shit at me."

"What did you expect him to say?" Maris asks. "Especially after all the flak he took when he arrived here, *invited*. You tell him to leave Stony Point and you think he'll just be like, *Oh sure, Jason. I'll get right on that for you?*" As she says it, the cardigan falls from Maris' hand. She scoops it up and tosses it on the bed, along with her still-rolled sundress. "No matter what, like it or not," she continues, "Shane's nothing more now than an old beach friend. One who, as far as I know, actually did nothing wrong." She walks to an open window facing the distant bluff. After taking a long breath of the humid August air, she turns back to him. "Every story about Shane seems to be a twisted web of *he-said, she-said*."

"What about Kyle and the whole thing with their father?"

"None of our business. That's between the two of them."

Jason looks at Maris as she zips up her now-empty

suitcase. His is still full, but he can't stand here and unpack.

Can't keep talking.

Can't keep it up.

He's so exhausted, there's just nothing left to give. So key and sunglasses in hand, he heads out into the hallway, then down the stairs.

"Okay. Just leave," Maris yells after him. She runs to the top of the staircase. "Don't say goodbye. Don't tell me where you're going," she shouts down the stairs.

Jason stops at the bottom of those stairs. Stops and turns to face her. Though her words are angry, he's surprised by the hurt in her eyes. Her striped blouse is limp now, and her brown braid is barely holding on. "Close the damn windows if you're going to yell like that. Don't need all the neighbors hearing this going on." He walks to the kitchen without waiting for her response. Instead he just calls over his shoulder, "I'm going to get the dog."

﹏

Maris stamps her foot, swipes her face and rushes back to the bedroom. Once there, she stops. Stops and looks at her utterly clenched fist. Slowly, she opens her fingers. They barely want to straighten—she'd clenched them shut for so long. Nestled inside them is that diamond-studded sailor's knot ring from Shane. She touches it, gently, before walking to the bedroom window. Pressing aside the sheer curtain, she sees Jason leaving in her golf cart. He drives it down the driveway, running over a few twigs littered there.

But there's more, as she's standing at the open window. The hot afternoon is still, and she hears distant waves breaking out on the bluff. Seagulls are crying, their call piercing the summer air. All of it makes Maris feel like her own heart is crying, too. Just sobbing.

Minutes later, her cell phone explodes with dings, over and over. So she pulls it out of her purse and reads the endless text messages from Eva.

*Supposed to leave for Martha's Vineyard in a few days.*

Then, *Will cancel if you need me, because I just saw that husband of yours.*

Then, ding, with no pause. *No Vermont trip?*

Ding again. *Are you unpacking?*

Another ding. *I'm coming over.*

"No, no," Maris says as she calls her sister's phone. "Calm down, Eva. Calm down."

"Calm down? What the *hell* did Jason do this time?" Eva asks. "Because he was just here, and … and he took the dog and left! Just like that. I'll be over in ten minutes, Maris. We'll talk."

"Eva, Eva. Stay put. Please."

"What? But something's wrong."

"Listen, you're *going* to Martha's Vineyard with Tay and Matt—like you planned. And I'll still water your deck pots while you're gone. This is nothing with Jason. Nothing that won't blow over."

"But you're not in Vermont? That's not nothing. It's serious stuff," Eva insists. "That trip means the world to you two. What's going on?"

Maris clears her throat, takes a breath and lowers her voice as she sits on the edge of the bed, right beside Jason's still-packed suitcase. "It's been a really crazy week, Eva. Jason's so beat."

"Well, I could *see* that. He looked shot. Does the guy even shave anymore?"

"He does, yes." Maris lifts one of his button-downs from his suitcase, then drops it back in. "It's just that, with everything happening here lately, his heart's not in the trip. But don't worry," she quickly adds just to keep Eva calm. "It's in our marriage."

Even though Maris knows that's not true, she had to say it. Having Eva cancel *her* trip just to hover around her and Jason will do no one any good.

Still. Ever since Jason learned that Maris had actually been engaged to Shane? No, Maris isn't sure that Jason's heart *is* in their marriage. Something about that one personal secret she'd kept really got to him. And nothing she says convinces him otherwise.

So okay, great. She broke Shane's heart years ago, and now she's working at breaking Jason's, too? That's something heavy to live with. Not everyone breaks someone's heart in their lifetime.

She doesn't believe Jason ever has.

Maris walks to that open window, leans her hands on the sill and tries, *tries* to inhale some of that sweet salt air. *Cures what ails you*, Neil would always say. Well, if it even gives her own heart the slightest salve, it'll help. Out on the bluff, the seagulls are still crying, their calls carrying on the summer air.

Standing alone in her hot, sticky bedroom, her hair and clothes in shambles—her life, too—Maris finally does it. The whole day led to this moment. The moment when she puts her face in her hands and, like the seagulls soaring over the bluff, she cries, too.

# *thirty*

## Saturday Afternoon

THEY CARRY THEIR LUNCH STRAIGHT from their vehicles, down the planked walkway alongside the little beach bungalow. Wild dune grasses sweep close by, the green blades thick and lush. As Celia and Shane climb the olive-painted steps to the open back porch, Shane feels it. Feels the oppressive heat today. The salt air is heavy and still.

What it all is, the August warmth and hazy sunshine and tang of salt air, is this: a day custom-made for eating outdoors.

While Celia's inside getting napkins and paper plates from the kitchen counter, Shane sets out the grinders on the porch table. Next he straightens its wooden chairs, mismatched and worn smooth by their time beside the sea. But something's missing. So he lifts his happiness jar off a crate top and puts it with their food on the faded white

270

table. The seaweed pieces Lauren had tucked inside the jar days ago are dried now. They edge the golden sand. Shane's skimming stone is also in there, nestled against a silver tea-light candle.

Standing there out on the big porch, he thinks, *Yes, this will do.* That's the cottage name, after all: This Will Do. And on days like this, he gets it. A sea view, summer afternoon, good food and company … what more could you need? Old candle lanterns—tarnished bronze and distressed black—are scattered around: one on the top step; a few on the half-wall; one on a crate table. Beach grasses cut from alongside the cottage spill from a rusted milk can, near the screen door.

Celia's coming outside now, her arms full. "I think I've got everything," she's saying as she shoulders open that door. "Except for the soda bottle."

"Here, let me help." Shane holds the door open, then goes inside for the soda. When he returns, the screen door slams behind him.

"What a view you have here," Celia says from the half-wall, where she leans and looks out at Long Island Sound. Beyond her is nothing but blue sky, blue sea.

"That I do. Especially in the morning. The sun rises right over that spit of land there," he says, walking closer and nodding to a smaller inlet. "Casts the Sound in a golden light that, well … it's something to see." He points to the left. "That's Back Bay, over there."

"Where Kyle and Lauren's place is?"

"Guess so. The trains go by a lot. It's a nice sound.

Reminds me of when Kyle and I would flatten nickels on the tracks there … well … anyway," Shane says, waving off the thought and turning to their lunch now.

Celia joins him at the table. "Do I recognize this happiness jar from the inn?" While setting their unwrapped grinders on paper plates, she stops and slowly turns the Mason jar.

"You do."

"I see some trinkets inside. Happy memories from your stay?" Celia asks.

"Some." He notices a slant of sunlight hitting their table beneath the porch overhang. "Here, let's move this over into the shade. That sun's strong, and your shoulders will burn," he says, motioning to the white peasant blouse exposing her skin.

Together they lift the table and shift it over. That done, Shane pulls out one of the mismatched chairs for Celia. When she sits, he does too, across from her.

They're quiet as they start eating. Shane bites into his salami grinder while Celia empties a bag of chips onto a plate between them. Settling in her chair, she lifts her sunglasses to the top of her head and gives him a small smile.

"The seaweed in that happiness jar?" Shane says around a mouthful of food. "It's from Lauren."

"Oh. From the day she visited you?"

"She picked the seaweed off the beach, over there," he explains, pointing toward the tiny private beach down below the back porch. "Said the seaweed's as tangled as all of us are."

"Isn't that the truth." Celia's digging into her own grinder, the back of her hand catching a dribble of oil from her chin. "Whatever happened between you and Kyle, all those years ago?" she asks. "It must've been pretty bad, the way everyone's avoiding you."

Shane quiets, glancing at the water first, then Celia. "I figured you'd eventually ask."

"Loaded question?"

"Yeah." Shane drags a hand along the shadow of whiskers on his face. "And, you know … I'm as surprised as you are by everyone's reaction to me here. Especially the anger—from Kyle, Jason. It really threw me, after all this time."

"Hey, if you don't want to get into the nitty-gritty, I totally get it," Celia says in between bites.

"No, it's okay. It's just that … no one's ever really asked. And it's hard to put into words." Shane picks up a piece of his grinder, then sets it back down.

Celia nods. That's it, just nods.

Well, Shane reckons she knows all about difficult, private stories. She shared her own with him during yesterday's rain. "What happened between me and my brother?" Shane repeats, reaching for the soda bottle. "Arrogance," he begins while pouring the fizzing soda into their cups. "Grief, after our father died. And a really big misunderstanding." He takes a long swallow of his drink. "My father was living with me in Maine when he passed away. And Kyle blamed me for Dad's death, in a misguided way. We fought about it, briefly but harshly. Said some nasty things and went our separate ways without ever resolving the issue. And when I say separate ways, I mean not a word between us. So that one misunderstanding has simmered for many years."

Celia sets down her grinder half and looks out at the Sound beyond the porch. "Grief, emotional misunderstandings and time?" She looks at him now. "A pretty potent cocktail."

"Absolutely. The kind that can take down anything in its path. Just like that," he tells her with a snap of his fingers.

And somewhere in there—as he and Celia swap sandwich tastes; and compare which is better, salami or ham; and debate the merits of toasted versus cold; and polish off another bag of chips between them; and as she dabs a crumb from his chin; as he takes off his sunglasses and sets them on the half-wall behind him—the truth of his and Kyle's rift comes out.

Not *all* the details, but the truth. It's the first time Shane's ever admitted it to anyone.

"That emotional cocktail? It was more like a grenade. And the firing pin that detonated it? Sadly? Long story, but it was money." He shrugs. "Took down two good brothers."

"I'm really sorry to hear that," Celia says, sipping her soda. "Seems like, unfortunately, a lot of things happened at the wrong time for you and Kyle."

"It is what it is. But you know, Kyle and I? We had good times growing up. A strong past together. I'm hoping it's enough to overcome the rest in these next few days."

Celia nods. "The good wins out over the bad. Most of the time, I believe that," she says, then nudges his way what's left of her ham grinder. "Sal used to love these."

Shane picks it up and takes a bite. "The good?" he asks, holding up the piece dripping with shredded lettuce and olive oil. "A good memory?"

"Don't get me wrong. I have those, too, with Sal. Good memories," Celia quietly tells him. "Not just the anger you saw when I came undone during that rainstorm."

"I figured, Celia. I figured. No matter what, even with anger, and frustration at being left alone, we always miss old loves, no?"

"Now you say that like somebody who knows all about it."

"I do. It was Maris for me."

"I kind of thought so."

Shane reaches for a handful of potato chips. "What have you heard, through this Stony Point grapevine?" he asks, then tosses a few chips in his mouth.

"A little. Only what Lauren's mentioned, actually. That you and Maris were the real deal back in the day."

"We were." Shane stands and looks out at the Sound. The midday sun shines high above it; someone's tubing behind a motorboat blowing past. When Shane turns back to Celia, he leans against a porch beam and folds his arms across his chest. "What Lauren *doesn't* know is that Maris and I were engaged to be married."

"What? Honestly?"

He nods.

"*Engaged?* Now that's a hard one to wrap my head around."

"Why? Don't think I'm marriage material?" he asks, tossing a wink her way.

"No. I ... That's not what I meant." Celia opens another bag from the pizza shop and pulls out two chocolate chip cookies wrapped in tissue. "It's just that around here, well, it seems like it's always been Jason and Maris."

"Huh. Still getting used to hearing that myself."

"And not sounding too happy about it?"

"You don't understand, Celia. Stony Point? This beach where we all summered as kids? Pretty much came of age? It's the furthest place I'd thought Maris would land—permanently. Never even *imagined* I'd run into her at my brother's vow renewal—"

"Let alone this whole world of hers here," Celia finishes. "With her aunt, sister ... Jason."

"Right."

"So when were *you* two engaged?"

"Her senior year of college. Planned to get married right after New Year's. Even bought a place of our own in Maine." As Celia sets a cookie on each of their plates, he continues. "Lobstering was there, and Maris had a job opportunity with MaineStay, designing a new clothing line."

"So what happened?" Celia asks, breaking her cookie in two.

"At the last minute? Maris changed her mind."

"About moving to Maine?"

"About us." Shane takes his grinder wrappings and stuffs them in a bag. "Back then, I thought we had a whole new life ahead of us," he tells Celia before finishing off his soda. "And we did. But a life separate from each other."

"Shane. I never knew."

"It's true. Last I'd heard, she became a denim designer, and I never looked back once I learned the lobster ropes out on the Atlantic. Which, believe me, was like night and day compared to my start here in Connecticut."

"How so?"

"With Maine lobstering, everything's bigger, badder, faster. The waves, the weather. The boats, the crew. The egos, the trawls."

"So lobstering probably saved you … Got you through that time and missing Maris?"

"Yeah. And when I wasn't hauling traps a hundred-odd miles offshore—too busy to even think—that's when I got to hone the blues." He stands and picks up his harmonica from a nearby vintage crate. Sitting sideways on an old whitewashed bench, he draws up a knee, props an elbow on it and plays a short riff. "I'm good with it all now," he says, loosely holding the harmonica and looking out at the sea view. "Maris had her reasons, and I respect that." He glances at Celia, then fiddles with the harmonica. "Still. Arriving at Stony Point last week and finding out she lived *here*—and married my old beach friend—well, it was like a sucker punch, on top of everything else. Including the shunning from my brother."

277

Celia begins clearing off the table, stacking their plates and cups. "Sounds like one heck of a dirty day to me."

"You know it. I mean, learning my old flame traded the fashion world for a writing shack by the sea? Back with the gang at the beach, living that casual life?" He looks over to Celia at the table. "The same life I'd offered her a long time ago?"

"Now that's a little sad," Celia says while wiping off the tabletop with a napkin, then twisting the cap onto the soda bottle.

"Time softens things, though," Shane tells her from where he sits. "You know, like it does on that sea glass you talk about. Softens the edges. Maris *is* an old love, but after all these years, nothing more than a friend today." He brings his harmonica to his mouth and plays another short riff, a bluesy number, the lonely sound rising on the muggy summer air. "But that Jason Barlow is a lucky man," he admits.

Celia stops wiping the table and looks back at him, tipping her head. Then she picks up his plate with the chocolate chip cookie and walks closer. Shane watches her—her sandaled feet crossing the painted porch floor; her peasant blouse pretty over her denim shorts; her perched sunglasses holding back her auburn hair. When she gets to him, she hands him the plate.

"Thanks," he says, still sitting sideways on the old bench.

But when she doesn't move away, Shane looks up at her again. A quiet moment slips between them. A summer moment, with the cry of a seagull in the distance, and the waves lapping on the little beach beyond the porch.

And Celia, standing there too, *in* the quiet moment— until she repeats his words. "Jason Barlow's a lucky man?"

There's another pause as Celia strokes Shane's tattooed arm.

As she leans down and gives him a kiss that starts on his cheek before her hand moves up to his neck and the kiss moves to his mouth. "Or maybe," she whispers then, "maybe Maris made a mistake."

# thirty-one

## Early Sunday Morning

SOMETIMES ONE SOUND IS STILL unfamiliar to Kyle: the crying gulls swooping out over the bay, across the street. Especially compared to the neighbor's rooster he used to hear in their old Cape Cod house back in Eastfield. But waking up to the seagulls proves that he and Lauren did it. After a year of beach-house hunting, they finally bought one of their own. It's still hard to believe, given the pathetic turns his life can take. Especially the turn it took this past week.

But here he is, in his own shingled house on the bay. The gulls prove it, their wild song over the sea music to Kyle's ears.

This morning, the gulls even beat his alarm clock. Their caws and wailing wake him up right as the sun breaks the horizon. Lying in bed, Kyle scratches his shirtless chest and looks toward an open window. He can just picture those white birds, dipping into the bay, feeding on small fish or crabs. Warm air drifts in through that open window, and he takes a long breath.

Salt air, if only it really worked. If only it *did* cure what ails you. Hell, doesn't hurt to try. So Kyle takes another deep breath.

Because it's Sunday. One week since his vow renewal fiasco. Every passing week will be a time marker from that nightmare day. And when Kyle thinks of that lost day, and the regret of it all, it still stings. The feelings haven't faded. Even now. So he takes yet another breath, still decompressing.

At least his normal life, normal routines, weren't lost to that day. He looks over at Lauren asleep beside him. She's wearing her satin nightshirt; her blonde hair is a tangled mess.

But she's here.

And he has his house on the bay, too. And his kids—both asleep in their rooms now.

And Ell, he thinks again.

Ell, who doesn't stop nudging him to reconcile with his brother. She tucks Shane into dinner conversations; mentions him on walks on the bay.

But Shane will have to wait. His kid brother's got that cottage of his rented another week, anyway. There will be time to deal with him later.

For now, Kyle reaches over and touches a strand of Lauren's hair. Heck, the vow renewal was one day. But marriage is a series of days, right? And this is one of them. So he'll make it nice.

Or he'll try, at least. Carefully, he folds back the sheet and gets up to heat a blueberry muffin and make coffee for Lauren. Even better? He'll bring it to her in bed before the kids are up and he cooks their breakfast. This way, Lauren can sleep in and enjoy the morning. Then maybe they'll have a family beach day, beneath the big umbrella, waterside.

Walking barefoot across the room, he quietly heads downstairs, closing the bedroom door behind him.

⌒

Jason calls this his paradise: Sunday mornings in bed, windows open to the sea breeze, waves breaking out on the bluff, golden sunlight streaming in.

It's true, too. Maris knows it. Most Sunday mornings, she wakes up to the gentlest touch of Jason's fingers tangling in her long hair. Or stroking her shoulder. Her every new week starts off sweet in the cocoon of their bed.

But not today.

No, this is one of the few times in their two-year marriage that she wakes up on a Sunday morning to nothing. No touch. No whispers. It was the same last week, when he was simply too exhausted after all he did to help Kyle and Lauren.

Yet today is different. Without opening her eyes, Maris can sense the weight of Jason in bed with her. Motionless. He's not making a move. No arm reaching around her; no words murmured; no kiss left on her neck.

This week, he's not even trying.

It's funny, how that makes her feel. Alone, somehow.

She turns on her side and looks at Jason asleep. Deep asleep. He's been more tired than ever lately; she sees it on his face. Even now, lying on their bed with his eyes closed, the fatigue is apparent. Any other time, she'd stroke his cheek, his whiskered jaw, the shadows beneath his eyes. Whisper, *I love you.*

But instead of reaching over and kissing her husband's face, touching his shoulder, she leaves him be. Just lifts her robe off the end of the bed, glances back at him once, then goes downstairs to feed the dog.

So quickly it can turn, Jason thinks as he opens his eyes and watches Maris leave the room.

Day turns to night.

The tide of the sea turns.

He thinks of the motorcycle accident ten years ago on a scrubby strip of turnpike that hot summer day. Life turns quickly, too.

Right now, if he had to say so, it's his marriage turning. It's in a slack water for the time being. But oh, he can feel it—and that scares him. His marriage is about to change, just like the sea between tides. In that slack water, there's no motion, no movement. The water is idle, waiting.

Jason sits up and reaches for the crutches propped against his bedside chair. Before standing on his one leg, though, he sits on the edge of the bed, listening. Outside, distant gulls cry, their piercing caws carrying on the warm August air. Finally, he hooks on the forearm crutches, stands and goes to the window. Wearing a loose tee over his pajama shorts, he just leans into his crutches and looks out. Another noise finally comes to him, too. It's the waves breaking out on the bluff. Again and again, rhythmically, a sound familiar as his own breathing—those gentle waves sloshing easy against the rocks.

It's the sound, too, where he sometimes finds his brother's spirit.

"Shit, Neil," he whispers. "What the hell's happening?"

In her little guest cottage behind the inn, Celia wakes up to silence Sunday morning. It's an odd feeling because usually the sound of Aria stirring in her crib comes through the baby monitor. The baby's coos, and movements as her little body kicks off any lingering slumber, softly reach her.

But today, Celia didn't turn on the monitor, nor set her alarm. With her father watching Aria back in Addison, it's the first time in a long time that Celia simply slept in.

The problem now is that her mind instantly fills in the silence. The day's itinerary—being a mile long—ticks past. Because, believe it or not, the Ocean Star Inn will be open in mere weeks.

So that checklist takes shape as Celia lies beneath the cool sheet. Finalize continental breakfast options. Review and confirm guest ledger. Plan seasonal activities: rowboat rides through autumn's golden marsh; leaf peeping through the wooded path to Little Beach.

A ding suddenly interrupts her imagined checklist. Celia reaches for her cell phone on the nightstand and smiles when she reads the text message from Elsa.

*BYOB – Bring Your Own Bandana! We're going to get dirty today. Dusting, polishing, sweeping, mopping. Join me first for breakfast … before we kiss those cobwebs goodbye.*

Without getting out of bed, Celia sets down the phone. One word of that message stays with her: *kiss*. Lying there, she turns toward the open window and thinks of another kiss—one with a man so different from anyone she's known. Different, especially, from Sal.

Feeling the salt air drift in the window, it brings her right back to sitting on Shane's porch yesterday. The salt air lifting off the Sound was warm and sweet. She thinks of Shane, and his tough exterior. The tattoos covering his arms. His way of pulling no punches when he talks about Kyle, and even about Maris.

But here's the thing. When Celia kissed him on his open porch overlooking Long Island Sound, she saw something else.

She saw a change in his eyes. Saw it happen, with their kiss. It was almost sad, she thinks now as she runs a hand along her own arm, the way his eyes softened.

~

*Where are the boys?*

It's a question Shane thinks while perched on the half-wall of his back porch. Sitting sideways and leaning against a tall post, he's having his morning coffee there, beside the Sound. Its waves lap easy down on the private beach beyond the porch. To the east, the sun rises, a golden globe emerging above the horizon.

But it's the sound of those waves that has him think of the lobster boat on calm days, when the sloshing seawater hits against the hull. Over and over again. So he wonders where the boys are right now. Is the crew somewhere on Penobscot Bay? This time of year, the water's like glass there, and the boat skips it like a stone. He reaches to the crate table beside him and lifts his cell phone. After nudging up his newsboy cap, he scrolls through the phone screens. There are no text messages, no emails from the boat.

Of course, there wouldn't be. The boys are on their own, working that sweet summer season. After catching some sleep, they're fed and ready to roll. Hauling lobster pots as that spectacular August sun breaks the horizon. Pulling those traps dripping from the depths of the ocean. There's no better feeling—one any landlubber would never fully understand.

Something that never changes, though, whether on the Atlantic or on a Stony Point cottage porch is this: dirty laundry. After being out on the lobster boats, he comes home with a duffel of it. Same here. All these years later, there are still no washing machines in these ramshackle cottages. And being here a week now, he's got a pile of clothes to clean.

So his day's booked. He'll be doing time in the local laundromat.

But not yet.

For now, he'll just sit here beside the sea. He tugs the brim of his cap low against the rays of the rising sun. Over on the bay, seagulls swoop and cry, their calls carrying on a slight morning breeze. An early train chugs along the distant tracks, too, its whistle lonely sounding. After setting down his coffee cup, Shane takes a deep breath of that sweet salt air they all talk about, and stretches his arms. Running a hand over the tattoos on his forearm, he can't help but think of Celia's touch on them the day before.

Remembers her surprising, gentle kiss, too.

The thing is? Shane's not really sure what to make of Celia, *and* her kiss. He picks up his coffee again and takes a good swallow of the steaming brew.

Actually, he's not sure of a lot of things here. Not sure what to make of his arms-crossed brother, either. Or of the Barlows.

Come to find out, sitting on his porch half-wall facing a golden, sunlit Long Island Sound, Shane Bradford's not quite sure what to make of Stony Point altogether.

All he knows is this: He's got only one week left in this little beach bungalow to figure any of it out.

# thirty-two

## Sunday Midmorning

*A*LL THE WATER OF THE *sea can't sink a ship, boys. Not unless that water gets inside it.* Jason can just hear his father's low voice telling him and Neil that. It was one of his father's favorite bits of sea lore. *Think about it,* he'd say. *A ship will go on happily sailing the seven seas, doing its own thing. Unless what?* His voice would drop to an ominous whisper. *Unless that ship gets a hole in it. Then? Well, then you've got trouble.*

How about if there's a hole in a marriage? Jason sits with a coffee out on the deck and watches Maris across the table from him. Can something get inside a marriage, he wonders, and sink it? Because it feels like something is. Like Shane Bradford is.

He tells Maris that. Tosses it across the table to mull over with their breakfast outside. Tells her the whole thing, sea lore and all. And that some unresolved entanglement with Shane feels like it's sinking their marriage.

288

"Jason." She leans close, breakfast dishes and coffee cups between them. Her brown hair is straight and tucked behind an ear. Her dark eyes, serious, hold his. "That's all *done*, what Shane and I had. It's in the past, for God's sake."

"A secret, unresolved past. It's obvious. Especially from the heated encounters I've witnessed between you two this past week—on the beach, in the shack. And it worries me."

When she just shakes her head, he repeats the same words he told her three years ago when she learned she might have a sister she'd never known. A sister who turned out to be Eva.

*Do you know what happens if you leave the past alone? I can tell you, from experience. It'll chase you down, Maris. That's what the past does if you turn your back on it. It hides behind corners, all the time. And when you catch sight of it, it scares the hell out of you. Don't leave the past alone*, he told her then, and tells her once more now on their deck.

"Are we really going there *again*?" she asks him back. "The past, the past. What about right now? You and me, right now."

To which he says nothing.

Their whole conversation goes like that. For half an hour, they sit there with buttered cinnamon toast, a bowl of fresh berries and coffee cups between them. Shade from the tall maple tree in the backyard falls across the deck, but the air is warm still. A robin persists in its singing, then stops—as though listening in on their talk. A talk that amounts to not much more than a comment here, a question there. Then, nothing. Maris toying with her etched-star necklace. Both of them sipping their coffee. Half-eaten toast between them. Thirty minutes laced with doubts, tension, few words and much silence.

Until Jason breaks it.

"Fix it, whatever it is, Maris," he quietly says, drawing his knuckles along the raised scar on his jaw. "Just fix it. With you. With Shane. Whatever's still there between you two." He pauses when her eyes fill with tears, moving him to reach over and touch her cheek. "Or it will haunt you, you know that. And haunt us."

She looks at him without saying a word. Not until she stands and pushes in her chair. "I have to go grocery shopping. There's nothing in the house because we were supposed to be away in Vermont."

Minutes later, she comes out wearing a lace cardigan over her tank top and cropped jeans, purse looped over her shoulder, keys in hand. Walking past him toward the deck stairs, she barely utters a hushed *See you later.*

⁓

As soon as Maris backs out of their driveway, Jason's cell phone rings. He's surprised to hear Ted Sullivan on the line. Ted, the man who had a heart attack at the wheel ten years ago and drove his car straight into the motorcycle Jason and Neil rode. Straight into Jason's life, obliterating it to pieces.

A life Jason rebuilt a year at a time; a month at a time; a day at a time. Sometimes all he could manage was an hour at a time. Days were that bad—between the horrific loss of his brother, and Jason's own ravaged recovery. If he got through sixty minutes intact, he'd worry about the next hour only then. And for the first eight of those years, he'd never sought out Ted Sullivan. Never talked to him. Never wanted to. It was too painful a situation. Jason *did* leave the past alone.

Until Ted reached out to him two years ago, asking Jason to renovate his old, run-down cottage at Sea Spray Beach. Lord knows, he was asking so much more.

Jason knew it, too. Knew that Ted was trying to make peace in both of their lives. That unless Ted reached out, they'd be stuck in one violent day forever.

So Jason did it. He faced his past. By taking on Ted's cottage renovation, Jason confronted his demons. What he never saw coming was that through it all, he'd find an unlikely friend in someone he'd once thought an enemy.

"Ted," Jason says into the phone now, sitting beneath his patio umbrella. "What's going on?"

"Glad I caught you, Jason. You free this morning?"

# thirty-three

### Late Sunday Morning

AﾠND SO IT IS THAT the talk begun on a phone call continues on a walk along Sea Spray Beach. It didn't take Jason long to load the dog and a few things in his SUV. In no time, he picked up the highway to Ted's cottage, twenty miles down the coast. Wearing a tee, gray camo shorts and hiking sneakers intended for his Vermont weekend, now Jason walks side by side with Ted along the ragged beach.

He's always noticed that about Sea Spray—it's ragged. More on the wild side. Reaching along a straightaway of the coast, there is no forest or rocky outcropping to protect it from the open Sound, like at Stony Point. Here, the waters run deeper; the waves break stronger; the wind blows sharper. One thing that never changes, though, is that salt air. Jason deeply inhales it, remembering his brother's mantra: *Cures what ails you.* Maddy's loving it, too, running ahead and barking into a salty onshore breeze.

"So good to see you, Jason," Ted tells him as they walk near the water. The sun shines bright. A gull soars overhead. "We'll have a nice brunch on the deck."

Jason nods. "How've you been, Ted? It's been a while."

"Enjoying these August days, but we're closing up the cottage today and heading home."

"Today?" Jason looks over at Ted beside him. "How come?"

"Going out of town next weekend for a wedding. And, you know, summer will be winding down after that. Which is why," Ted says, stopping at the water's edge, "I could not let this month go by without getting in touch."

"It's been a hard month." Jason admits. He picks up a few stones and skims one over the choppy water.

"For both of us."

"True. It feels different this year, the anniversary. There's something about that ten-year mark. The accident almost feels fresher."

"I get it," Ted says. "Because listen … So many days this summer, I'd wake up feeling sad." When he pauses, Jason gives him a skimming stone. Ted joggles it in his hand. "Been ten years since my heart attack, too, right at the wheel of my car."

"I know."

"Your poor brother. Still breaks my heart that he died that day. Been thinking about Neil a lot. *And* you. We didn't stand a chance with the cards fate dealt us all. Not one blessed chance."

To that, Jason only nods.

"I'm in my seventies now. And sometimes, Jason? Sometimes I wonder how my old ticker goes on with all that sadness."

"Life does, though. It goes on, Ted." Jason skips another stone, watching the three jumps it manages on the rougher water here. "Every day, the God damn earth spins on its axis."

"That it does." Ted sends his stone skimming atop the water, then looks over at Jason. "Your wife good?"

A difficult question, indeed. One Jason can get into with all the tangled details, or one he can skip past just like the stones he's skipping over the water.

Ted decides for him, picking up on his hesitation. "Something wrong?" he asks, brushing aside a lock of his silver hair lifting in the sea breeze.

"Yeah, now that you ask. We've actually been having a tough time, Maris and I," Jason tells him as he starts walking the beach again. He keeps to the firm sand beneath the high tide line.

"Really. What's going on?"

"A lot of personal things. Started about a week ago. Someone came into town and stirred up the past." Jason bends and picks up a stick of driftwood. "Stirred up things no one really wanted to face."

"Hate to hear that."

"I know." Jason takes a regretful breath. "Me, too."

"Do you want to talk about it? Sometimes it helps."

"The thing is …" Jason whistles to his German shepherd, getting her to lope back across the beach. "Maris and I?" he says over his shoulder to Ted before flinging the stick for the dog. "Well … Ah, hell. We're actually taking a breather."

As Maddy bounds after the stick, Ted stops in his tracks. "*What?* You and your beautiful wife?"

Jason turns back to Ted. Seeing his face—weathered from years beneath the sun, beside the sea—reminds Jason of his own father, who passed away not too long ago. There's some life experience there, some knowledge behind Ted's wrinkled skin, his hooded eyes, which Jason really needs. So he speaks freely. "We can use some space, Maris and I, that's all. It's complicated. And … I don't know. Time apart might do us good."

"Might, and might not. Because time apart is time you're not talking things out, my friend."

"But that distance lets us see things more clearly sometimes."

"*Jason.* Time apart? You mean, permanently?"

"Not sure yet." Jason steps into the shallows, scoops up a handful of the sea and splashes it on his face. He feels the whiskers on his jaw; feels the cold water soothe his tired eyes. "For now, a few days apart anyway. Maybe a few weeks. Don't know."

"This does *not* sound good."

"It's not."

"Where would you go?" As Ted asks, Maddy runs close and drops that driftwood stick at his feet, so he picks it up and throws it down the beach for her.

"Where would I go?" Jason drags a hand through his

hair. "Motel? Maybe find a short-term rental somewhere."

"No, no. I don't like the sound of *that*."

They walk further along the high tide line. Or the *driftline*, as Neil called it. Even named his book after it. Waves splash on the sand, reaching for them before retreating back to the Sound.

"I have an idea. Now hear me out," Ted says then. "Like I mentioned before, my wife and I are leaving today. We're going home."

"Got it. A wedding invite next weekend."

"That's right. But, well, I didn't mention that we're also shutting off the refrigerator here, closing windows, sweeping up."

"For the season? This early? It's only August."

"One of those years ... We've got that wedding next weekend, and there's more." Ted clasps his hands behind his back and drops his head while talking. "I'm taking my wife on a cruise, too. Afterward. A few weeks later. It's ... It's an *anniversary* cruise," he says, nodding slightly. "So, you know. Between packing and traveling, well ... everything we need is at home. Luggage, clothes. We'll be away far too much to be coming here, too."

When Jason tries to object to where he suspects Ted's taking this, Ted simply holds up a hand to silence him.

"We'll be gone for a month. At *least*," Ted continues with a nod. "Thought we might come back for a few weeks in October, maybe. It's a nice time on the beach. But with that wedding and cruise? Place will be empty till then."

"What are you saying?"

"You're staying here, Jason." Ted stops and turns back, motioning to where his beach house sits on the street beyond the dunes. "We won't close up the cottage today. And heck, you know the place inside and out, after that renovation you did. I'll leave you the key."

Beneath the midday sun, Jason looks back at Ted's stately cottage. Its cedar shingles are the color of golden honey. From here, he can make out the egret stained glass window on the second-level loft. Jason also notices people setting their gear on the beach. Colorful umbrellas have gone up; blankets are spread out; sand chairs snapped open. So he whistles to the dog, and she runs back to him, tail swinging. "Thank you, Ted. But I really can't impose on you and your wife like that," he says while clipping on Maddy's leather leash.

"For Maris, you will," Ted says right back. Insists, actually. "She needs to know where you are, and that you're in a good place. You'd be doing me and my wife a favor, too."

"A favor? How so?"

"Keep an eye on things while we're gone."

Jason starts walking back across the beach again, Maddy at his side now. "Are you sure?" he asks Ted. As he does, he thinks about the suitcase intended for Vermont that he never unpacked yesterday—as if he knew. Knew that he'd be throwing that suitcase, along with his crutches and some dog things, in the back of his SUV today.

Which he did when he'd left home an hour ago. He tossed those items in his vehicle, shut the liftgate and hit the road. After their breakfast ended in a tense stalemate, he needed some time alone. Time away from Maris, away from their troubles.

He just never dreamt it would be time spent *here*, at Ted Sullivan's cottage.

"Yes, I'm sure," Ted's telling him. "Just let me know when you'll be back with your things. But I'll give you the key today, after our brunch."

Jason rubs a knuckle across his jaw and takes a long breath. Before committing to this, *he* has to be sure it's the right thing, too. Because Stony Point's always been his haven. Just last week, sitting out on his deck, he couldn't picture ever being away from there.

He'd thought he could never leave the gabled house; the old framed seascape paintings on the living room walls; the photographs of Neil, and Neil's leather journals; the stone bench overlooking the Sound—the bench Jason's father built when he got back from 'Nam. A bench where his father could drop his head, close his eyes, hear the waves breaking on the bluff, breathe the salt air—and quiet the incessant sounds of choppers, shellings, insects, gunfire … that still played on in his mind.

Yes, like his father, Jason had thought that in his life, every answer, every comfort he could need, was right on his one patch of coastal land, at his home by the sea.

Now? Now he's not so sure. Not after walking in on Maris and Shane alone in that shack Friday night. The heated moment he'd interrupted between those two blindsided him. And it's enough to change Jason's mind about the peace he finds at that very home by the sea.

Enough to get him to walk away from Stony Point. To try to find a different perspective on his marriage, his life.

"I can stay today, actually," Jason says.

"Today?"

"Everything's in my truck already."

"What? You're kidding."

Jason turns up a hand. "Afraid not."

"Oh, Jason." Ted stops and pats Jason's shoulder. "I'm truly sorry. Things are that bad?"

"Kind of."

"Then it's settled." Ted extends his hand for a shake. "You'll stay here until you work things out with Maris."

Jason takes his hand and clasps it for a moment. "What about Maddy?" he asks, pulling the dog close beside him. She sits at attention, her ears tuned to Jason's voice. "You don't mind having her in your cottage?"

"Not at all. Listen, I will *not* take no for an answer." Ted leans down and scratches the German shepherd's head first, then reaches around and claps Jason's back. "I'd do anything for you."

⁓

While carrying two overloaded grocery bags, Maris opens the screen slider on the deck. She noticed that Jason's SUV was gone, so she glances around the kitchen for a note. Setting down the bags, she looks on the counter, the table. No note, anywhere. Regardless, it's obvious he went out.

So she goes back to her car for a few more grocery bags, which she quickly brings in and drops on the counter. The house is awfully quiet. "Maddy?" she calls out.

Nothing. No dog scrambling down the stairs. No license tags jangling.

"Okay," Maris whispers while checking her watch. "He took the dog."

After bringing in the last two bags of food, she closes the screen slider and cranks open the window over the kitchen sink. Any air coming in on this hot day will help. She also plugs in the tower fan and turns it on. It blows around the warm air in the room. Maybe someday they'll install central air.

Or not, she thinks. The last thing Jason wants is to close the house up tight, blocking out every whispering breeze, every rustle of the trees, every splash of the waves breaking out on the bluff. Because those are the very noises in which he hears his brother's spirit. Lifting out a package of deli cheese and sliced turkey, she stops and looks toward the slider. How many times has she spotted Jason standing there at the screen, just listening. Head tipped, hand to his jaw. Sensing his brother in the sea breeze.

No, central air will never happen.

Digging into another bag, Maris pulls out a package of strawberries and a watermelon half. As she loads them in the fridge, it strikes her how quiet the house is. Oh, there's the birdsong drifting in the open windows; a neighbor's door slams. Still, in the quiet, she briefly thinks of their talk this morning.

But remembering the things Jason said about the past only gets her tense again. And fed up. Mostly, though, his words leave her unsettled.

So instead she sets cans and boxes and packages of cups and paper plates on the table. She folds up the paper bags. Brings them to the pantry stockpile. Neatly aligns yogurt containers in the refrigerator. Gets a dishtowel and wipes fingerprints off the fridge handle. Puts a loaf of bread and hamburger rolls in the bread drawer. Tosses the week-old stale rolls.

Stays busy, busy.

It doesn't work, though. No matter how much she rattles the paper grocery bags; no matter how carefully she stacks olive oil and coffee filters and jars of peppers in the cabinets; no matter how many rolls of tinfoil and paper towels she stacks in the pantry, she gets a funny feeling.

The house is too quiet. Too vast.

So she pays attention. Cautiously, softly, she puts a carton of eggs in the refrigerator. And a box of tea bags on a shelf.

"Wait a minute," she whispers.

This morning, Jason left his forearm crutches in the living room when he put on his prosthetic leg there. So Maris walks to the living room. Turns in and goes straight to his upholstered chair near the fireplace. No crutches are to be seen. Not leaning against the chair. Not set near the hearth. She slowly turns around. Not anywhere in the room.

"Come on, Jason," Maris says.

It takes her only a second to begin piecing things together. She hurries to the pantry and it's just as she feared. Maddy's kibble bag and dog bowls are gone. A few of her chew toys, too.

"No. He didn't," she tells herself.

Again Maris looks outside. She actually opens the slider and steps on the deck. Leans her hands on the splintery railing and looks out over the driveway—as if by some miracle, Jason would be driving up. *Please, please*, she thinks while bending over and straining to see around the side of the house. Because she'd rather he be here, arguing, than be away, silent.

After a minute, she goes inside and runs upstairs. The whole time, she's thinking of one thing: the full suitcase he never unpacked yesterday when they came home angry from Vermont. Jason just couldn't get his clothes put away.

Maris rushes down the hallway until she turns into their bedroom and just stops. From the doorway, she looks to where he'd left the suitcase yesterday—near his bedside chair.

The luggage is not there.

So she walks around the bed. But his bag's not shoved aside, out of the way somewhere. Well, surely it's because he unpacked it and his clothes are all put away. She checks the closet and brushes through the shirts hanging there. A gray chambray shirt; a few short-sleeve button-downs— plaid, a blue linen. Then she turns to his dresser and opens drawers. Her hand sifts through some shorts, tees. *Some*, but not all.

Because nothing's been unpacked. Nothing. And his luggage is nowhere to be found.

"Damn it," Maris says. Standing there with her hands on her hips, she brushes a wisp of hair from her perspiring face. Again she goes to a window and looks out. Leans on the sill and feels the warm air coming through the screen, touching her face. Carrying a hint of saltiness to her.

But there's no use. No use looking. No use wondering. Because she knows it. Something about the house was too quiet, too empty all along.

Jason left.

Quickly she turns around and scans the room—his dresser, hers, the bedside tables. There is no note, anywhere. No advance warning. He left with no discussion, no small talk with her.

And that gets her mad, because what can she do? She won't call him, won't argue anymore. So her only option is … nothing.

Nothing more than to stew on it. To think she was wrong yesterday, when she believed Jason's never broken anyone's heart. Because there he goes now, breaking hers.

Walking out of the bedroom, Maris heads downstairs and returns to the kitchen. There, she reaches into another paper bag and pulls out a half-gallon of orange juice and a bottle of ketchup. She sets those on the table and lifts out mayonnaise and a container of sea salt. Opening the cabinet near the stove, she sets the salt on the shelf before putting away the rest of the groceries.

# *thirty-four*

*Sunday Noontime*

AN HOUR LATER, MARIS IS back upstairs changing into something more comfortable in this heat. She puts on frayed white shorts with her fitted black tank top, twists her hair in a low bun, and stops at her jewelry box. The engagement ring Shane gave her all those years ago sits there, front and center. The white gold shines; the diamond glimmers. After running a finger over the sailor's knot, she tucks the ring in her shorts pocket. And checks her watch. Then her cell phone. Changes her earrings, too, picking thin silver hoops.

Does *anything*—until there's nothing left to do.

Because damn it, there's no denying it. She's drawn to that old fishing shack as though under its spell. That little shingled shack calls to her with its windows and painted door open to the sea air. With Neil's leather journals around her. With dusty lanterns aglow as she sits there and writes.

Nothing else matters. Not that Jason's left. Not that Shane's here at Stony Point. No. She can't do anything about them anyway.

Oh, she knows something else, too, as she finally crosses the backyard and unlocks that shack door. Knows it as she turns on the computer and lights a hurricane lantern.

What she knows is this: As her life falls utterly apart, the manuscript she's finishing for Neil takes the best shape it has yet.

All when she finally stops resisting.

When she takes Shane's engagement ring out of her pocket.

When she polishes the sailor's knot with the hem of her tank top and sets the ring in clear view beside her computer.

When she flips the pewter hourglass to get the Stony Point grains of sand falling ... and begins typing the next chapter of DRIFTLINE.

～

*When he opens the cottage door, he holds it with all his might. Otherwise the hurricane-force wind will slam it against the wall. One of his hands clenches the doorknob, the other grips the door edge, as he gets himself inside. Afterward, he nearly falls against the closed door in some odd relief—especially after his world came undone this week.*

*So this is what it feels like when someone leaves you. Now he knows. There's a weight, a heavy weight as sodden as his wet clothes. And everything crashes down around you, like the storm outside.*

*Just then, something—a tree branch, maybe—hits against a*

305

*boarded-up window with a sudden bang.*

*Leaning against the closed door, he looks into the dark cottage. With the windows shuttered and the power out, the rooms are shadowed. The sound of the roaring wind comes in, though, along with the thrumming of rain pelting the cottage's shingled walls. Blending with that, barely discernible, are voices from the kitchen and dining room. The talk is hushed, rising and falling. Some laughter comes, too. Silverware clinks against dishes.*

*He still stands against the cottage door. Every fiber of his clothing—his jeans and jacket and button-down shirt and boat shoes—is sopping wet. Soaked right through and dripping off of him. To the side, a lit candle sits on a table at the foot of the stairs. After another glance toward the dining room, he pushes away from the door and goes up those stairs. In each bedroom he passes in the second-floor hallway, a candle flickers on the dresser tops.*

*Once in his own boarded-window room, he closes the door behind him. Enough candlelight lets him make out some details: an extra blanket folded at the foot of the bed; an antique three-drawer dresser; on that dresser, the austere white envelope with his name and address neatly typed on it, postmarked this past week; on the wall, a framed assortment of nautical knots.*

*And he is alone.*

*Stopping in front of those miniature nautical knots, he recognizes some beneath the glass: the entwined rope of a reef knot; the looped rope on a bowline; rope wrapped over and under a miniature cleat in the cleat hitch knot. He glances from the framed knots, to that plain white envelope on the dresser, to his wet hands. Who knows when— or if—he'll ever tie one of those sailing knots again.*

*While standing there and peeling his drenched jacket off his arms, a soft rap sounds at the door. He looks over just as it opens. She's the last person he expected to see. A candle she holds throws soft light on her face, her eyes. And barely, past the howling wind and waves crashing just outside the cottage, he makes out the sound of her voice.*

*"I heard you come in."*

Maris sits back and looks at the computer screen. *Write what you know.* Even those nautical knots make it into the novel. With a deep breath, she scoops up her sailor's knot engagement ring and walks around the shack's little room. There's no putting it off. Like the characters in the passage, Maris is minutes away from facing the inevitable. She stops at the open door and looks out toward the bluff. The August day is so still, the sound of easy waves breaking on the bluff comes to her. Crossing her arms, she leans in the doorway and just stands there, looking out on the summer day.

Until a moment later, when she turns and looks into the shack.

Stands there in the exact spot where Shane stood Friday night. From the doorway, she sees her worktable, her open laptop, the lacy cardigan still draped over her chairback. It's everything that Shane saw. And her heart breaks. Because it's actually all that he wanted, fifteen years ago. In Maine. He wanted her to live in their shingled harbor home and create. Design clothes. Spearhead a new fashion line. Be with him. That's it.

Nothing more.

He just wanted *then* what he saw here Friday night.

Apparently she did, too. It's the life she ended up choosing all these years later. The life she lives now. With someone else.

Maris opens her fisted hand and looks at that white-gold ring there. So much story, and love, is in the intertwined sailor's knot. So many thoughts and feelings are twisted up inside her, too—just like the twisted knot of the ring. She gently slides it on her finger, holds her hand at arm's length, then takes the ring off.

The day is warm and humid. The air in the shack, stifling—pressing in on her like the recent days have. Standing in Neil's beautiful fishing shack filled with his journals and salty seashells and old tarnished cups and stargazing guide and dusty lanterns … her eye is drawn to something on her desk.

To something all Jason's: the pewter hourglass beside her computer. Only a few grains of sand remain in the top bulb.

And she knows.

Time is running out on more than her hour of writing. It's running out on so much else.

She glances at Shane's engagement ring in her hand. Mostly, though? Time is running out on her marriage.

# *thirty-five*

### *Early Sunday Afternoon*

MARIS CLOSES UP THE SHACK and leaves.

Walks straight across the backyard, straight down the driveway and straight onto Sea View Road. Walking takes more time than driving. Walking gives her precious more minutes to change her mind. To wonder what the hell she's doing. To turn around and go back home.

But she doesn't.

The little beach bungalow Shane rented is at the other end of the street. On her way there, she says hello to families trekking to the beach, sand chairs in hand, packed wagons in tow. Still, Maris continues on. Several blocks of cottages distract her with windows open to the summer day; with geraniums and vinca vines spilling from decorative planters; with hummingbird feeders and spinning garden pinwheels in shady front yards. To the east, those cottages face Long Island Sound. Its blue water

309

sparkles beneath the afternoon sun. *Ocean stars*, Maris thinks. Oh, if only she could wish on one of those fallen stars flickering on the sea.

She can't, though.

Because she's actually out of wishes this August. Out of dreams. No stars—celestial or ocean—can shine their magical light on her life. Any wish Maris might make, might plead to those glimmering stars, would evaporate as quickly as a sea mist.

And there's only one way to get her wishes back.

To get her happiness back.

It won't be easy. Quite the contrary. What she's about to do will be one of the hardest moments of the summer.

Her step slows when she spots Shane's cottage up ahead. Its cedar shingles are weathered beneath the sun. As she nears, she can't miss that the cream trim paint around the windows and front door is cracked and peeling. A planked walkway leads around to the open back porch and a private beach below. Wild dune grasses sweep alongside that makeshift walkway. But the grasses are still today; there's not even a whisper of a breeze rustling them.

The bungalow has a small front porch, too. One with a shady overhang, beneath which there are a couple of rocking chairs and small table. The cottage name—*This Will Do*—is painted on a piece of driftwood. It's strung with twine and hangs beside the door. And yes, it *will* do. It's perfect, actually, this little beach bungalow, for what *she's* about to do: tell Shane how she really feels. Here, beside the sea.

Maris climbs the few steps to the front porch, pulls Shane's engagement ring from her pocket and sits on one of those wooden rocking chairs. Her hand joggles the ring; her fingers feel the twisted white gold beneath them. Finally she stands, puts the ring back in her shorts pocket and goes to the front door. Its top half is paned glass, giving a view to the living room. Maris cups her hands to her eyes and presses close to the glass. The room's walls inside are white, but the slatted ceiling is unpainted, the wood a natural brown. Exposed beams crisscross it. A gray rattan sofa is covered in white pillows and cushions. She steps back, looks the door over from top to bottom, then gives a sharp rap on the glass.

Standing there, her ears strain to hear the fall of Shane's footstep. Or the sound of a door closing. Something indicating Shane is inside. She knocks again, more urgently this time. While she waits, she looks through one of the paned front windows. Even though the living room is in shadow, she can make out glass fishing floats hanging from ropes in the corner. And a tin pitcher filled with dried beach grasses sits on a table.

But there's no Shane rounding a corner. No Shane unlatching the door.

So she hurries down the front steps and peers around the side of the cottage. "Damn it," Maris whispers when she sees that Shane's pickup truck is gone. He went out somewhere. She takes a long breath, looks behind her to the street, then looks at that planked walkway winding through the beach grass. Well, surely he'll be back soon. It's enough of a hope to get her walking to the open back porch. The lush beach grasses beside the walkway brush the skin of her legs. Grains of sand are gritty beneath her sandaled feet. She climbs several olive-painted stairs to the porch, then stops. Beneath a shady overhang there, she sees a white table with mismatched chairs; an old bench near a rusted milk can; vintage crates, some with tarnished lanterns on them. And wait ... On one crate near the screen door sits a happiness jar. It's unmistakably one of Elsa's, from the inn.

Still standing on the porch stoop, Maris can't take another step. Not one. The back porch feels too personal. Too much Shane's, and not hers. She doesn't really belong here.

So she sits herself down on the top stair, instead. From her seat, she looks out at Long Island Sound. Its blue waters waver all the way to the distant horizon. But in a moment, she's leaning forward from where she sits, craning around to see the front of the cottage again. Hoping against hope that Shane's pickup is turning in.

It's not.

Minutes pass like that. She fidgets. Looks behind her at the porch that's so clearly Shane's. Looks at the half-wall perfect for sitting on. Looks at that happiness jar again—squinting to make out what's inside it. But still sitting on that top stair, she doesn't dare move closer. Doesn't dare put herself that intimately into Shane's world yet.

With her arms wrapped around her knees, she leans forward again to see if his truck's returning from some random errand. Some Sunday drive. Maybe a stop at a farm stand.

"Come on," Maris says to herself. "Come on."

The four words have her close her eyes against sudden tears. Because oh, she remembers the last time she said those simple words in succession like that. It was fifteen years ago, to be exact.

That day is still clear. Though every minute of it is etched into her mind, she's kept the memory well tucked away. Buried it beneath everything else in her life: denim designing, relocating around the country, settling her father's estate, marrying Jason, novel-writing, reuniting with a long-lost aunt and sister. Anything and everything, keeping herself too busy to ever think much of that one day again.

Until now. Until her heart brings her to Shane's doorstep.

But on that long-ago afternoon, her heart kept her from Shane. She was newly engaged to him then. Had been for four days. It was December 30, weeks before she and Shane were to elope. In Stony Point, she'd stopped at Eva's house to show her the ring—and swear her to secrecy. Only then would she ask Eva, her best beach friend, to be a witness at her private wedding.

Problem was, Maris was on winter break from college. And before seeing Eva, she had first spent two days at home with her father in Addison.

Two days that changed everything.

Two days that had her show Eva her diamond ring,

313

while telling her a heartbreaking story—not a happy one.

*Come on. Come on*, she'd whispered after leaving Eva's home. *Come on. Come on*, Maris had pleaded fifteen years ago from Stony Point's only coin-operated payphone by the creek.

Back then—like now—she was desperately waiting for Shane.

⁓

*The winter wind whipped off the Sound that afternoon,* Maris remembers. *It was biting cold, hitting her face with a hint of icy sea spray. She had to turn her back against it, the best she could. Maybe she should've made the call from Eva's house. But Eva had just put her baby, Taylor, down for a nap.*

*"Are you sure you don't want to call Shane from here?" Eva asked while dropping several quarters and dimes into Maris' hand. "I'll go in the other room to give you privacy."*

*Maris shook her head. "I'll use the payphone near the beach. It's better this way, and I don't want to wake the baby."*

*Once Maris was there, standing at the payphone, it was too late to change her mind. The call couldn't wait any longer.*

*But Maris could hesitate, and look around to buy some time. To build her courage. It was colder out than she'd thought. The grassy area around the payphone was snow-dusted. So was the boardwalk, behind her. She hadn't counted on that wind coming off the water, either. Even wearing a wool hat and heavy winter jacket, the wind went right through her. She bounced on her toes to stay warm. Finally, she picked up the receiver of the public phone and talked with the operator. After depositing the appropriate amount of coins, the operator put through the call.*

*Maris stood there alone, the phone pressed to her ear. The creek beside her babbled along as it always did, flowing to the marsh. But Stony Point was a ghost town. The nearby cottages—a low blue one on the corner, a two-story brown colonial behind her—were boarded up for the winter season. Their windows were shuttered. Their yards, barren. So much about this corner right near the beach was the same, familiar. And so much was about to change.*

*Huddled beside the payphone, Maris listened to each ring on the other end. They sounded so far away. Though she was calling Shane in Eastfield—several towns over—it might as well have been a world away.*

*One ring, then quiet. Two rings … still nothing. Not the clatter of someone picking up, not a quick hello. Three rings.*

*"Come on. Come on," Maris said into the phone. She quickly turned into the wind and brushed blowing strands of hair off her face.*

*Four rings, and the moment that she dreaded finally came. It began.*

*"Hello?"*

*"Shane," Maris said, turning away from the wind again and bending into the call.*

*"Maris? Hey, what's going on?"*

*She briefly squeezed her eyes shut. "Shane." A pause, then, "We have to talk."*

*"Now? What's up?"*

*Another pause, when there was only a biting wind, and the distant waves breaking on the beach. "I can't do it, Shane."*

*"What? What are you talking about?"*

*"I can't do it. Can't elope with you."*

315

*"What do you mean? Is everything okay?"*

*She shook her head. "No," she managed to say, pressing a balled-up tissue to her eyes. "It's my father."*

*"What's wrong? Is he sick or something?"*

*"No. No. He's upset about our engagement and doesn't approve."*

*"Your father? Well … Well, it doesn't matter. You're an adult. You'll be twenty-two soon. And finishing college."*

*"I know. But Shane …" She took a sharp breath. "He told me it would be a mistake."*

*"Louis said that? A mistake? But I love you, he knows that. And I'll take care of you. We'll have a home together. And you'll have a good job there. So what's his problem?"*

*"I don't know. He thought we should maybe wait a year or two. And Shane? It's just that he's my father."*

*When the operator interrupted, requesting more coins for the next few minutes, Shane's voice got cut off. Maris quickly dug loose coins out of her coat pocket and deposited them in the phone.*

*"Maris," Shane was saying. "Where are you?"*

*"No." More tears ran down her face and blurred everything. The boat basin across the street—was it ice-coated? Or were her horrible, burning tears clouding the sight? "No. It doesn't matter where I am. I just can't marry you. I'm sorry."*

*"That's bullshit, Mare. You love me, I know you do."*

*Though she was nodding, though she wanted him to know that she did love him—she did—she couldn't talk past the lump in her throat.*

*"You've got cold feet. You'll feel better after the ceremony," Shane insisted. "It's a couple weeks away. You're just nervous."*

*"No. My father got me thinking, and … I don't know anymore. Shane. He's all I have."*

*Silence. A long silence that ate into her coin-funded minutes.* "You have me," *Shane's voice finally said, low and serious.*

"You don't understand. I'm all my father has, too."

"Louis is just being overprotective. I can talk to him. Is he there? Put him on."

"He's not here, Shane."

"Where are you?" *His voice grew angry.* "Tell me. I have to see you, Mare."

"No. It's over, Shane. I just wanted you to know that … I can't go through with it. With us." *Sobs lost to the wind stopped her words. Painful sobs she wasn't sure she'd ever felt the likes of before. Again she pressed that tissue to her eyes, and tried to breathe some of the biting salt air. But that hurt, too. Talking hurt. Breathing hurt. Everything hurt.*

"Where are you, God damn it? We have to talk more."

"It doesn't matter. There's nothing left to say."

"What about Rockport?"

"I can't do it."

"But I bought the house, Maris. I bought it. When you were at your father's, I drove back to Maine and closed the deal. We're all set."

"Too fast, too fast. It's all too fast, Shane." *A gust of wind blew so strong, Maris felt spray from the distant water. When she looked out toward the Sound, whitecaps were rolling in.* "My head. My head is just spinning."

"Where are you? I hear waves. Are you at the beach?"

*She squeezed her eyes shut and nodded. Oh, she knew what seeing him would mean. Shane would rush to her, take her up in his strong arms, kiss away her sadness. Convince her this was the mistake. This moment. This phone call.*

317

*"Operator," a woman's voice cut in. She requested more coins before the call could continue.*

*"Okay," Maris said. "One second." Her hand dug deep in her coat pocket again, and a dime fell to the ground. Just one dime. "Wait," Maris insisted. She switched the phone to her other ear to check her other pocket. But there was no money there.*

*"Maris, for the last time, where are you?" Shane's voice came through the phone.*

*"Shane, wait. I'm getting more money." She cradled the phone to her neck and dug into her purse. Her fingers, they were so frozen it was hard to maneuver them. But she managed to pull out her wallet.*

*"Where the hell are you? I'll just come get you and we'll——"*

*And like that, it was over. Shane's voice was cut off when the operator ended the call. The phone went dead. In the jarring silence, Maris dropped her purse to the ground.*

*"Operator," the woman's voice said. "Will you be calling again? Reverse the charges, maybe?"*

*Maris, well, she looked through tears at her empty wallet. Turned and looked at the churning, wind-blown water.*

*Felt that wind blow right past her, taking her every happiness with it. Whisking and swirling it far, far away. She paused another long second, then gently hung up the phone.*

~

"Where are you?" Maris asks now. "*I made a mistake, I made a mistake,*" she whispers so quietly, the words fade in the sea air.

Standing, she finally walks onto Shane's back porch—

into his world. The floorboards are painted the same olive green as the steps. Tall cream-colored posts reach from the half-wall to the roof overhang. The open-air view out to Long Island Sound is breathtaking. The stuff of seafaring tales. On any other day, she'd love to sit right on this ledge and take it all in: the salt air, the sparkling water, the gulls swooping low.

But not today.

Today she paces. And checks her watch. And tucks a fallen strand of hair back into her low, twisted bun. She rushes down the seven painted steps to see if Shane's truck is back. When she sees that it's not, she trots along the planked walkway, past the sweeping dune grasses, to the driveway and up to the street. There she looks first one way, then the other. Two teenage girls in bathing suits walk by, their flip-flops flipping, their hair wet from a swim. Every bit of the beach road is checked, but there's no Shane in sight.

Finally, Maris returns to the back porch and does it. She hoists herself up onto the half-wall, leans against a post and pulls Shane's old engagement ring from her pocket. Sitting there, she slips it onto her finger. And takes it off. Then puts it on once more.

Time stands still. It locks her in uncertainty. Casts doubt on her decision.

Her desperation—to see Shane, to talk to him—is all-consuming. She can think of nothing else. No one else.

So now she knows. Sitting here and waiting for someone who might or might not want to see her, yes, she knows.

319

It's the same desperation Shane had to feel fifteen years ago. The day she called him from the payphone—long gone now—by the creek.

The day she might as well have pulled the deep blue sea out from under him.

After rushing to the steps and checking the driveway once more, she returns to her perch on the half-wall. Here at this little beach bungalow, the sea, the sweet sea that Shane lobsters and loves, spreads out before her. The afternoon sun scatters a constellation of ocean stars across it. Stars she dare not wish upon until she sees Shane again.

Sitting alone on this hot August afternoon, Maris pulls her knees up close, looks at the sailor's knot ring on her finger and only hopes she's not too late.

The beach friends' journey continues in

# EVERY
# SUMMER

The next novel in the Seaside Saga from

New York Times Bestselling Author

# JOANNE DEMAIO

# Also by Joanne DeMaio

**The Seaside Saga**
*Blue Jeans and Coffee Beans*
*The Denim Blue Sea*
*Beach Blues*
*Beach Breeze*
*The Beach Inn*
*Beach Bliss*
*Castaway Cottage*
*Night Beach*
*Little Beach Bungalow*
*Every Summer*

**Countryside New England Novels**
*True Blend*
*Whole Latte Life*

**Wintry Novels**
*First Flurries*
*Cardinal Cabin*
*Snow Deer and Cocoa Cheer*
*Snowflakes and Coffee Cakes*

For a complete list of books by *New York Times* bestselling author Joanne DeMaio, visit:

Joannedemaio.com

# About the Author

JOANNE DEMAIO is a *New York Times* and *USA Today* bestselling author of contemporary fiction. She enjoys writing about friendship, family, love and choices, while setting her stories in New England towns or by the sea. Joanne lives with her family in Connecticut and is currently at work on her next novel.

For a complete list of books and for news on upcoming releases, please visit Joanne's website. She also enjoys hearing from readers on Facebook.

**Author Website:**

Joannedemaio.com

**Facebook:**

Facebook.com/JoanneDeMaioAuthor

Made in the USA
Middletown, DE
29 November 2022

16438311R00198